30

30

Book One in The Lost Relics Series

BRAD OWENS

Superbia Publishing

CONTENTS

This book is dedicated to my family,
biological, chosen, and yet to meet.

You are my heart.

CHAPTER 1

Part 1

Prelude

The little silver bell, a hold over from the days before electric chimes, tinkled softly as the front door to Woods Department store opened. It tinkled again as the door closed and Lonnie Woods walked from the back room, still thumbing through a stack of dollar bills he had collected from the cash drawer. He liked the bell. It made him think of the good old days, before the big box stores had pulled all the customers to the outskirts of town and away from downtown. Luckily, the novelty of those giant retailers seemed to be wearing off because the day's totals were good, better than they had been in months, and he had a bounce to his step. He looked over the clothes racks and between the shelving units.

"Hello?" he asked and got silence in return. "I must be hearing things," he whispered and returned to his work, but there was the echo of a feeling that pulled at him. He wanted something, he wasn't sure what, but the desire was there like a tickle on his brain. It wasn't hunger, not precisely, and he had eaten a large lunch. The phone rang and he nearly jumped out of his skin. He picked up the receiver of the old rotary phone that had come with the building and waited until the ringer stopped reverberating inside the ancient plastic casing. It was old and rickety like everything else in the store, including Lonnie, but he liked it for the same reasons he liked the doorbell. He lifted the olive green receiver to his ear and pulled at the impossibly kinked cord. His wife had been suggesting a cell phone, or at least a cordless one, but Lonnie was opposed to the idea. He liked his old things. "Just a fad," he would joke with Elizabeth every time she suggested updating anything.

"Yep," she would always agree. "Just like color television and the internet."

"Hello," Lonnie spoke into the receiver, and smiled at the sound of his wife's voice. He tried to unkink the cord enough so he didn't have to bend over. It didn't work, so he pressed a hand to his lower back as he crouched. "Yep, I'm closing up now...we did pretty good today...Yep, meatloaf sounds good. I'll be home in a little bit. Love you too."

Unbending himself with a grunt, he placed the bound stack of money on top of the closed register and began to fill out a deposit slip when a sound, like a piece of metal dropping on the parquet floor, suddenly poked at the silence. He looked at his feet, but he hadn't dropped any change. Another sound scratched at the silence; it was like the wheeze of a wounded animal near the front door. Tentatively, he made his way around the counter and toward the sound. The feeling he had before, the desire for something, was stronger now, so very much like hunger, but deeper, darker, a desperate need, but fear had clawed in too. He inched closer, strained his ears, looked through the bottoms of his trifocals to get the most focused view, and pulled back a bunch of long sleeved shirts on the sales rack.

Having never seen a dead body, nor ever having expected to see one on his floor under the half priced flannel shirts, Lonnie was very confused. A man, dangerously thin, lay face down just inside the door, his arms stretched out and one hand was lying open, the palm to the ceiling. He was dressed in filthy rags like those hikers last year that got lost on the backwoods hiking trails. After a week and a half wandering in the woods, they had looked almost as bad as this man. Lonnie stood gaping and holding his breath for a long moment before he bent and pushed at the man's neck, where he thought he might find a pulse. He had seen plenty of people do similar things on television shows, but he had never thought he would need to do it, and he wasn't sure he was doing it right. There was no pulse, at least none that he could find, and the man's skin was abnormally cold. He pushed at the man's shoulder, rocking him gently back and forth with no reaction. He felt the man's neck again, and his wrist, and still nothing but cold, clammy flesh.

"You okay?" he asked in a voice that sounded similar to his own, but this voice was shaking and a little too loud. Lonnie knelt beside the body a moment more, images from television shows were replaying in his mind, people giving CPR, one movie where they performed a tracheotomy, several where they zapped people with those defibrillator things. He didn't know how to do any of that. He returned to the phone behind the counter and quickly called the Sheriff's office, mentally kicking himself for not taking that CPR course they offered every year at the volunteer fire house. "CPR's just a fad," he had joked with Elizabeth. He definitely wasn't laughing now.

"Yes, I need the Sheriff down at Woods Department Store," his shaky, somewhat familiar voice echoed through the quiet. "No, not a robbery. There...well, you might want to send an ambulance too. Someone's...hurt maybe? Dead, I think."

After an awkward question and answer period, with far more questions than answers, Lonnie was assured that help was on the way. He replaced the receiver and looked toward the door where the body lay hidden from his line of sight by strips of flannel. *It's odd*, he thought, *that this man would just walk in and fall dead right in front of the sales rack.* Then, he thought it would have been just as odd if the man had fallen dead anywhere else in the store, but the sales rack? It was especially odd, but Lonnie didn't know why. He could just see the tips of the fingers, framed by flannel, of the outstretched hand lying upturned on the wood floor. There was an old episode of Miss Marple where she held a mirror under the nose of a corpse. He had a compact mirror on the counter for customers trying on reading glasses. Maybe he should try the mirror?

He walked over and knelt once more, rolling the man as gently as he could onto his side. He tried holding the compact just under the man's nose, but his hands were shaking so much that he kept hitting the man's cheek. "Sorry, sorry, sorry," he repeated and looked at the mirror. There was no reaction. Then, he wondered what the reaction should be. He held the mirror to his own nose and breathed out. A brief fog painted the mirror. He touched the man's wrist again, and the skin was noticeably colder. He jerked his hand back and sat next to the body. "Who are you?" he whispered.

Lonnie thought he knew everyone in town, and this man did seem familiar, but his face was so drawn, his body so withered. *There had been a sound,* Lonnie thought. The man's palm, the loose skin of his hand, showed an angry, red impression of something small and round. Lonnie lowered his head and stared at the open palm. It looked as if the man had been clutching a coin. *A coin dropping,* he thought. *That was the sound.* He sucked in a long, tense breath and followed the line of the man's hand to a piece of metal in the aisle.

He crawled, wincing three times as his knees ground into the wood floor, and picked up the coin lying between the other clothes racks. It was old. The worn edges of the aged metal were lipped with rough-hewn tool marks where it had been flattened long ago. The image on one side of the coin was the indistinct profile of a man, nearly rubbed smooth but still yet there. The other side was too worn to make out. He began to rub the coin between his thumb and forefinger, feeling the formulated sludge of time on the metal. The sensation sent sparks throughout his body. His eyes grew wide, hungry. The coin was so beautiful, so precious. The feeling he had before, the desire for something indistinct, was now fulfilled.

The faint sound of a siren sounded in the distance, and a sharp thought pierced Lonnie's mind. They were coming to get his coin. He couldn't allow that. He closed his hand around the metal so tightly that blood began to trickle as the rough edges stabbed into his skin. He ran out of the store and disappeared into the night.

CHAPTER 2

The kiss was rough, deep, and flavored with bourbon. This man tasted of lust and Brady wanted more. His hands found the back of the man's head and the buzzed cut hair toyed with his fingers, and as the man's tongue found his own, he wrapped himself in sensation, pulling and pleading with the sexual physics of the moment, wishing for something deeper, closer to love, but sex was enough—for now, and for a few hours more at least.

Clothes fell away and Brady luxuriated in the heat between them. They tumbled onto the bed, hands exploring, a welcome torrent of fingers and tongues, skin and breath. The taste of this man's skin sent electric spikes through Brady's entire being. He arched his back as he licked down, ever downward, finding one nipple then the next amidst a shock of chest hair and the scent of desire.

The man's stomach fluttered as Brady continued his descent prompting a quick, playful nibble of hips and a deeper exploration of the exquisite line framing the man's torso pointing to the promise of pleasure. Brady followed the trail and arrived at the place he needed to be. Salty, musky sex filled his mouth.

Soon, much too soon, Brady tasted the culmination of the man's excitement. He needed more. He moved up the man's body, retracing his path as an ascent to something new, and found the man's own greedy face. This kiss was impossibly deeper, filled with a longing that Brady was happy to fulfill. He pushed between the man's thighs and the exploration continued.

Two became one, only momentarily, but it was exquisite, only momentarily. An electronic light filled the room and an annoying buzz interrupted everything. Brady paused, stumbling in his exploration, before continuing to completion. Spent, only momentarily, he rolled onto his back and allowed one final, fleeting instance of satisfaction before reaching for his phone.

"Really?" the man asked.

Brady smiled his most charming smile. "Sorry, it's work," he rubbed the man's chest as he listened to the voice message. He looked at the man and flashed an exaggerated frown, then he shot out of bed. "Got to go," he explained as he hurriedly dressed and headed for the front door.

"Can I get your number?" the man asked as he pulled on his own pants.

"I'll call you," Brady called as he hurried out into the night.

The man yelled from the doorway, "You don't have my number!"

"Yep," Brady waved as he got behind the wheel of his cruiser. The night was nearly giving into the morning by the time Sheriff Brady Edwards responded to the 911 relay operator. He had often thought that there needed to be a better system in place than someone in the town calling 911, the answering service operator then calling the station, and the voice mail system telling them the operating hours of the office, and informing them that if it was an emergency to call 911. The frustrating circle of the system meant that any emergency call outside of office hours took far too long to reach the Sheriff.

Even though the system was antiquated and redundant, Brady had gotten the message and arrived at the scene just forty-five minutes after the call. *A new record*, he thought as he smoothed and readjusted the front of his uniform. He looked at himself in the reflection of the store's glass door. The sheriff's badge on his chest never seemed to be in the right place, probably because the shirt was too big. He had meant to order a new one, just like he had meant to reorganize the phone system, but life in a small town moved slowly. In Richmond, before he made the move to simplify his life, things had moved much faster. Now, he took things in stride. He took off his hat, and tousled his hair, which he had always thought was the color of weathered brick but now was starting to be peppered with gray. He sniffed under his arm and he smelled like bourbon sweat and sex. He smiled and shrugged, nothing to be done now, as he walked into Woods Department Store, a pleasant bell tinkled above him.

He had returned to Potter's Field, Virginia, after nearly ten years in Richmond, and had found his hometown exactly the same as he had left it. The small town was in the middle of nowhere, but somehow within five hours of everywhere. In high school, and then college, he would travel up to DC, or down to Atlanta for long weekends, which was exciting and prompted his move to a city after graduation. City life did not fit, however, so he returned to Potter's Field and a simple, stress-free existence. The most stressful situations he faced now were people dying under mysterious circumstances, like walking into a department store and dropping dead, but this was just the latest example.

As he surveyed the scene, he was reminded of the first mysterious death. It had been just a few months earlier when Penelope Ivey had a heart attack in the middle of the town's only supermarket. She had been acting strangely, and, according to witnesses, she had started screaming at the other customers. She was angry to the point of being frantic, and then she just fell over in the produce section. The coroner had found an old coin clutched in her hand so tightly that he had to break her fingers to retrieve it. No one thought much about the coin, at the time. After all, Penelope had been an antiques collector, but the coroner had called several times to ask if he could see the coin again, just a final look. That was the only thing that had seemed odd. Why was the coroner interested in an old coin? Was it valuable? Was he trying to steal it? In any event, Brady had not released it from evidence.

Then came the second death, which truly irritated Brady. Arnold Fuller, a retired history teacher, had committed suicide by jumping off of the State Line overlook just outside of town, a cliff that faced a hundred foot, sheer drop. Witnesses of the incident had said he was raving about people stealing from him just before he jumped. Brady had found an old coin, still clutched in Arnold's fist, and his mind had gone into overdrive. Two coins, nearly identical, and two deaths, equally troubling but explainable, with a multitude of witnesses. Penelope had a history of high blood pressure, and Arnold had always been a bit paranoid. He could have easily dismissed the deaths as a rage induced heart attack and schizophrenia resulting in suicide, but the coins suggested there was something else going on here. His near-atrophied police mind knew there was something, and he had become focused on the coin almost immediately. He had actually gone to the bar and met, what's his name, he really should have paid more attention when they had met, but the bar trip was in order to stop thinking about the coin, the death of Arnold, for just a minute.

And now, a third death. John Yates, the postmaster and the town's only historian, but the body looked emaciated, barely recognizable. John had always been thin, but this was something else entirely. And, of course, there was the indentation about the size of a coin in the palm of his hand, demarcated by puncture wounds, evidently created by the jagged edges of a coin very much like the other two. Brady had searched the entire store but couldn't find a coin. And he couldn't find Lonnie Woods, the owner of the store who had made the emergency call. Something was going on all right, and he would bet his, always in the wrong place, sheriff's badge that it was not easily explained away.

Brady left the store as the coroner was loading the body into the ambulance and stood next to his patrol car. He could hear the rumblings of a storm off in the distance as he pulled his cell phone from his front pocket and re-dialed the number he had already called three times in the past ten minutes or so.

"Any word?" he asked as Elizabeth Woods answered. "No, there's no need to worry just yet. It's still only been an hour or so...yes, I know your house is five minutes away, but...yes, we're looking...yes, make sure you call if you hear from Lonnie. O.K. Bye."

Brady dropped the phone back into his pocket. Where was Lonnie? What was going on in his town? The questions were beginning to take over any other thoughts, and these coins. He wanted to look at the coins again. Both of them. All three of them? The glint of the metal in the late afternoon sun when he had held it up out of Arnold's hand, the shimmer of the silver, the intensity of...what was it about these coins? He wanted to go back to the station, get the coins, and protect the coins, but he needed to find Lonnie. He was so distracted that although he saw the shadowy figure in the alley across the street watching him intently, he did not register anything as strange about him

The morning dawned quickly in the small sheriff's office where Brady took a shower and changed out of his soiled uniform that still smelled of the bar and the man's cologne. *I really should have gotten the man's number, or his name,* Brady thought as he finished dressing and returned to the coroner's report on John Yates, where a phrase in the otherwise mundane paperwork caught his attention. *...indentation of a circular object, roughly the size of a dollar coin, in the right palm...* He retrieved the evidence packets from the other two recent deaths and took the coins out of their respective cardboard boxes. He laid them side-by-side. He couldn't remember the last time he had seen a dollar coin, but these looked roughly the same size to him. They were also very similar and obviously not machine made.

He picked up one of the coins, still encased in the heavy-duty plastic evidence bag, and looked at it closely. It was old, just the sort of thing that Penelope would collect and both Arnold and John would have been interested in studying. But old coins? Penelope usually focused on furniture, Arnold loved the Civil War Era, and John was mainly concerned with the town's history. What were they doing with old coins? And what, if anything, would Lonnie have to do with this? Lonnie ran a department store and had no known interest in history, ancient or otherwise, as far as anyone knew.

The plastic-shrouded metal in his hand glimmered in the fluorescent light of his office. The silver sparkled hauntingly, enticingly, with beautiful sparks of brilliance. His analytical mind said it was the oil from the hands of the people who had held it that made it shine so brightly, but there was something about the coin, the coins, something he couldn't place, something that tickled the back of his mind, like a half remembered dream. He liked to call that tickle his mystery sense, which was really his memories of previous cases or case reports or even books he had read. Whatever it was, his mystery sense told him when there was something not quite right, and it had been working overtime recently.

But it was the glow of the coins that held his attention much more than the feeling that a possible mystery was developing. That glow dominated everything else. It filled his range of vision; it poured into his mind; it made him feel important. The phone rang suddenly and Brady jumped, letting go of the plastic bags and allowing the coins to drop onto his desk. He grabbed for the coins, he needed to hold the coins. He...the phone rang again. He closed his eyes tightly, swallowed hard, and then reached for the receiver.

"Hell...o?" he said, his voice breaking. He cleared his throat and settled the receiver against his ear. The coins glinted on his desk. His free hand went out to them, but he stopped and said in a decidedly stronger voice, "Hello? Elizabeth? Is that you? Calm down...he what? O.K. where? The truck stop? Yeah, I know it. What was he...? O.K. I'll head over right now." Brady replaced the receiver and leaned back in his chair. Things were getting stranger and stranger, and now Lonnie had been seen at the truck stop just off the interstate.

What was Lonnie doing heading toward the interstate on foot? he thought. He was suddenly aware of something in his hand. He had picked up the coins, still in their individual plastic bags. Thoughts, dark and a bit paranoid, kept invading, but his mystery sense had been engaged. He shook his head and shoved the two individual plastic bags, each holding a coin, into another plastic evidence bag and slipped the whole bundle into his front pocket; he headed to his car.

Brady saw a man step out of the shadows of the alley across the street. Even from a distance, Brady could see the man had gray eyes. *Strange*, Brady thought as he pulled his car into the street. He glanced in his rear view and saw the man, a toothy, gray smile on his face, his hands in the pockets of his gray tweed sport coat, step out of the alley and begin walking behind the car with a slow, easy stride.

Really strange, Brady thought but then turned his attention to the task at hand.

CHAPTER 4

Tulia's Diner was a small truck stop just off I-83. It had been eclipsed in size by other such establishments at various exits along the interstate, but there was a steady stream of loyal locals who frequented the place, enough to keep the business afloat. Tulia Destin, the owner, was now in her late sixties, but she was still active in the day-to-day operations of the diner. She was the best cook around, and Brady wished he could eat her gravy and biscuits for breakfast every morning, but that might make his oversized uniform much less oversized.

Brady pulled up to the building, an old fashioned diner that would have looked ancient in the sixties, and quickly made his way to the counter. Tulia was pouring a cup of coffee for the one lone customer perched on the stool at the far end.

"Brady. 'Bout time you showed up," Tulia said before the door even had a chance to close behind him.

"Just got the call from Elizabeth, Tulia. If it was an emergency then you should have..."

"Called 911 and then you still wouldn't be here. So I called Lonnie's wife. Figured she'd come take care of it herself, but I guess she thought you needed to be involved, even though nobody can reach you after dark."

Brady thought about pointing out that there were no funds in the town's treasury to upgrade the 911 system and that he had been trying for months to get the mayor or the state or anyone to increase the funds, but he determined that, right now, a prolonged argument about funding was not going to be productive. Instead, he asked, "What happened?"

"Just a minute," Tulia said as she motioned toward the back wall and went to the pass-through to get her customer's food.

Brady looked at the pay phone near the restrooms hanging from its cord, bits of plaster on the floor, and a large hole in the wall. He made his way to the phone and waited for Tulia to finish serving her customer and join him.

"He was crazy last night. Tore the phone right outta the wall," Tulia said as she sauntered up behind him.

"Lonnie Woods?" Brady asked, although he knew the answer. He just couldn't see Lonnie, the kindly department store owner, doing anything like what Tulia alleged.

"It was him alright," Tulia said, popping chewing gum between her teeth.

"Anything set him off?" Brady asked as he examined the phone, more for show than for any clue he thought he might find.

"Don't know. He walked in, sat back here, acted like...well, like he was hiding from someone or something, y'know, looking over his shoulder, staring out the window, all squirrelly. Then, he got up to make a phone call and went crazy-like and ripped it off the wall. I asked what was wrong and he looked at me all wide-eyed and ran out the door."

Brady listened to Tulia, but he had a difficult time putting Lonnie into the scenario she was describing. The Lonnie Woods he knew, the Lonnie Woods everyone knew, was the most non-violent, mild mannered man he could think of. If Mr. Rogers had a less verbose brother, Lonnie Woods would be that man. "You're sure nothing set him off?"

"Not that I could see. No one even talked to him, 'cept me. And all I asked was what he was doing here so late?"

"What'd he say?"

"Nothing really. At least nothing I could understand. He just said 'they want it' over and over. And when he looked at me...it was like those kids on drugs, you know? Those crazy eyes?"

Drugs? Drugs would explain the odd behavior. Maybe he got a prescription mixed up? Elizabeth would know what he was taking. And who was he trying to call? In any case, he needed to find Lonnie to make sure. "And you didn't see him holding anything?"

"He might have had something in his pocket," Tulia admitted. "He kept one hand in his pocket the whole time, now I think of it."

"Did you see which way he headed?"

"Toward the interstate."

"O.K. Thanks, Tulia. I'll head out, see if I can catch up with him. Anything else you can think of?"

"Well," Tulia began and seemed to be searching for the right words, the correct tone. "I think he did say something right before he ripped the phone off the wall. I'm not sure, mind you. I was all the way over near the pass-through, but I think he said, 'she wants it too' and then he went crazy."

"So, he didn't actually call anyone? Just started to and then freaked out?" Brady asked, thinking the "she" in the scenario was probably Elizabeth.

Tulia shrugged, "Yep, I think that's right."

"And that's it?" Brady thought about jotting down some notes for the report he would have to write later, but decided he could remember everything. Adequately describing it was going to be the trick, not getting the facts right.

"That's it." Tulia nodded and went back to work.

Brady pushed the pay phone back into its place on the wall and then let it fall forward again, the cords taught and straining. "Ripped it off the wall," he whispered to himself. He returned to his car and started driving toward the interstate, one hand on the steering wheel and the other absentmindedly gripping the plastic bag of coins in his pocket.

CHAPTER 5

The interstate slithered through the trees and hills like a black snake zeroing in on its prey, which was any town beyond the borders of Potter's Field. Lately, more and more, it seemed that all roads were leading out of Potter's Field. The boarded up businesses downtown were evidence of that. Lonnie's department store was one of the few businesses that seemed to just keep going year after year. It was an institution. Lonnie was an institution. *None of this made any sense*, Brady thought as he slowed his car to a near stop and looked from side to side, trying to spy any trace of Lonnie.

The interstate cut over his path, elevated by a bridge on top of solid-looking retaining walls made of concrete. Maybe Lonnie headed to the other side, under the bridge, but that didn't make sense. Nothing but cow pastures for miles past the interstate. If he headed north then the interstate ran by several small towns, eventually making its way to DC. He couldn't imagine Lonnie was planning to walk the nearly five hundred miles to DC. Then, with a mental kick to his head, he realized that he hadn't been able to imagine anything since this case began. He needed to just go with his gut and find Lonnie. Follow the evidence, not his feelings.

A rustling in the tall grass near the southern retaining wall caught his eye. It was most likely a deer or a dog, but he needed to check anyway. He stopped the car and got out.

A chill wind was blowing in from the East and he shivered just a bit before he donned his hat and called out to the field as he stood awkwardly on the gravel just off the pavement, "Hello?"

The rustling grew frantic, pulsing with activity, for just a moment and then stopped all together. He could see an area of grass, roughly the size of a full-grown man, bent and flattened against the ground at the end of a long trail of similarly bent grass.

"Lonnie?" he called toward the flattened grass. The low rumblings of the cars passing on the interstate above were punctuated by the loud grumbles of semi trucks on the bridge above, otherwise, the night was silent.

He stepped over the embankment and walked into the grass. As he neared, he could hear labored breathing that sounded human. "Lonnie? That you? You okay?"

The rustling started anew but quickly died down. Without meaning to do it, Brady placed his palm on the handgun at his side. He had never even touched his firearm in the line of duty before, but now he was glad he had it. Everything about this day put him on edge. He squeezed his other hand around the plastic covered coins in his pocket, and he could feel the rough edges threatening to pierce the plastic. He squeezed a bit harder and stepped closer to the place where the rustling had been. He could see the red and blue plaid pattern that Lonnie wore so often. He quickened his pace.

Lonnie lay face down in the grass. His arms bent under his chest as if he were clutching something underneath him, like a running back protecting the football after a tackle. Brady bent and placed a hand on the man's back.

"No!" Lonnie screamed as his head bucked backward and he tried to scramble away on his belly.

"Lonnie! Lonnie, it's Brady!" Brady placed both hands on Lonnie's shoulders and tried to hold the man in place. Lonnie bucked for a moment but then fell quiet, panting erratically. Brady recognized the signs of exhaustion.

"You can't have it," Lonnie muttered weakly into the grass.

"It's okay, Lonnie. I'm here to take you home."

"It's mine, it's mine, it's mine..."

Brady watched as Lonnie eventually settled, appearing to melt into the earth. What little energy remained finally gave out, but his arms, still folded tightly under his body, remained tense, strained. Brady rolled Lonnie over and looked at the half-conscious man's chest. Both of his hands were locked around a small object pressed against his breastbone. Brady pulled at Lonnie's hands, but the muscles were so tight that they would not loosen. Brady tried again. The fingers of Lonnie's hands slackened as a sigh escaped from his mouth. A small metal object fell free. Brady grew a bit frantic, a bit desperate and he began to paw at the grass, like a wild animal after prey. He snatched and pulled at the weeds, he slapped at the ground and dug his fingers into the earth. One of his fingers found a rock and the pain shocked him back to a semblance of reality.

"What the hell is going on?" he asked the wind as he fell back on his haunches and squeezed his throbbing finger with his other hand. He gazed at the grass but couldn't see anything. In truth, his eyes were barely focused on anything. His mind was reeling, working overtime to try and explain what he was feeling. A pained gasp erupted from Lonnie's prone body, then he began to convulse.

Brady was fully a trained sheriff again. He tried to move Lonnie onto his side, making sure his head was away from any rocks or solid objects. He loosened his shirt to allow better air flow. Soon, Lonnie's body slackened, becoming still. Brady grabbed the radio at his side and called for help.

The ambulance arrived quickly, one nice thing about living in a sleepy town—emergencies were rare and response teams were quick to arrive. Brady knelt in the tall grass and watched the paramedics attend to Lonnie. He looked up at the sun, now high in the sky, and wondered how this elderly man had kept moving, running, for nearly, he looked at his watch instead of the sun. It was just after noon, so he did the math in his head. The department store closed at seven. So, Lonnie had been on the move for over seventeen hours. It didn't seem possible.

"He okay?" Brady asked the nearest paramedic, a man he knew but couldn't place. Lonnie moaned, and Brady saw the shop owner's usually kind, exuberant face was drawn and contorted in pain.

"He's passed out from exhaustion, looks like. What has he been doing?"

Brady shrugged and took off his hat to scratch his head. The ambulance, loaded with the unconscious form of Lonnie Woods, soon pulled back onto the highway and disappeared over the rise. Brady sat and listened to the drone of the interstate and thought about Lonnie. He slipped his hand in his pocket and closed it around the plastic bag. He felt the comforting solidity of the coins, and he felt so grateful that he had found them. They were his now. He could protect them, keep them safe from all the people who were trying to get them. He sighed contentedly, and his hand closed more firmly. The coins began to press into his skin. It was a slight pain, but it was delightful. Brady shook his head and struggled to remember that he had a job to do. He reached for his cell phone and dialed Elizabeth.

"Elizabeth? We found him. He's on the way to the hospital," Brady listened to Elizabeth sob into the phone and mutter words of thanks, but his eyes were fixated on a glint near the fuzzy impression of Lonnie's body in the grass. "Yeah. You head on over. I'll check on you in a bit."

He knelt down near the glint. It was a coin. He could see the jagged metal partly hidden by broken grass blades. The same glow emanated from it as the others. That glow was so beautiful, so enticing. He reached out, but then stopped, pulling his hand back quickly. This was evidence. He pulled a pair of latex gloves from his pocket and slipped them on.

The coin was surprisingly cold, even through the latex. It felt nice, soothing. He retrieved the plastic evidence bag containing the other coins and dropped the new one in. The silver was dazzling. The design, the same as the others, an indistinct impression of a man's head, was intriguing. Flipping the coin over inside its plastic shroud, revealed a great bird, maybe an eagle, stamped onto the back. The eagle was even more intriguing than the man's head. He wanted to touch it. He needed to feel the metal against his skin. He wanted to hold it tightly in his hand. He grabbed a hold of the top of the bag, pinching each side, preparing to open it. He pulled. The plastic strained. He just wanted to touch the coin. Just a little touch.

He shook his head. "No," he told himself. "This is evidence. I collect the evidence. It's my job." The words lingered in the air, refusing to settle. Then, he took a deep breath, then he exhaled completely and stopped pulling at the plastic. He straightened his badge and balled up the heavy plastic bag and slipped it into his pocket where it suddenly became much heavier than it should have been. Fuzzy thoughts hung on the corners of his consciousness. He wanted to protect the coins. He needed to protect them. Everyone was after these coins, they…he shook his head again.

He stood up to leave and swooned. His mind felt foggy, like he had just awakened from a deep sleep. He stood on shaky legs, turned his face to the sky, and breathed deeply. He closed his eyes and breathed again. He unclenched his fists and breathed once more.

When he opened his eyes he saw the figure standing in the shadows just behind his car. The man seemed so out of place in his gray tweed sport coat and matching gray slacks that it took a moment for Brady to understand he was real and not some memory he had of a college professor from an old black and white movie. He wanted to call out to him, this strange man, but he couldn't find his voice. Instead, he closed his eyes to keep from fainting. When he opened them again the gray man was gone.

"I'm just tired," Brady whispered to the air. "That's all. Tired." He got into his car and pulled out, feeling weak but more in control. He needed to check on Lonnie anyway. There was no point in chasing daydreams. In his rearview mirror he thought he saw a man standing near the spot where Lonnie had been. But then the man was gone. He chalked it up to being tired again and drove on.

CHAPTER 7

Potter's Field Hospital was little more than an emergency room, but there were a few beds for patients awaiting transfer to other, larger, better equipped facilities. Brady went to the nurse's station to find out which one of the rooms Lonnie was in.

"I need to find Lonnie Woods' room," he said as he flipped through his notebook looking for anything that might give him an idea of how to proceed.

"Sheriff," an oddly familiar voice said in a severe monotone. Brady looked up from his notes to face the man he had just had sex with standing at the nurse's station dressed in scrubs.

"You're a nurse," Brady exclaimed, looking at the name tag, he added, "Mark."

"Yeah, I told you that last night. Good memory."

Brady tried his most charming smile again, "Sorry, I'm just a bit distracted. Work, you know?"

"Uh hum," Mark did not seem charmed. "Room 4, end of the hall." He turned and walked away.

"Thanks," Brady called after him, waving to the back of his head. He received an over-the-shoulder middle finger in return. "Guess I won't need your number after all, huh?" He produced a tight-lipped smile and a shrug before going back to work. *It's for the best,* he thought. *I do not need a boyfriend right now.*

Brady walked into the hospital room and was greeted by the sight of Lonnie lying in bed attached to more wires and tubes than he thought was possible. Elisabeth was perched in a chair pulled close to the bed. Her head was lowered to the mattress and she was sobbing weakly.

"Elizabeth?" Brady spoke softly.

Elizabeth raised her tear streaked face and smiled a weary half-smile. "He's going to be okay. He's dehydrated and suffering from exhaustion, but he should recover."

"Good. That's good," Brady had so many questions about Lonnie, but he knew Elizabeth had fewer answers than he did. She looked near exhaustion herself. He decided his investigation could wait for a better time.

It was Elizabeth who propelled the investigation forward. "He's been going in and out of consciousness. He hasn't spoken. What happened, Brady? Why did Lonnie...what happened?"

"I'm not sure," Brady said, his hand involuntarily going into his pocket and grasping the plastic encased coins. "Had he been acting strange at all?"

"No. You know Lonnie. He's the most predictable man on the planet..." Elizabeth paused a long, thoughtful pause. "His grandmother had...Alzheimer's."

The statement felt accusatory. Brady considered for a moment and then pulled the bag of coins out of his pocket. "Have you seen these before? Or anything like them?" he asked, holding the evidence bag out toward Elizabeth.

The coins dangled in their clear plastic prison, and Brady felt the need to free them. He could take them out to show Elizabeth. That would be fine. Just take them out and let Elizabeth see them. *No, Brady* thought. *She wants the coins. She wants him to take them out of the plastic.* Brady jerked the bag backwards and the fluorescent light caught the metal and shot a glint toward Lonnie's unconscious form.

The man in the hospital bed came alive. He lunged for the bag, pulling wires and cords with him as he moved. Instruments crashed to the tile floor. Elizabeth screamed. Startled, Brady threw his arms back and the coin bag flew through the open door. It produced a muffled clink, hitting the floor tiles outside the room, and Brady felt his heart ache.

The coins needed him. He stepped forward and Lonnie, now sprawled out on the floor, clawed and scraped at his legs. Brady stumbled back, fear and shock keeping him from acting, but his eyes returned to the plastic bag just outside the room. Lonnie turned his attention to the bag as well and began to claw his way toward it. Brady dropped down and held the man still. He would not let Lonnie get the coins. They were his coins now.

Elizabeth was screaming for help. Hospital staff members came flooding into the room and took Brady's place on top of Lonnie. Finally, orderlies and nurses were able to wrestle him back into bed and administer a sedative.

Brady rushed into the hallway, snatched up the bag and shoved it back into his pocket. A wave of relief sent a shiver through him.

"What...?" Elizabeth cautiously moved into the hall and stood close to Brady.

Brady didn't have an answer.

Mark came out of the room and shot Brady a severe look, "What was that?"

Brady shook his head and watched Lonnie slowly succumb to the drugs. Order, and silence, returned to the room and Elizabeth followed the staff down the hallway to discuss what had just happened.

"You okay?" Mark asked, the severeness tempered with true worry.

Brady's face ached from the intensity of his frown and furrowed brow. "I really don't understand what's going on in this town."

Mark looked to him and then to Lonnie and back to him, "I guess you do have a lot of work, huh?" He patted Brady's arm before he strolled down the hall.

Brady watched him go, a twinge of guilt fluttered briefly and was replaced by a sharp pain in his hand. He had been clutching the coins so tightly that his fingers were cramping. He forced himself to release the coins as he inched his way back into Lonnie's room.

He watched Lonnie for a moment, he pondered the man's tight faced slumber and wondered if he dreamed of the coins. He began to finger the sealed flap of the bag inside his pocket. It would be so easy to pierce the plastic, to rip it open and hold the cool, gleaming metal to his skin. It would feel so good, so welcome, to have the coins in his hand and not in the plastic. He should touch them, he thought, in order to fully understand why Lonnie wanted them so badly. He should hold them. That was really his job. It was his duty to touch the coins.

Everyone wanted these coins. Lonnie wanted them, that was clear, but Elizabeth and the doctors and nurses, even the janitors, they all wanted the coins. He needed to run. He needed to protect them. He needed to...He shook his head violently, and then another time, and once more. He held a clenched fist to his temple and pressed hard. The encroaching thoughts were so powerful, so real. He tried breathing again. It had worked before, hadn't it? It was not working now. He raised his hand and the bag was in it.

He could not tear his gaze from the metal. The shine flickered across his face. Lonnie began to buck and convulse. Two nurses rushed back in and tried to calm him, to hold him. Brady thought about his training. The first responder training told him what to do in case of seizures. The first step was to time the seizures. He thrust the bag back into his pocket and then held his watch up.

The convulsions stopped. Brady continued to stare at his watch. He stared as the nurses checked Lonnie's medication, his oxygen, his vitals. He stared as they straightened his sedate form in the bed. He stared as they left the room. He stared until the ridiculous thoughts he had been having about these coins dissipated slowly. He finally lowered his watch when he decided it was time to find out more about these coins.

CHAPTER 8

With the comparatively low crime rate in Potter's Field, Brady felt confident leaving his senior deputy in charge even with the recent mysterious deaths, after all, everything about them could be explained, except the coins. He needed to find out more about these coins, and Pete Daily was a capable deputy. If there was trouble, which should be unlikely, he could handle it. And, of course, if there is another death, he would just be a phone call away. He huffed at the thought of a 911 call to the service, to the recording, to the...It didn't matter. He needed to investigate.

So, Brady carefully made sure that each of the coins were contained in their own evidence bag, and that all three bags were secure in another bag, then he put them in one more bag just to make sure. He thought briefly about wrapping them in aluminum foil or something more substantial than plastic, but he decided he was being childish. They were just coins. They were evidence, and they were just coins.

He felt the pull of the coins only once after that. It was a sudden impulse that took hold of him as he was reading a web page about ancient coins. He suddenly thrust his hand into his pocket and grabbed the coins in their plastic bag. He needed to see them, to make sure they were still there, to make sure they were safe. He wanted to take them out of the plastic, but they were evidence. He couldn't tamper with evidence. It was his duty to maintain his professionalism. He took his academy oath seriously, even in the face of ridiculous circumstances like an unnatural desire to hold a coin.

He kept repeating his academy oath in his head until the compulsion ended. *On my honor, I will never betray my badge, my integrity, my character or the public trust.* It helped to get his mind off the coins, but the fact that everyone wanted to take them from him still remained. *I will always have the courage to hold myself and others accountable for our actions.* He tried deep breathing and he was able to let go of the plastic bag in his pocket. *I will always uphold the Constitution, my community, and the agency I serve.* After repeating the oath three times, he felt better. The coins were safe in his pocket. No one even knew he had them. He was going to solve this mystery. Everything was fine.

He returned to the webpage and reached the end of the article with no new revelation, except that the page was published by Taylor College, which was a small, private liberal arts college about fifty miles from Potter's Field. Brady had gotten his Bachelor's from there, and he remembered the faculty being more than competent. If he was going to find out about these coins quickly, the college was his best bet. Otherwise, he would have to take the day, go to D.C. and hope to find someone there. Taylor College was faster.

Friday afternoon saw very few students milling about campus. Brady had no trouble finding a parking space in front of what he knew was the history building, one of the oldest buildings on the campus, and the place he hoped to begin to find answers. Inside, it was an easy matter to find an office belonging to a history professor, and luckily there was one professor sitting alone in his office. The nameplate on the door read, "Dr. Richard Stanley, Ph.D." This one would have to do for a start.

He knocked on the door and a man's voice told him to come in. The office was not what he had expected. He remembered from his time at college that professors were notorious for having the most cluttered offices with books and student papers piled to the ceiling, but this office was neat and orderly. There was one bookshelf in the corner behind the small, neatly organized desk. A man, about Brady's age, sat at the desk gazing into a computer screen. He was dressed in a clean, pressed polo shirt. His dark hair was close cropped and neatly styled. He had sharp features, but not too sharp, just enough to add interest to his face. His shirt was just a bit too tight too, which allowed a clear view of his nipples. Brady frowned and swallowed hard. *Professionalism*, he told himself.

"Professor Stanley?" Brady asked tentatively, hoping this was a graduate student or an intern. He didn't need the added distraction of a good looking expert.

"Can I help you?" The man responded calmly without looking up from the computer screen.

"I'm Sheriff Brady Edwards, from Potter's Field. Are you Dr. Stanley?"

Richard stopped looking at the screen and turned his curious brown eyes toward Brady. He pursed his lips, but then he quickly smiled, stood, held out a hand in greeting, and asked, "Yes, I'm Richard Stanley. How can I help you, Sheriff?"

Brady suppressed a gasp at the smile, which seemed to fill the entire room. This man was going to be a distraction all right. He took Richard's hand and squeezed a little too tightly. The other man's eyebrows rose just a bit. "Hi, sorry, you're just not what I was expecting," Brady said quickly, slurring a couple of the words.

"What were you expecting?" Richard asked, the smile on his face becoming a little strained but no less beautiful.

"I don't know," Brady began and then suddenly realized he was still holding Richard's hand. He quickly let go and dropped his hand to his side. "You know, like Einstein, crazy hair, paper everywhere."

"Ah," Richard's smile was now merely a polite formality. He motioned to the chair across from his desk. Brady sat and immediately began to fidget. "What was it I could do for you?" Richard asked with a marked professionalism.

Brady chastised himself, *he's not that hot. Get a grip,* he thought and then said, "I have this case that I hope you can help with."

Richard's surprise was evident, and Brady knew that it couldn't be often that the police asked a history professor for help on a case. This whole thing was crazy, and he knew it was crazy, but what other choice did he have. He could try to solve this craziness on his own or he could ask the handsome professor for help. He chose the handsome professor.

"I will, of course, do what I can, sheriff," Richard said, still with an air of surprise.

"I found these coins at, well, possible crime scenes," Brady said, producing the plastic bag from his pocket and holding them out to Richard. The metal gleamed as it always did, and Brady wanted nothing more than to stare at the shiny metal until he got his fill. Instead, he forced his eyes away from them. "I was hoping you could tell me something about them. You know, what they are, where they're from, that sort of thing."

Richard took the bags and looked at one of the coins through the plastic. "Ah, okay. Well, they are Roman, I think. Pretty old. Maybe Antoninianus, possibly older, Denarius, maybe."

"What?" Brady asked, frustration and anxiety mixing into a slight tone of anger. Richard was holding the coins up to the light, and Brady wanted to snatch them back. He was breathing heavily, sweat began to trickle down his forehead.

"Sorry," Richard said and smiled a sweet, friendly smile. Brady relaxed, but only a bit. "Those are classifications of Roman coins. Named for various...it doesn't matter right now."

Brady nodded and tried to smile back. He had the distinct impression that he had grimaced instead. "Is there anything odd about them? Anything off?" Brady asked, willing himself to calm down. He began to recite his oath of office again.

"Well, they are an odd size, roughly like a modern half-dollar, dollar coin, maybe," Richard admitted. Brady sighed loudly. He already knew how big the coins were. Richard's eyes darted up and looked at Brady, but then he continued, with more emphasis on less general knowledge, "And they seem to be of a consistent metal. So many Roman coins were made of mixed materials, but these...I'll need to research a bit. Can I keep these for a couple of hours? I can spend some time now, but I have a class starting in a bit. After that, I can research some more. I should be able to have some preliminary information for you around two. Would that be okay?"

Brady thought about the question. He eyed Richard carefully. The professor was gazing intently at the coins, and Brady struggled to keep from grabbing the evidence bag. After all, the coins were evidence, and he shouldn't leave evidence with a civilian, even a handsome one. Evidence should never leave his possession, even evidence that didn't seem to be that important, not really. Then again, there was no real crime that he could identify and tie to the coins. The coins weren't important at all, not really. He could just take them and keep them. No one would know. Part of his oath repeated in his head, *I will not betray the public trust*. The desire to hold the coins, to feel the coolness of the metal against his skin, to slake the deep pain of being separated from them - it was becoming a hunger—a desperate hungry need that was weighing him down.

Then, a new thought occurred to him. He could be rid of the coins, if only for a little while, a couple of hours. The thought was suddenly so very delightful. He could trust Richard, the handsome, friendly professor. He knew that, but he wasn't sure how he knew that. But he did, in fact, know that. He began to tell Richard to take them, but with a moment of professional clarity, he said, "I can give you two hours. As long as you don't take them out of the plastic, and you call me as soon as you have something."

"Of course," Richard said as he began fingering the books on his shelf. He dropped the coins onto his desk and Brady nearly swooned, but he controlled himself. "Do you have a card?"

Brady fumbled inside his coat pocket where he kept a stash of business cards and handed one to Richard. He watched the coins sparkle on Richard's desk, wrapped in plastic, and the urge to grab them and run flared, and much like the glint from the silvery metal, it faded quickly. He swallowed and tore his gaze away from the coins and looked, instead, at Richard's face. The professor had kind eyes and a welcoming smile, a beautiful smile. Brady liked this man immediately, but there was a nagging thought bouncing around the base of his skull. The thought was weak, but tenacious. *This man wants the coins*, Brady thought. Then, ideas of violence entered his head.

"I'll give you a call as soon as I find something," Richard said, jarring Brady from the dark thoughts. He stared into Richard's eyes and found only curiosity and a glimmer of caring wonder.

Brady nodded, wanting to say thank you, or give more of a warning, but, in that moment, the need to leave was stronger, and he turned and exited the office. The corridor seemed lighter, brighter somehow. No, it wasn't the corridor. It was him. He felt lighter without the coins in his pocket. He chanced one quick glance behind him and saw a man dressed in a gray suit, with gray hair, standing in front of Richard's office. *Did he want the coins?* Brady thought and then forced himself to turn away. He was being ridiculous. No one knew the coins were here. He was sure of that, much more so now. He shook his head, rubbed his eyes, and hurried out of the building.

CHAPTER 9

The next hour passed so quickly that Brady didn't really notice that he had stayed in the coffee house an extra thirty minutes. He had planned on staying there for an hour and then making his way back to Richard. He had walked a good fifteen minutes from campus to find the coffee shop. It was now late afternoon, and by the time he got back to the professor's office, he figured it would be early evening and he would have to take the coins back. The thought of having the coins again filled him with dread, but he had to do it. If nothing else, he needed to make sure the professor hadn't taken them out of the plastic. He wished he had been more clear when he had warned him not to do that. He should have been insistent. He should have made sure that Richard knew the danger, but what would he have said, really? Would he have told the college professor that the coins were cursed? That he suspected that the coins had the power to make people commit suicide? Those were ridiculous thoughts.

However, the feelings, the urges, he had been getting since finding the coins were real. They were dangerous. He suddenly realized he should have stayed with the coins. He should never have let the coins out of his sight. He...the recriminations continued until Brady rose to his feet and began a steady, purposeful walk back to campus.

He found it difficult to lift his feet on the walk back, as if he were walking through waist deep water, and he had to force his gait. Then, he began trying desperately to walk faster, but the feeling that his feet were too heavy and his legs were too stiff was strong. Secretly, in a barely heard corner of his mind, he wished that the sun would move faster and night would fall and Professor Stanley would think he forgot and would just go home, and then he thought about what might happen if the Professor touched one of the coins. His mind cleared as he became more determined to keep the coins out of people's hands, and he discovered he had stopped walking.

It was difficult to start again, his feet were even heavier than before, as if a weight had been attached to them. To add to the difficulty of walking, the dread was building with each step, and the campus seemed to be getting farther away instead of closer. He tried to jog. His feet hit the pavement much harder than they should have and his legs ached with the effort, but he began to make forward progress. *The coins are my responsibility*, he thought, and his sense of duty propelled him forward. He got back to Richard's office at the same time that the professor rounded a corner with an armful of old looking books.

"Good timing," Richard said as Brady greeted him at his office door. "I just got back from the library, and I think I found some good information for you."

Brady just nodded and tried to smile. The trepidation was building with every tick of the clock. His heart pounded, threatened to jump out of his chest, and he fidgeted waiting for Richard to open his office door. He desperately wanted the coins back. He needed to feel the weight of them in his pocket. He didn't feel right without it. Richard fumbled with his keys, and slipped the correct one into the lock easily, but it was taking too long. Brady felt a strong desire to shove the professor out of the way and do it himself, but, finally, Richard opened the door and stepped into the office. Brady followed a little too closely.

"Well, to begin, I was right. The coins are Roman, and they are old. Maybe around the first century. Maybe a little earlier. Most probably made from zinc. They almost look like silver, but that would be less probable. These are some of the books from our library collection on the subject," Richard began and indicated the pile of books he had heaped on his otherwise orderly desk. "I've marked the pages to show you. This one in particular is of interest," Richard held up a book and flipped it open and he just kept talking. He was describing the pressed image. It was the emperor, evidently, or possibly a governor, Brady was only partly listening. This was taking far too long. Where were the coins? He just needed to know where the coins were. That's all. Brady performed the now familiar action of shaking his head to clear his mind as Richard talked. *Something is wrong*, he thought as he shook his head again, and again. Everyone who knew him remarked on Brady's exceptional patience. He had often considered it his greatest virtue, his most attractive feature. Where did all that patience go all of the sudden? "Hmmm? That's odd," Richard said, holding two of the coins in front of him.

Brady saw the silver glint and his hand reached for them, to snatch them back, but he forced his arm into a semblance of politeness and gently took the coins from Richard's outstretched hand. Everything changed then. It was like taking a breath after being underwater too long, and then being shoved immediately back down. The air went into his lungs, to capacity, but then he found he couldn't release it. His conscious mind, the part with the police training, recognized the signs of hyperventilation and he tried to force his breathing to deepen, but his unconscious mind was not cooperative. He kept trying, the air came out in staccato, as if he was breathing through a grate. It was just enough to avoid collapsing, through sheer force of will.

Richard was shifting the few papers on his desk when Brady finally was able to focus on something other than his breathing. Richard was lifting and looking under the books that were now piled on the surface. "Where did I...?" Richard asked.

"What?" Brady responded, trying to sound light and friendly, achieving frightened and exhausted. He looked at the plastic bag in his hand. Two coins. There were only two in the bag.

"One of the coins," Richard said as he opened and closed every drawer in his desk. "I'm sure they were all together, but one of them, well, it's gone."

"What!" Brady exclaimed and rushed forward. Richard jumped out of the way just in time as Brady began to rummage through the desk.

Papers flew in all directions until Brady turned to Richard, rage evident on his face, "Where is it?"

"I...uh, are you alright?" Richard asked, and Brady felt the room swirl. He felt a sinking sensation, like missing a step while going up a flight of stairs. Richard was there supporting him, but the darkness soon engulfed him completely.

CHAPTER 10

Brady woke with a strange, cold sensation on his forehead. He put his hand to his temple and felt the damp cloth that had been placed there. Then, a warm hand covered his and a soothing voice was speaking to him. He couldn't quite hear. He tried to sit up.

"Take it slowly," Richard said, helping Brady to rise to a seated position. "Looks like you just fainted. Probably stress, but you'll be woozy for a little bit."

Brady felt Richard's hand take the cloth away and then press it to his cheek, the side of his neck. It felt wonderfully cool. "I fainted?"

"Yes, just after you attacked my desk," Richard smiled a tight, wide-eyed smile before he patted Brady on the knee and picked up a pile of papers near the sofa where Brady now sat.

The memories came back fresh and unbidden, "Sorry about that."

"What was that, exactly?" Richard deposited the papers on his desk and bent for the books and pens.

Brady didn't have a good answer. He remembered being so angry that he couldn't control his body. He remembered wanting, no, needing to get...the third coin. The rage had fueled him, propelled him, compelled him. "Did you find the coin?" he asked calmly yet with an obvious tinge of anxiety.

"I think so, yes," Richard said. "I have to apologize for that. If I had known how seriously you would take the coin missing I never would have left them here and I would have told..."

"Where is it?" Brady sucked in air and tried to calm down. The rage was rising again, but he would control it. He had to. "Please, it's important."

"I had my graduate assistant helping with the research," Richard continued as he finished putting the errant contents of the floor in the appropriate piles on his desk. "The department secretary said she went over to the Geology department to ask a question. I suppose she took one of the coins with her."

"Oh God!" Brady exclaimed and shot up off the sofa. He regretted that immediately as his head swooned and his vision blurred, but only a little. He swallowed hard and set his feet. "We have to find her. I think she might be in trouble."

"What kind of trouble?" Richard asked as he followed Brady out into the hall. Brady shuffled from foot to foot, he began to walk in one direction then swiveled toward the other. Richard pointed, and they hurried down the hall. "I can assure you that Carrie had no intention of stealing..."

"No one ever does until..." Brady started but decided to save the rest of his thought for when they found the coin. Instead, he shoved his hand into his pocket and felt the other coins there, wrapped in their protective shrouds. He could feel the coolness of the metal through the plastic and he was able to exhale more easily, but then a twinge of something unwarranted emerged. Anger flared from deep in Brady's chest and directed itself at Richard. It took every last vestige of will power Brady possessed to keep the anger from consuming him, from igniting into a rage. His fingers tightened around the coins until they ached.

Richard asked as they left the building and headed across the lawn out front, "What are you not telling me?"

"It's...these coins...they have...it's hard to explain. I..." Brady stopped talking as he noticed several campus police officers running in the same general direction they were heading. With effort, he released his grip on the coins and immediately felt more focused. "Where are they going?"

"It looks like, oh no, the Science building," Richard responded as Brady broke into a run.

They arrived in front of the Krammer Science Building amid a flurry of activity. The campus police had erected a barrier of orange cones and hand-held stop signs at the front entrance. Brady immediately went to the closest officer, hoping his own uniform would grant him access to information. "What's happened?"

The officer looked at him and his uniform and seemed to quickly come to the conclusion that Brady wanted as he said, "A student has a gun in one of the classrooms, she's threatening to kill anyone who comes in."

"Which student? Do you have a name?" Richard asked from behind.

The officer just shook his head and turned away from them. Brady pulled Richard to the side of the building, away from the campus police. "It's her," he offered.

"How could you possibly know that?" Richard asked.

"She has the coin." Brady headed around the corner of the building looking frantically up and down the brick walls. His eyes landed on a half opened window on the ground floor. He pushed the window up enough to squeeze through. Once inside, he crept to the door and opened it slowly.

A voice behind him made him jump. "There's something wrong with these coins. What is it? Radiation? Some kind of contact drug?" Richard asked.

"You can't be here," Brady said and pointed back to the window.

"What is wrong with Carrie? What did you give us?"

Brady sighed wearily and thought about his response, "I think it'll be better if you just see it for yourself. Just...prepare yourself, and stay back, out of the way." He turned and headed toward the sounds of shouting and lamented that, after this, the handsome professor would never go to dinner with him.

CHAPTER 11

They jogged upstairs and into a hallway but stopped as a loud sound, like a pop, reverberated off the cinder block walls.

"Was that...?" Richard started.

"A gunshot," Brady finished and stood in front of the other man. "You should go back. Let me..."

"No," Richard said, his jaw clenched, his eyes wide and frantic. "I am coming with you. She is my student, and..."

Brady held up a hand and Richard took the cue to stop talking. Brady recognized the fierce, determined look on Richard's face and nodded, "Just stay behind me."

They slowly made their way to the end of the hall where Brady stuck his head around the corner and pulled it back in one quick movement. "They've set up a barricade at this end of the hall. Looks like the shooter's in a room near the middle, maybe a bit toward the other end." Brady watched as Richard's brow furrowed and his eyes darted from side to side. "Do you know this building?"

"What?" Richard was breathing erratically.

"Tell me about this building, what's at the end of the hall? What's above us, below us." Brady had a hand on Richard's shoulder and was squeezing firmly, consistently.

Richard's breathing began to calm and he turned his head upward and pointed as he talked. "All the floors of this building are identical. Stairwells at each end. We can go back down a floor and then up on the other end, should be right across from the, yes, I think, there's a geology lab."

Brady nodded. It was as good a plan as any; of course, the campus police had probably already considered the layout of the building. They were more than likely getting people in place to do the same thing, but they would need to be more cautious. That was an advantage they could use to get to the girl first. He turned back toward the stairwell and Richard followed. They quickly made their way to the lower floor and ran, full-tilt, along the length of the hall, around all the necessary corners. The other stairwell was still empty. They had made it in time, before the police. Brady flung open the door and they headed up, nearly slamming into a young woman running down toward them, pursued by angry shouts.

"Carrie?" Richard shouted a bit too late as the woman raised her gun and pointed it at Brady's chest. Brady didn't hesitate. He rushed forward, pushing her outstretched arms up. The gunshot flashed above him but the echo was devastating in the close quarters, bouncing off concrete walls, piercing his brain. Brady winced but was able to slam Carrie's hand into the railing and the gun clanked down the stairwell.

"It's mine!" Carrie screamed and began to claw at Brady's face. She was a slight girl, barely weighing a hundred pounds. Brady worried about hurting her, but the ferocity of her attack made up for her seeming lack of physical strength. She twisted her wrists suddenly and broke a hand free. Sharp nails stabbed at Brady's eyes. He jerked himself away, and the two fell backward, tumbling to the landing below.

Brady had fought his share of criminals in his early days, and this fight brought to mind several drug fueled battles that had caused him to seek employment in a quieter locale. Carrie's features were twisted into a mask of rage. Her strength belied her small frame and was troublesome, frightening.

"Grab the gun!" Brady yelled to Richard who was attempting to lift his legs over the railing to get to them. Brady could see movement and knew that Richard was passing them, but he couldn't stop concentrating on Carrie. She writhed and contorted herself out of every attempt at being held down. Brady was tiring fast and this young woman seemed stronger than ever. He needed to end this fight quickly. A fast slap to the face forced a shocked calm in Carrie's struggle, enough that Brady was able to get the handcuffs from his belt and around one of her wrists. She was screaming incoherently as he roughly pushed her to the railing and fastened the other cuff around the metal bar. He jumped back, out of the reach of her remaining hand as it continued to claw at his face.

Pressed against the opposite cinderblock wall, Brady watched the seething rage distort Carrie's otherwise pretty face. He tried to slow his own breathing. His head was pounding, his face was burning, and he worried that he might be bleeding. He touched the scratches on his cheeks, one very near his eye, realized that her nails had not quite broken the skin, and he sighed.

His energy left this body with the breath he exhaled. Carrie had renewed her attempts to break free of the restraints, and Brady worried that she would break her own wrist, or even her arm trying to get out of the handcuffs. He would need Richard to help him subdue her further. He looked down the stairwell and saw that Richard was crawling on his hands and knees toward a glint of metal on the landing.

"Don't touch it!" Brady screamed and scrambled down the stairs.

"It is so beautiful," Richard whispered and continued to reach for the coin. Brady lurched forward, wrapped his hand with his coat sleeve, and landed between Richard and the coin. Richard looked at him, rage inching into his face, as he raised Carrie's gun, slowly leveling it at Brady.

Pulling his arms free of his jacket, Brady wrapped the cloth, over and over, around the coin. As the cocoon grew, Richard sneered, hissed, made a half-growl, but then he blinked once, twice, lowered the gun, and let out a long, halting breath. "Wh..what...?"

Brady lifted the bundle that was his jacket, pressed it tightly together into a ball, and imagined the coin deep within the overlapping layers of cloth, safe and harmless. He kept the bundle firmly under one arm, steadied by his other hand and looked deeply into Richard's eyes.

"Are you okay?" Brady asked and received a nearly imperceptible nod in return. He scanned the other man's face, looking for signs of rage, an indication of the effects of the coin, but he only saw the kind eyes he had seen before. "Can you take this and not touch the coin?" Brady asked and watched Richard's eyes grow large and fearful, but, to his credit, the professor nodded slightly, and a little defiantly. Brady handed the bundle to Richard, taking the gun in return. "Take this back to your office. We need to keep the coin safe. Remember, do not unwrap it. I'll deal with the police and meet you back at your office."

"But..." Richard began, his trembling arms clutching the bundle of fabric.

"Can you do this?" Brady asked, grabbing Richard firmly by one shoulder.

"I...think so."

"Do not unwrap this," Brady reiterated and finished by placing a hand on the bundle in Richard's arms.

Richard nodded. He stood, slapping a steadying hand against the railing before heading off down the steps. Brady exhaled, trying to slow his breathing. There was no question about the coins now. They were the cause for all the mysterious deaths in Potter's Field. The only question now was what could be done about them.

Brady hurriedly dealt with the local police; his own credentials helped with that. He suggested that the young woman must have had a breakdown of sorts, which both the campus and city police accepted too readily for Brady's taste, but he was still relieved that they did. The charges were serious, but since no one was injured, Carrie would be taken to the hospital for evaluation, and Brady was pretty sure that the remnants of the coin's effect would appear like a mental break. She would probably be sentenced to psychiatric evaluation at the local mental hospital instead of prison. At least he hoped that would happen. He couldn't help but feel responsible for the whole incident.

The sun had since set, and the long night was nearing its end when he finally made it back to Richard's office. He rushed through the door and saw Richard staring intently at the lump of cloth on the desk, several open books were strewn haphazardly around the room.

"You okay?" Brady asked.

"What is this thing?" Richard couldn't seem to tear his eyes from the bundle. Brady stepped forward and took the other man by the shoulders and roughly pulled him away from the desk. Richard blinked and let out a jagged breath. "I'm okay. I promise. This is my curious face, not my deranged face. They are similar, I admit."

Brady smiled and the two shared a nervous laugh.

"We need to figure out what's going on with these coins, and fast," Brady offered.

"So, what's your best guess? Do you have a best guess?"

"Not even a bad guess," Brady admitted.

"Why not just give them to the police here? Let them figure this out," Richard said as he began to inch back toward the desk.

"And how many more people will die while they waste time not believing me?" Brady took Richard by the arm and pushed him toward the door. "Stay there. Look out into the hallway." He waited until Richard turned away, then he carefully unwrapped his coat like it was a sinister present. He slipped his hand into an evidence bag, turning it inside out, then he took the coin and encased it in the thick plastic. He could feel the air thicken around him as he sealed the bag.

"People have died?" Richard asked, staring out into the dimly lit hall, breathing through the open doorway like a drowning man gasping for air.

"I think so, yes," Brady admitted. "They looked like accidents at first, weird, unexplainable accidents, or suicide, but now I know more."

"I think I know someone who might be able to help," Richard offered. "It is a bit of a drive. She lives in DC."

"Let's get started then," Brady said and shoved the coin deep into his pant's pocket where it mingled with the others. The weight felt strangely familiar, oddly comforting. Too heavy for such small objects, but it was his burden, this unnatural weight. He would bear it to the end.

The day dawned heavy. Brady struggled to extricate himself from the remnants of the night that he had allowed for sleep. The light of a new day was too harsh, too difficult, but he forced his eyes to open, his body to move, his mind to settle. It was a meditation technique a therapist had taught him years ago. *Center yourself and breathe,* she had told him. And he had to admit that breathing worked. It was calming when the daylight was not. For some reason, he felt he needed to repeat his oath of office again, so he did. He felt stronger.

Brady stretched and flexed his neck. Richard's couch was comfortable enough, but the tension from the incident on campus was too much to allow for relaxation. He went into the guest bathroom that Richard had offered him and tried to erase the night completely with soap, water, and toothpaste. Richard had a stash of unopened toothbrushes that he kept for guests. Brady liked that idea and thought about doing it himself when he got back home. It would make the "mornings after" go more smoothly. He washed with the provided wash cloth until he felt similar to himself. He stepped from the bathroom, no shirt, his pants unbuttoned, his hair tousled and nearly ran into Richard emerging from the bedroom.

"Oh," Richard exclaimed when their eyes met. He watched the man struggle to keep his gaze on his face, and he smiled. It was Richard's turn to be discomforted by the handsome sheriff. Brady enjoyed the turn of events. "You want breakfast?" Richard asked, clearing his throat and glancing down just for a moment.

Brady felt much more comfortable with this new arrangement. He took his time drying his chest, pulling on his t-shirt, buckling his pants. He noticed Richard lick his lips at least twice as he moved around the living room. "I usually just have coffee in the mornings."

"Yep," Richard said and hurried into the kitchen. Brady watched him brew coffee as he finished dressing and the power he felt from tempting Richard shifted. The professor was dressed in very form fitting jeans that showed much more of what his dress pants the day before had kept hidden.

"Uh oh," Brady said as his mouth went a little dry. He tried not to stare at Richard's ass, but that was going to be difficult.

"How do you want it?" Richard asked and Brady choked back a dirty response.

"Black," Brady said and then tried desperately to be professional once again.

They stood in the kitchen and sipped coffee and talked of their pasts, their childhoods for some reason, and their love of mysteries.

"Is that why you became a police officer, the mysteries?" Richard asked.

Brady nodded, "I suppose so. I like solving mysteries. Nothing like it. What about you? History for mysteries too?"

Richard laughed, "Yeah, kinda. I love a good artifact and discovering what it is, what it means, what it meant to the people who made it. That's like solving a mystery, right?"

"Absolutely," Brady took the last swig of his coffee and then leaned forward to put the cup in the sink. He brushed Richard's arm and had a sudden desire to kiss him, but he cleared his throat and stepped back, an awkward smile etched on his face. "Yu ready to go?" He asked quickly.

The drive to D.C. typically took five to six hours, but Brady pushed the speed limit, trusting that his out-of-town cruiser would allow some professional courtesy. He needed to find out about these coins quickly. Lives depended on it. He knew that for certain now.

The afternoon was just giving way to the early evening as they came into D.C. He should have been tired, Brady knew, after just a couple hours of sleep, after the incident yesterday, after the drive today. Instead, he felt energized. Alive. Pulsing with power. He relished the feeling but feared it too. *Was this the influence of the coins again? Was this how Lonnie Woods was able to run for miles and miles until he finally collapsed from exhaustion?*

"She lives in those apartments just over there," Richard said as they took the last exit and entered a residential area. He was pointing to a row of brick buildings that stretched along the street.

"Who is this we're going to see again?"

"She is an expert in...well, artifacts of a...spiritual nature," Richard said.

"Spiritual? What does that mean?"

"Surely, you can feel it," Richard began. "The coins. They speak to the mind in a way that, well, let us just say it is not normal. I think she might be the only person I know who might be able to help."

Brady nodded, hesitantly. He wasn't sure about the spiritual thing, but he had no better ideas. It wouldn't do for him to close his mind off this early in the investigation, but he made a decision that if this woman was a quack he'd just take the coins and throw them in the nearest blast furnace and be done with it. The thought of the coins melting into slag was at once exhilarating and terrifying. Would he just be creating one giant block of cursed silver instead of several little disks? It was the first time he allowed the word 'cursed' to make its presence known in his analytical mind. It made him feel uneasy, frustrated, and intensely curious.

Richard led the way to the correct door. He knocked while Brady stood back, nervously gathering the fabric of the pocket of his pants into a lumpy bundle before releasing and then grasping again. The repetition annoyed him, but he could not stop. Instead, he kept clenching and unclenching his fist around the coins and waited for the apartment door to open. There was no answer to Richard's knocking, no sound, from behind the door.

"Maybe she's not home," Brady offered.

"Katie is a shut-in," Richard explained with a bit of frustration and anxiety. "By definition, that means she has to be home." He walked to the front window behind a low hedge and tried to look through the curtains.

Brady stepped closer to the door and put his ear to the cold metal. He couldn't hear anything, but a faint smell found its way to his nostrils. "Something's wrong," he said and pushed at the door. The door swung open about an inch and a half, and the smell flooded the small stoop.

"Oh God, what is that?" Richard said, holding his nose as he rejoined Brady.

"Decay," Brady said softly as he pushed the door open further. The apartment was dark, save for a sliver of light fighting its way between the curtain panels. The odor, now fully expressed, was a mixture of human waste and rot. Richard gagged involuntarily, but he was able to keep from throwing up. Brady reverted to cop mode. He shut off his mind to everything except the task at hand. There would be time to vomit later. Now, he needed to keep focused. He lingered at the doorway, his hand on his sidearm, until he spied the light switch next to the door. He flipped it on.

"Oh..." Richard exclaimed and ran outside to release the contents of his stomach onto the grass.

Brady listened to him wretch but kept his mind focused. "She's not dead," he whispered as he stared at the hulking figure spilling over the sides of an oversized recliner. Her massive chest was rising and falling in erratic intervals. Her feet, purple and swollen, were nearly obscured by the human waste and decayed food that had piled up around the base of her recliner.

CHAPTER 12

The paramedics arrived quickly and confirmed what Brady suspected. Katherine "Katie" Share had suffered a heart attack about a day and a half ago. Not quite long enough for her neighbors to report anything wrong, especially considering she was a shut-in.

"She worked from home, taught classes online," Richard reported to one of the officers, solving the mystery of how she earned a living and how she could go missing for a couple of days and no one took notice.

The paramedics had some trouble stabilizing her due to her size, and then they had an even more difficult time getting her out of the apartment. Luckily, Katie lived on the ground floor and had a backyard patio door. Brady noticed the gathered paramedics and police officers forcing their professionalism. He knew they were making conscious decisions to keep from making comments about Katie's condition. He appreciated their respectful attitude.

"She was in a bad car accident," Richard was telling an officer. "Her fiancé died and she was badly injured. After that, her anxiety was too much for her. She..."

The officers worked diligently and Brady helped where he could. Words jumped out from Richard's interview with the officer, "...kind...brilliant...loving..." and Brady began to see Katie's humanity through his words. It became harder to be objective. After several long moments of silently frantic work, hastily delivered medical interventions, and whispered brainstorming sessions, Katie was freed from her apartment and on the way to the hospital.

"You friends of Dr. Share?" the building's superintendent asked Richard and Brady as they all stood in front of the wide open door of the apartment. The older man eyed Brady's uniform curiously as he kept a handkerchief over his nose and mouth to keep out the smell.

"Yes," Richard said through shallow breaths.

"Then, you'll lock up after you leave," the man said and walked off leaving the pair alone, obviously relieved to exit the stench.

"Should we just head on to the hospital?" Richard asked.

"Let's just have a look around first," Brady said as he stepped back into the dimly lit apartment. The smell had not lessened with the door being opened, but the fresh air mingling with the stale made the small space bearable. Brady went straight to the laptop on a t.v. tray next to the recliner. The open web page showed a grocery store's delivery site, so he clicked on the browser's history. The computer was in the middle of a routine update, and Brady decided to search elsewhere while that took place. He tried to rummage through the debris near the recliner, but the motion of his gloved hand moving anything merely caused the stench to rise. He exhaled as much as he could and went to a different area of the room to search.

Brady watched as Richard went to the book shelf and took out a copy of a book called *Ancient Coins*. He saw that the author's name was Dr. K. Share. *That might tell us something.* He thought, *nice job, professor.*

"She loved research, y'know?" Richard said as he thumbed through the book. "Relics. She loved ancient relics. It was a passion. She used to go on these expeditions to recover relics. You should have seen her then." As he spoke, he flipped through the book and a small metal object was nestled between the pages. "I found a key," he announced.

Brady was bent over, looking under the sofa. "Is it to a lockbox?" Brady asked.

"Maybe. Why?"

"I just found a lockbox," Brady said and pulled out a heavy metal box. He hefted it onto the couch cushions and it sank deeply into them. Richard handed him the key. The lock clicked and the box sprung open.

Inside, amidst a well-used notebook and some loose papers, was three silver coins. "Oh God," Brady exclaimed and tried to close the box, but the pull of the coins had him. The act suddenly became difficult, nearly impossible. He wanted to lock them away. He knew that he should. Instead, he reached out his hand toward the glinting metal. He could feel the tug, familiar yet frightening, on the fraying edges of his mind. He knew he had to take these coins. If he didn't, Richard would get them and he'd never see them again. He could not let that happen.

"What are you doing?" Richard asked and pushed the other man backwards. The contents of the box flew across the room and disappeared into the rotting remains of takeout food on the floor. Brady bucked and fought, but Richard held him fast until the frantic look in his eyes subsided. He held him a moment longer after that, just to be sure. "You okay?"

"I...uh, yeah. I think so," Brady said as Richard helped him to a sitting position on the sofa. "Three of those...I just wasn't ready."

"I know," Richard admitted. "I could feel them too."

"But you saved me. Thank you."

"You would have done the same," Richard offered.

"It's my job, but you...just, thanks," Brady said and placed a grateful hand on Richard's shoulder. Richard's hand covered his own and the touch of skin to skin sent an electric jolt to Brady's stomach. He ignored the feeling as best he could and said, "Let's get those coins wrapped up in something."

Richard agreed. They each steadied themselves, Brady tried calming breaths again, but the smell made that difficult. He, instead, tried to focus on his thoughts. pushing one this way, another that, until his thinking became ordered, calm, focused. Richard had obviously done something similar and Brady found himself in awe of this man's coping capabilities. Then, he imagined what Richard would look like without so many clothes. He smiled, licked his lips, swallowed hard, and then went back to work as he retrieved a couple of pairs of latex gloves from his cruiser, and they were as ready as they were going to be.

Carefully, they rummaged through the empty food containers and assorted trash. Several times, Richard gagged as his fingers closed around something mushy and slimy, but he maintained his composure, barely. When he found the first coin, Brady gasped.

He could feel the metal through the latex, the coolness, the reassuring solidity. He wanted to take it so badly that other thoughts became indistinct, misty, unimportant.

"Here's the bag," Richard announced beside him, forcing the indistinct thought into a more congealed form, at least enough to drop the coin into the thick plastic.

"Thanks," Brady said with a relieved expulsion of air.

The process of finding and bagging was repeated once, twice, and Brady had the idea to store the coins back in the lockbox. The metal seemed to provide more insulation from the coins' effects, and they assumed that Katie had discovered that as well. The trunk of Brady's car would allow them to put the coins a little further out of mind, they hoped.

"We have got to figure out what to do with these things," Brady began, taking the three coins in his pocket, and with more effort than the action should have required, placing them with the others into the car's trunk. It was like pulling a juicy bone away from a hungry dog; no, it was more like a hungry dog letting go of a juicy bone, but he managed it. With all six coins in Katie's lockbox, he closed the lid and then the trunk. The pull of the coins lessened, but it was still there. He could feel it in the furthest recesses of his mind. It was a desire unlike anything he had ever felt before, like a physical need, as if he would die without them. He thought of the bodies back home, the look on Lonnie Woods' face, and the pull of the coins, the longing, slackened. Then another thought invaded and he said, "We really need to figure out how many of these things there are."

They walked back into the apartment and a barely perceptible bell-like sound tinkled from the laptop near the recliner. Brady looked at the now open list of web pages Katie had recently visited. One caught his eye and he clicked it open.

"I'm gonna say thirty, there are thirty," Richard said as he thumbed through one of Katie's notebooks that he had picked up from the sofa.

"What makes you say that?" Brady asked, carefully making his way around the coffee table while holding the laptop. Richard simply held up a photocopy of Rembrandt's *Judas Repentent*. A deep red circle of ink surrounded the thirty coins near the bottom center of the page.

"Well, that explains this," Brady offered and turned the laptop around so that Richard could see a digital reproduction of the very same painting. But this version was blown up so that the coins were the dominant feature. Katie had placed digital arrows pointing to the individual coins. Three of the arrows had captions that read, "Mine!"

CHAPTER 13

"Thirty of those things out there?" Richard said as Brady drove the two of them to the hospital. "This is bad."

"We have six of them now," Brady offered, trying to keep the trepidation out of his voice. He often practiced his authoritative manner, hoping he could inspire confidence as a sheriff. He never seemed to get it quite right. "I can't believe Katie survived this long, on her own, with three."

"What are we going to do with them now?" Richard asked and Brady could see his eyes darting back toward the trunk of the car every few minutes, and he knew that Richard was feeling the pull of the coins just as he was. It took a tremendous amount of self control for him to keep driving and not pull over just to look at the coins, maybe touch them, take them and keep them safe. Richard wanted them for himself. He was going to take them and ...Brady shook his head.

Familiar dark thoughts bumped against the facts littering his brain. *Richard was a friend. He was helping. He did not want the coins. Well, he did want the coins, but that wasn't his fault. I'm a police officer. It is my job to stop this.* He felt a little bit better, a little stronger, and a lot tired. He had shaken off the pull of the coins more easily this time. He could feel his resolve returning. He offered his current thought to Richard, "It seems Katie's lockbox blocks...whatever it is these things do. I say we head to the hospital to check on Katie. We know the coins are safe, for now. We'll just not let the box out of our sight until..."

"What?" Richard asked, still glancing toward the back of the car anxiously, as if the coins would sneak up on him if he wasn't looking.

"I...don't know," Brady admitted and turned his full attention to the road ahead of him.

"Maybe it is the iron," Richard said, seemingly from out of the blue, but with more force and focus than he had been displaying just a moment before. Brady knew the type of man Richard was. Knowledge was comforting to him. He felt better about a thing if he knew something about it, and Richard must have been rolling around ideas in his professor's brain the same way the police techniques were filling Brady's mind. Staying busy was the key, Brady convinced himself. Keeping your mind on the task at hand. Not giving into the impulses that the coins promote. He could fight this, and Richard could fight too.

"What about iron?" Brady asked, hoping for a bit more knowledge that would fill in the quiet areas where the coins were seeping in.

"The lockbox. It might be iron or an iron alloy. Legends say that iron negates..." Richard stopped, seemed to consider something, then spoke again, "I can't believe I'm about to say what I'm thinking out loud."

"What? Negates what?" Brady prodded.

"I am not sure, mind you," Richard said and Brady recognized a delaying tactic in the man's demeanor. He knew that people who had something to say, but did not want to say it, often clarified what they were about to offer with phrases like, 'I don't really remember,' or 'I don't really know,' or 'I'm not sure.'

"Just say it," Brady instructed.

"Magic."

"Magic?" Brady said through clenched teeth.

"I think the coins are magic of some kind," Richard continued.

"Some kind? What kinds of magic are there?" Brady said and immediately wished he had softened the sarcasm in his tone. "I'm sorry. I don't mean to sound dismissive, but magic? Really?"

"Do you have a better explanation?" Richard asked and there was a tinge of anger to his words that swiftly softened to resignation. "Look, I get it. In grad school, whenever I brought this stuff up, people looked at me like I was crazy. Science and magic are not compatible, in their estimation, but I've seen things, I've noticed things. Here be dragons."

"What are you talking about? Dragons?"

"It was the way medieval peoples marked the unexplained. The place where their understanding became insufficient. Something unknown, unexplored. Do you see, we've ventured into a place with dragons."

"Dragons?"

"Not literal dragons," Richard began. "It's just a way to describe something we don't fully understand."

"Yeah, I get the metaphor," Brady offered, slightly offended that this college professor confused his momentary inability to absorb this new, outlandish information with an inability to understand it. "I get what you're saying, but I've seen quite a bit too. I would hazard a guess that I've seen more on the police force than you've seen in the classroom." Brady paused. His anger was getting the best of him. He was about to insult Richard. He stopped himself, sighed, and began again. "Usually, there is a perfectly rational explanation."

"I agree," Richard hurriedly explained. "I've found that to be true too. Even in the classroom." Richard said it and Brady winced. He thought about apologizing, but Richard continued, " Sorry. I know you didn't mean to insult my profession. I'm finding it difficult to keep my anger in check."

"Me too," Brady agreed. "I'm sorry too. Let's just make sure we understand each other clearly."

"Agreed," Richard took a deep breath and said, "I was just trying to say that right now, until we figure this out, it's a dragon. And it might stay that way for quite some time. Maybe forever for us."

"What?"

"Science, rationalism, can only get us so far. Even today. Scholars in the Middle Ages knew that. They knew their limitations. We should understand ours. Are you a religious man?"

"What does that have to do..." Brady's anger was rising again. He swallowed it down and waited.

"I just mean that many modern scientists say that instead of dragons, it's God. Maybe that would make you feel better. Here be God."

"That doesn't make me feel better, at all. God, dragons, I don't believe any..." Brady allowed his words to trail off. He didn't want to offend Richard, so he just stopped talking.

"I know, believe me, I know, but the supernatural, magic. Maybe that's just another way of describing a force that we don't understand...yet. Don't you think that could be possible? Look, all I'm saying is that we shouldn't just dismiss theories out of hand. Don't you agree?"

Brady didn't answer. He didn't have an answer for any of Richard's questions, or he didn't want to give the answer that sprang to mind. He couldn't really tell which. Instead, he thought about police procedure. Should he call someone? Backup? But who? The FBI? And say what? That some coins, possibly magic coins, were causing everyone to go insane? No, he would have to take care of this situation to the point where something made sense. With Richard's help, of course, because he was now feeling that he was entering into some startlingly uncharted territory where there might be dragons, or God, or coins that make you want to kill yourself or others.

"Tell me about iron and magic," Brady prompted, trying his best to adopt a professional tone and failing miserably.

"It's all throughout literature, throughout history," Richard began, a slight tinge of excitement painting his words. Brady wanted to tell him to calm down, to be professional, but he was feeling his own emotions, not excitement, but not particularly controllable either. "There are fairy tales dating back thousands of years."

"Fairy tales?" Brady said, his voice dropping too much to sound sincere. "Sorry," he said and consciously forced his voice to some semblance of respect. "So, these stories are from what? Ancient Rome? Greece?"

"Even before that," Richard said, the excitement dulled, seemingly more professional, but still present. "Before written language, maybe before spoken language."

"How does that work? Telling fairy tales without words."

"Cave paintings. This is all speculative of course, but some scholars believe that cave paintings, some dating back 40,000 years, told stories, or were instructive in some way, just like the fairy tales we know today."

Brady nodded and forced his mind to consider this possibility. He was trying desperately to keep an open mind. "Alright, so what about iron?"

"Right," Richard's voice became even more animated. "It relates to blood. Or some believe it relates to blood. Blood contains iron. You can smell it, if you smell blood. It is that metallic smell. Anyway, just like blood is the key to life in animals, many believe that minerals, such as iron, compose the blood of the earth."

"Wait, blood of the earth? People believe the earth is alive?"

"Brady," Richard said with apparent disbelief in his tone. "Of course the earth is alive. Maybe not like you imagine life, but there are many forms of life that do not necessarily conform to strict classification."

"Alright, alright," Brady acquiesced. "For the sake of argument, I will agree that the earth is alive and that iron is the blood of the earth. That still doesn't get me to magic."

"Well, just as blood has been used in ceremonies of a spiritual nature for centuries, maybe for all of human history, minerals have been used in similar ways. To heal, to wound, and to protect."

"So iron is a protection against, what exactly?" Brady asked, his memories conjuring stories from children's books. One in particular stood out. It was a picture book he had as a child that told the story of King Arthur. He remembered magicians in that story, and something about a powerful sword. "Wait, is this something like King Arthur?"

"Maybe," Richard began. "That is one interpretation of why the sword Excalibur was so powerful in the tales. So much of the story is propelled forward by magic. It would make sense that an iron alloy would...wait, and I remember my literature professor explaining parts of Beowulf too. The swords that fail to harm certain magical entities in that story could have been weak iron or an impure alloy, that kind of thing."

"Swords?" Brady spoke loudly to get Richard to focus, "What about the coins?"

"What?" Richard asked, obviously roused from deep thought. "Well, that's simple. The coins, if they are magical in nature, would be impacted by iron, or as you point out, iron alloys, like steel."

"Okay, so we just keep the coins in the lockbox and we're safe?"

"Yes, but that seems to be a temporary solution, at best," Richard offered. "We need something more permanent."

"You get on that," Brady instructed as he turned the car into the parking lot of the hospital where Katie Share had been taken.

CHAPTER 14

The hospital was cold and smelled strongly of antiseptics. Brady kept wiping his nose, but the smell had already penetrated. It felt like it was part of his nose now. He hated hospital smells. They reminded him of illness and death. As sheriff he had seen his fair share of the insides of hospitals, so he had gotten used to the sights and sounds and, especially, smells, of hospitals, at least as much as anyone gets used to hospitals. However, every now and again he would catch a whiff of something metallic and he couldn't stop thinking about blood, about violence, about death. Now, he also thought about magic and swords and dragons, about cursed objects and sacred quests.. He shivered, shook his head, and tried to focus on the task at hand.

"Do you think she'll even be awake," Richard asked as they neared the nurse's station.

"I hope so," Brady responded. "We need to know what she knows if we're gonna figure this out."

Brady walked with purpose. He, they, needed to talk to Katie Share. She was the ancient coin expert. She had managed to gather three of the coins, seemingly without leaving her apartment. They definitely needed to talk to her, but...magic? The Supernatural? God? This was not the direction he had imagined this case heading when he had left Potter's Field looking for answers.

Richard entered Katie's room first. Brady followed closely, making a mental note of the room number, 413. There was probably no reason to memorize the room number, but he felt it necessary anyway. Inside the room, there was space for only the oversized bed, where Katie breathed softly, and a single chair near the window. The curtains had been drawn and the lights were off. The antiseptic scent mingled with a soapy smell that reminded Brady of lavender and citrus, but a lavender-citrus smell that made his stomach churn just a bit. It was off, this smell, unnatural, too hospital-y. He tried to focus on his training, something solid instead of all the curses and magic swirling ephemerally through his head. He walked to the side of the bed and leaned in. Katie's eyes were closed tightly, swirling and twitching underneath her lids.

"Seems to be dreaming," Brady said as he walked to the window and opened the curtains enough to let some light in. The beam of light fell directly on Katie's unconscious face.

"Katie?" Richard whispered as he leaned over the bed. Katie's eyes fluttered open, and she screamed. The oxygen mask muffled the sound, but the panic on Katie's face was more frightening than any scream should have been. Richard stumbled backwards, nearly knocking over the moveable dinner table that was behind him. He recovered quickly though. "Katie!" Richard shouted over the sound of the woman's screaming and positioned a firm hand on his friend's shoulder. Her frantic eyes darted toward him, full of fear. "Katie, it's okay! You're okay!" he continued to shout until the woman's screams began to quiet. "You're in the hospital. You're safe."

Katie mouthed the word 'safe' underneath the foggy plastic on her face and sighed. Her hand shot up and grasped Richard's in a death grip. She shook her head violently from side to side as she repeated, "No, no, no, no..."

"It's okay, Katie," Richard soothed, as he pushed the call button for help.

"Take them away," Katie suddenly hissed through labored breaths as her free hand snatched away the oxygen mask. She began to push at invisible things that seemed to be near her face. "Please, take them."

"Take what?" Richard asked as he tried to wrestle her flailing arms to her side.

"Take them, please. I can't have them anymore."

Brady left to look for the nurse as Richard continued to try and settle Katie down, he returned quickly. "The nurse is coming with a sedative," Brady announced as he reentered the room and flanked the woman. He tried to hold one side of her while Richard held the other, but Katie was so consumed with fear that no amount of restraint seemed to help.

Both men had seen this reaction before, with Carrie back in the stairwell of the college. And Brady had seen it with Lonnie back in Potter's Field. It was the pull of the coins, but there was something different this time. In fact, Brady noted that it seemed like Katie was not trying to get back to the coins at all. Her hands were not grasping as Carrie's had done. Instead, she was pushing.

"You can't let him get me," Katie whispered in her breathless voice, her arms jutting out at awkward angles, slapping at the two men by her sides.

"Who?" Richard asked. "Who's trying to get you?"

"The gray man," Katie said with such clarity that the words reverberated around the room. "Our Heavenly Father, protect me," she sighed. And then, she fell back into unconsciousness.

A team of two nurses and three orderlies streamed into the room, but the excitement was over, for the most part. They struggled to straighten Katie's unconscious form back into her bed as Brady and Richard walked out into the hall to give them room to work.

"That was..." Richard began.

"Yeah, it was," Brady responded.

"The gray man?" Richard asked, and Brady shrugged.

Brady thought back to the man he thought he had seen standing by the road in Potter's Field after he found Lonnie and again at the college where he met Richard. If he had been asked to describe the man he thought he saw, he would say the man was gray. But the memory of the man was vague, which made him question whether he had really seen anyone. There was nothing he could have said about the man's height, build, or face. He had been trained to see details, but where this man was concerned there was only gray. *It was stress*, he thought, *too much adrenaline, too much excitement. There was no gray man watching from the side of the road, no gray man standing in the hall of the college.* He forced his mind to return to the task at hand, to keep to the facts, and he moved back to the room. Richard joined him and the two men poked their heads back through the door.

"She'll be out for a few hours," one of the nurses informed them. "We gave her a sedative to help her rest."

Brady nodded as the hospital staff went back to other duties. The room fell into a tense silence. Richard sat in the chair pulled close to the bed and Brady perched on the window sill, his eyes narrow slits of concentration. The beeping of the monitors and the hiss of the oxygen machines languidly filled the space.

"She was different," Brady began and the silence shattered. "She didn't want the coins back. She wanted us to take them."

"Yeah, I was thinking that too. She did something that broke the curse's hold on her, or changed it somehow. We need to figure out what that was. She said a little prayer before she lost consciousness. Did you hear that?"

"Yeah, she's religious, so?"

"I'm not sure," Richard admitted. "Just a theory."

"This gray man though, what do you make of that?" Brady asked, not wanting to jump to any conclusions, but fearing that he knew what Richard's answer would be. He tried once more to conjure the image of the man he had seen, or had thought he had seen. It was too indistinct, and he could identify only the color gray. He concluded that his faulty memory would be useless information to share.

Richard thought for a moment, "I've been trying to mentally cycle through all the stories I've ever read about supernatural beings. I know it's illogical, but I really have no better explanation or frame of reference. Iron, sure. Coins, absolutely. Curse, yes. A gray man? I'm just not sure."

"Best guess?" Brady prodded. "Look, I just, well, you've been...these things are..."

"I know," Richard admitted. "I'm not exactly comfortable with any of this either, you know?"

"Alright, then what are you thinking?"

"I really don't want to…"

"Come on," Brady pushed. "I'm a big boy. I can handle it."

Richard paused and took a deep breath. "There are stories. Lots of stories, from literature, from philosophy, about a man who appears to people and…tempts them. The man is often described as a gray man, or a man in gray, or wearing black or…sometimes an animal."

"Wait," Brady interrupted. "Don't tell me you think this is…what do you think this is?"

"I don't think anything. All I'm saying is that there are stories about a gray man."

"Who tempts people?"

"Yes."

"With what? He tempts them to do what?"

Richard paused again, and Brady could see his mind at work. Richard was grasping for answers, looking to the only source of information that seemed to fit the situation. He was seeing dragons everywhere. Richard continued, "Lots of times he makes bargains with them. I'm sure you've heard some of the stories. They get fame and fortune in exchange for, sometime in the future, their…"

"No, nope, no, you are not trying to tell me that these coins are from…what are you trying to tell me?" Brady could feel his grip on reality loosening as the image of the gray man became just a bit more solid in his mind, and it frightened him more than even the coins.

"Their souls, Brady. The Devil tempts them to sin and takes their souls."

"The Devil?" Brady said, the disdain clearly evident in his voice. He had no argument against Richard's theory, but that didn't mean he had to like it.

"I know how it sounds, but the literature is…" Richard began.

"Is literature. The literature is just stories. Fiction. What's happening out there," Brady pointed his finger toward the glass of the window, "That's real, and we need real answers, not stories."

"I'm trying to suggest that maybe the...stories, since they seem to have elements of what is currently happening, might also have the answers you, we, need. Most ancient stories, especially myths, have a kernel of truth at their centers."

The room grew darker as the shadow of a cloud passed in front of the sun outside the half-drawn curtains. The hiss and hum rhythm of Katie's oxygen machine filled too much of the empty space, sounding like an engine of doom revving next to the recliner. Brady's imagination filled the rest. He imagined demons waiting in every corner, in every shadow, and then dread took over for his imagination. Dread and a nagging bit of anger.

"Fine," Brady finally said, pushing the anger down as far as he could, which only allowed the dread to rear its head. "What do you wanna do? Go to a library?"

"I have a better idea," Richard offered, shaking his head.

Brady kept from commenting on the quality of Richard's ideas because he knew that his words would sound unkind, and he was no longer sure whether he would mean them to sound that way or not; instead, he followed the man from the room. He was feeling lost in this new world of curses, of devils, of monsters. He could find no internal map to follow, even one filled with dragons, so he chose to follow the other man's lead for the moment at least, which eased the dread a bit. Of course, following someone else made him uneasy in other ways. He fell back on his training once again, and he had been trained to follow the clues wherever they might lead. He just never imagined the clues to any mystery would ever lead to the devil, but he needed to trust someone. Richard would do.

The second floor hall of the hospital was nearly empty with only one nurse at a portable medicine station, making his rounds. Brady watched the nurse gather a few small paper cups onto a tray and enter a nearby room. The quietness of the hospital, complete with the mechanical noises that seemed to take up physical space, pushed down on Brady. He felt the weight of the investigation, the deaths, the danger, and he paused in his march toward more of the same. He turned away from the direction Richard was leading, for just a brief glimpse behind.

At the far end of the hall, standing in a pool of yellow light spilling from the stairwell, was a man dressed entirely in a gray flannel suit, his gray face a mask of imperceptibility. Brady gasped.

"What?" Richard asked and spun in time to see the gray clad figure disappear through the open door.

"The gray man," Brady said and sprinted toward the far end of the hall. Richard ran behind him. The stairwell reverberated with the sound of the metal door hitting the concrete wall as Brady dashed through. Richard stopped the door from slamming shut and stood with Brady on the landing.

"Which way?" Richard asked, looking at the stairs heading both up and down.

"Shhh," Brady instructed and stood still, straining his ears. He heard the noise he was looking for, a door opening upstairs. "Up!"

The two men ran up two flights, three, then to the roof access. Brady pushed through the door and the flood of natural light after so much fluorescent illumination was shocking. Richard began rubbing his eyes, immediately. Brady drew his gun from his holster and leveled it at the haze shrouded figure standing near the edge of the building.

"Police! Hold it right there," Brady said, pointing his gun at the gray man. His mind raced and he knew, intellectually, that the man hadn't really done anything to deserve a gun pointed at him, but the action felt right. It felt necessary to have a gun between him and this man.

Brady stepped into the light, gun held firmly, ready to use, and watched as the gray man raised his arms dispassionately over his head. It was then that Brady realized how gray this man truly was. It wasn't just his clothes. His eyes were gray. His hair was also gray. Not white, as gray hair often turns, but gray, with streaks of blue that made his entire head look as if it was domed with metal. The skin of his face and hands were gray as well. Not pallid, not beige, gray, like he had been devoid of oxygen for far too long, like a cadaver, a corpse. Brady was breathing heavily, Richard tried to catch his breath too. The gray man seemed perfectly relaxed.

"I believe you have something of mine," the gray man said coldly, unnervingly calmly.

"Who are you!" Brady yelled. The gray man, still holding his hands high into the daylight made no sign that he even heard Brady's question.

"I would like them back please," the man said, his voice as steely as his eyes.

"Tough!" Brady responded and looked at Richard. "Search him for weapons."

"What?" Richard asked, clearly taken aback by the request.

"I have to hold the gun," Brady said. "Search his pockets, carefully, there might be something sharp. Pat his legs to see if there's a holster."

"I assure you I have no weapons," the man said, a slight laugh in his otherwise lifeless voice.

"Thanks, but I'd like to make sure," Brady said with painfully obvious sarcasm that stood in such stark contrast to the man's gray tone that Brady wondered if he had shouted the words too loudly. He nodded toward Richard and then the man.

Richard reluctantly stepped forward and behind the man.

"Wait," Brady called. "Be careful of..."

"Right," Richard answered, nodding at Brady. He gingerly patted the coat pockets first. "I don't feel anything. No coins either." Slowly, he began to press harder on the coat pockets and the man's trouser pockets. "I don't think there's anything at all in his pockets."

"Careful, I'm ticklish," the man whispered over his shoulder, his voice rough as gravel.

Richard pulled his hand back, but then appeared to gather his courage. Brady nodded at him, and he began to roughly rummage through the man's pockets. He pulled something out of the left breast pocket. It was cylindrical, smooth. He held up a vial of yellow liquid, and Brady got a good look at it.

"What is that?" Brady asked.

"Aromatherapy oil," the man said, bowing his head toward the vial. "Have a whiff." Richard held the vial to his nose before Brady could protest and sniffed.

Richard announced, "It smells earthy and sweet, like cinnamon mixed with dirt. It reminds me of something."

"We don't need that," Brady instructed. "Put it away. Look for weapons."

Richard nodded and bent, patted the man's legs, and he put a hand into each of his pockets.

"Nothing," Richard said loudly.

"Here," Brady said as he awkwardly reached to the back of his belt while still holding the gun, leveled at the man. He produced a pair of handcuffs and threw them to Richard. "Use these."

"Surely, there's no need..." the man began.

"Quiet!" Brady shouted. "Just till we talk!"

Richard reached up and pulled the man's arms down and latched the handcuffs around his wrists, the metal of the cuffs seemed to blend with the color of the man's skin. Once the man was secure, Brady lowered his weapon.

"What were you doing at Dr. Share's room?" Brady asked.

"Who?" the man retorted, and Brady couldn't help but shiver. The colorless tone of the man's voice gave him the creeps. It had inflection, intonation, but, somehow, no emotion. No, that wasn't accurate. It had plenty of emotion, maybe too much. He couldn't say for sure what the problem was, but he knew the man's voice was entirely too unnerving.

"Dr..." Brady began, but faltered. Was the man at Katie's room? He was at the stairwell near Katie's room. Maybe he was just standing there, an innocent bystander, but then, why did he run? No, this man knew something. Brady was sure of it. "Katie Share."

"Aw, dear Katherine," the man's voice changed from gravely to lilting, but in the same unnerving, emotionless, or too emotional manner. Brady focused on each sound, each letter, each intonation, and still he couldn't identify a single, solitary, reason that the voice was so unsettling, but he came to the conclusion that there was no other way to describe the voice than by saying it was gray. The man continued, "She's...an old friend. I came to check on her well-being."

"Who are you?" Brady asked, stepping closer to the man. Richard backed away, he was holding his stomach. Brady made a mental note to ask how he was when this was over.

"I think you know," the man responded. Richard began to wretch. He turned and bent at the knees, his head dangling precariously over the edge. His thighs rested against the low ledge, but the rest of his body teetered above a six story fall.

"Richard?" Brady asked, trying to keep the gun pointed at the gray man. Richard heaved and stumbled dangerously close toward the edge. "Richard? You okay?" Brady faltered and stepped around the man to help his friend. He rushed to Richard's side and pulled him away from the ledge, patting him on the back as the other man released the contents of his stomach onto the rooftop.

"I'm fine," Richard finally said. "Don't bother with me. Watch him."

Brady turned too late. The handcuffs dangled, unlocked, from one of the gray man's outstretched hands. "For my next trick," the gray man said and then with a flourish of his other hand, he produced, from seemingly empty air, a shiny, silver coin. He placed both the handcuffs and the coin on the rooftop and turned toward the door.

Brady's mouth suddenly went dry, his head throbbed, his heart beat faster. So fast that he feared it might leap from his chest. He wanted to hold the coin so badly, just touch it to feel the cool metal, the comforting weight of it, the importance of possessing it. Just one touch. That's all he needed to feel normal, to feel complete. Just a touch. He dropped his gun next to Richard's foot and stepped forward. He knew he shouldn't, he wanted to stop, but he stepped again. And again.

***

Richard wiped his mouth, pressed his hand into his still churning stomach, and steadied himself against the roof's ledge. He scratched at his nose, the smell of the oil, or whatever was in that vial, was still lingering, sticking in his nostrils, sweet and sickening. A clatter at his feet drew his attention. Brady's gun. He lifted his eyes and saw Brady, who was moving slowly toward a glint of metal. He could feel it then, the pull of the coin scratching its way into his brain. He swallowed hard then bent to pick up Brady's gun. He fired into the sky. Brady flinched but did not turn from his inexorable walk.

"Brady!" Richard shouted. "Stop! You have to stop!"

Brady heard the words. He nodded in agreement. He should stop, he wanted to, but he couldn't. He needed the coin. He wouldn't let anyone else get it. It was his and his alone. Richard was trying to trick him, trying to get the coin for himself. He wouldn't fall for it, but Richard was not like that. He was a friend. He could trust Richard, couldn't he?

***

"Brady!" Richard called. He stepped forward, awkwardly, gathered himself and stepped again. He dropped the gun and hurried in front of the entranced man. "Brady," he said, placing each of his hands on Brady's chest and pushing. "Our Father," Richard said and nodded at Brady. "Say it with me! Our Father!"

Brady blinked and tore his gaze away from the coin. "Our Father," he said softly.

"Who art in Heaven," Richard continued.

"Who...art in...Heaven," Brady echoed and a deep breath flowed from his lips with the words.

"Hallowed be thy name," Richard prompted.

***

Prayer? Brady thought. *Why is he trying to get me to pray? It makes no sense. Wait, he wants me to give up the coin. He wants me to make a sacrifice. That's why the prayer. He's trying to trick me.*

***

Brady pushed Richard hard, and lunged for the coin. Richard recovered quickly and grabbed Brady's arms. They both fell to the hard surface of the rooftop and began to grapple. Brady was strong, much better trained in fighting, but Richard was desperate. He wrapped his arms around Brady's chest and hugged him tightly.

Centering beliefs, he thought. *That's what combats the curse. But prayer is not working. What would work?*

They continued to wrestle. Brady freed one of his arms and began to grasp for the coin. His outstretched hand was nearly touching the metal.

"Brady, you have to stop," Richard pleaded and something sharp against his chest made him wince. Brady's badge was digging into his flesh. "That's it!" He called out. "Brady, your oath of office. Say it! Recite it now!"

***

Brady stopped struggling and turned inward. The oath, his promise when he put on his badge, began with "On my honor," he whispered it, like a secret. His heartbeat slowed, just a bit. Richard was trying to help him, he could see that now. He said it again, a bit louder, "On my honor..."

"Good," Richard said. "On my honor. What's next?"

"On my honor," Brady began. " I will never betray my badge..."

"I will never betray my badge. Good, keep going."

Brady relaxed into the surface of the rooftop. He could feel Richard's weight on top of him, and it gave him strength. He took a deep breath and said, "On my honor, I will never betray my badge, my integrity, my character, or the public trust."

"Yes," Richard said. "Again."

"On my honor, I will never betray my badge, my integrity, my character, or the public trust."

***

Then, they both said it together. Then, once more. One final time, and Richard felt Brady's body completely relax under him. He rolled off and flopped onto his back, breathing heavily and wanting to sleep for a week.

Brady was next to him, breathing easily. He rolled onto his side, propping himself on an elbow and stared blankly at Richard. "I'm better."

"Stay right here," Richard instructed and, retrieving a napkin from his jacket, he hefted himself up, knelt in front of the coin and scooped it up, stuffing it quickly into his jacket pocket. He stripped off his jacket and folded it as many times as he could around the coin.

"Why am I better?" Brady said, shaking his head, rubbing his temples, and rising to his feet.

Richard looked at him and shrugged, "Prayer worked for Katie, but you needed a different centering belief."

Brady exhaled. "Centering belief?"

"Yes," Richard continued. "Something you believe in that is stronger than your greed. Luckily, you believe in that." He pointed to Brady's badge.

"How do you know that?"

Richard shrugged and said, "It's in a lot of the literature."

"So, the big secret to overcoming this curse is to just repeat a personal mantra?"

Richard shrugged again and headed back through the still open door. "Come on," he called over his shoulder. "We need to check on Katie."

***

Brady stayed behind for a moment, looking for any trace of the gray man, finding none, but also pondering what had just happened. His rational mind was reeling, unanchored, searching for some mooring, some port of sanity. There was nothing. So, he retrieved his handcuffs and gun before following Richard back into the hospital.

CHAPTER 15

Richard and Brady went together to secure the new coin in the trunk of Richard's car, in the lead lockbox before heading back to Katie. The hospital room was quite a bit brighter when the two men re-entered.The shades had been opened, the lights were on, and Katie was sitting up and looking around excitedly.

"You did it," she said as Richard rushed to her side. She held out a trembling hand. He grasped it, patted it tenderly, and smiled.

"Did what?" he asked. Brady inched closer in behind him.

"You took them away," Katie continued. "I feel...so much better."

"You mean the coins?" Brady asked from the corner. Katie glanced around Richard and eyed Brady's uniform suspiciously.

"This is Brady, uh, Sheriff Edwards. He's been helping me, or I've been helping him to do, or maybe find..." Richard stammered.

"Good. Good. You'll need help, Richard." Katie interrupted and her head flopped back onto the pillow. "That was my big mistake, thinking I could do it alone. I've been fighting for so long, so long..."

"What do you mean, fighting?" Richard asked as he began busily fluffing her pillows and rearranging the sheets. Brady smiled at how he fussed, but quickly re-focused on Katie's words.

"The gray man," Katie said weakly. Richard turned and looked at Brady who had stepped closer. The two men hovered over Katie as she spoke.

"Who is he?" Brady asked, absentmindedly smoothing out the sheet on his side of her bed..

Katie's head struggled to rise again. "You've seen him?"

"Yes, here. He was here," Richard said before Brady had a chance to warn him that it might not be a good idea to tell her that the man who had been tormenting her was in the hospital.

"I could feel him," Katie continued, calmly, detached, her eyes darting from side to side. "But he's gone. You did something?"

Richard and Brady shared another look. Brady's brow furrowed and rose with a question. Richard shrugged in response. "At least he's gone now," Richard offered.

"But he'll be back," Katie said, her eyes welling with tears, her hands trembling. "He always comes back."

"Do you need police protection?" Brady interjected.

"He won't be back for me. You took them. You took the coins. He'll come back for you." Katie's eyes closed involuntarily, and she drifted off into a peaceful sleep.

Brady thumbed through the papers he had gathered at Katie's apartment as she slept and Richard fretted over her. He looked for any kind of clue to the gray man's identity, other than the one he'd been offered, but the papers were not as helpful as he had hoped. They began with cogent, solid, casual observations of the coins, and they seemed so much like the notes he would take when investigating a case. The notes mentioned the coins' composition, engravings, the possible minting dates, etc. Then the notes became peppered with the same paranoia he had observed in others, and had felt himself.

She wrote about a myth regarding thirty pieces of silver, tracing its origins as best she could, about a man who possessed the coins and grew so large with gluttony that when he died suddenly on a trip, he blocked an entire cart path. The myth was disturbing, even with its obvious, less-enlightened attempts at humor, but then her writing would veer off onto descriptions of the gray man standing outside her apartment window and worries about neighbors breaking in to steal the coins while she slept. At one point, she seemed to suggest that a stray cat had intentions of carrying off a coin. After that, the notes were difficult to decipher.

He moved on to her laptop files and confronted similar difficulties. He had hoped that the files would give some indication of how she had managed to survive so long, nearly two years, with a stockpile of coins when everyone else he had known to come into contact with even one had died shortly after. The only clue he got was that she offered prayers of strength, daily at first, then toward the end of the files, hourly, every few minutes, constantly. Her notes about the coins included her typed prayers, which often interrupted a thought she was having about the historical implications of the coins. One file was nothing more than a plaintive plea for help from any angel or saint that might be nearby or listening in.

Through the fog of paranoia and the distraction of prayer, he was able to determine that several of the myths regarding the coins were either, according to Katie's research, woefully inaccurate or completely fictitious. But there were some that seemed to, again according to Katie, have a basis in fact. Gems of truth hidden within mountains of exaggerations. How had Richard put it? *A kernel of truth at their center.* One thing remained consistent in her analysis of the stories though— there was always a supernatural entity bent on using the coins to foment chaos.

"This is pointless," Brady said after nearly two hours of silence. He was tense, needing to move, to do something, anything. "We need to talk to her."

"She needs to rest," Richard retorted and the room fell back into a tense quiet.

Brady broke the silence, but with a whisper, "So, the story I heard in Sunday school that Judas donated the coins to the church was, what? Wrong?" He tried to sound earnest and not sarcastic.

"Maybe, maybe not," Richard began cryptically. He had one of Katie's private journals open on his lap. He had pulled a chair from the hall and had squeezed in between Katie's bed and the various machines that surrounded her. Brady realized Richard had been studying the notes as well, nestled in his tiny crook of space. "Katie was investigating the various stories. It seems that quite a few of them were, at least partially, true."

"Yeah, I got that too, but how can that be? There's only true or not true. Isn't there?"

"Not when dealing with ancient history. Usually there's possible, probable, impossible, or varying degrees of all of the above."

"How can you stand it?" Brady asked, closing the laptop and placing it onto the floor next to his chair. "The uncertainty?"

"I don't need to be certain, just thorough." Richard's answer made Brady frown involuntarily. He wanted certainty. He craved it. In his line of work, certainty was the preferred state. Thorough, yes. Absolutely. Thorough, of course. But leaving open ended questions meant that a criminal was likely to go free. He couldn't abide accepting uncertainty.

"Richard?" Katie's voice pierced Brady's brooding. He jumped up and rushed to her side.

"I'm here," Richard said, jumping up and bending close to her head.

"We need to prepare," Katie said, her voice stronger than it had been earlier.

"Prepare for what?" Brady asked as he joined Richard in bending down to her.

"What I tell you next will mean that you will have to confront the gray man again. You need to prepare." Katie said as she struggled to lift herself into a sitting position. She struggled and then fell back into her pillow. "I keep forgetting how much weight I've gained in the past two years," she said, lifting her arms and grabbing the bar dangling over her. Richard steadied the bar as she pulled against her own weight. "I was never a thin woman, mind you," she continued as she struggled, Richard offering help where he could, Brady lending a steadying hand on her back.. "But this...this was a direct result of the coins' influence." She achieved a semi-upright position and tried to get comfortable.

"Tell us," Brady prompted. He had forced himself to stay calm through the readjustment in the bed, but his patience was wearing thin.

"What is it that you need to tell us?" Richard asked much more evenly than Brady. He held up a hand in Brady's direction, a clear suggestion to calm down.

"I need you to understand what you're dealing with here." Katie began, as she tried to rearrange her hospital gown to cover more of her. It was not working. Richard helped by pulling up a sheet from the side of the bed. "The hunger. Even through the lead of the lockbox, I felt it. I fought it, everyday I fought against it. And everyday I gave in. Don't you see?" Her voice became plaintive, agitated. "That's how he works. He finds a weakness and he picks at it and picks at it until...you give in."

"The gray man?" Richard asked as Katie fell silent. She nodded.

"Who is he?" Brady asked. Katie shook her head.

"I don't know who he is. I suspect, as I'm sure you do, Richard, but I'm not sure. But that's not what I need you to know. Who, or what he is is not important." Katie stopped talking long enough to make sure the men were paying close attention. "Now, I'm going to tell you where you can find the rest of the coins," she offered and exhaled a long, steady breath for the first time in nearly two years.

"You know where the rest of these coins are?" Brady asked excitedly. This was the break he had been waiting for. Getting a coin here and there, usually attached to a dead body, was not what he considered to be the preferred method of collection. If there was even a chance of wrapping up this investigation sooner rather than later, he was more than eager to get started.

"I do, but it won't be easy to get to them," Katie began. Her voice was strong and steady. She reached for a cup of water on her bedside table. "Water," she whispered, taking the cup from Richard who was already offering it. "One drink and my stomach settles. I'm not hungry. I might never be hungry again." She crossed the fingers on both hands and lifted them toward the ceiling.

"If we can get these coins out of circulation then we need to..." Brady began but felt his anxiety was showing too much. He didn't want them thinking that he was under the coins' influence. He just wanted the deaths to stop. He wanted to go home, and he wanted the world to be solid again.

"We've come this far. We've seen, well, we want to help," Richard offered.

Katie nodded. She paused, breathed once, then again. "There's a man. A horrible, greedy man. A collector. He has at least twenty of the coins."

"Twenty?" Richard asked, quickly doing the math in his head. "But we only have seven. That leaves three unaccounted for."

"You have seven?" Katie asked, her eyes wide and fearful.

"Yes," Brady responded. "I gathered three at crime scenes back home in Potter's Field. We got your three from your lockbox, and the...man left one on the roof."

"Hmm," Katie began. "That's bad."

"What?" Richard prompted.

"I knew that there were some out in the world. There was no way to track them until the deaths started in Virginia. The gray man kept me informed about the deaths. He loved to recount every detail," Katie began. "So I knew that there was someone gathering them, the gray man was getting desperate for mine, you see?"

"Yes," Brady interjected. "Like I said, I gathered three at crime scenes."

"Right," Katie continued, obviously deep in thought. "Your three, my three, the collector's twenty. The one you got from the gray man. That just leaves the ones in the museum."

"The museum?" Richard asked.

"The Smithsonian," Katie said firmly and her brow furrowed in thought.

"Then, they should be safe," Richard said with a hint of uncertainty.

"Yes, but if the gray man had one, then..." Katie began.

"How could he have gotten them out of the Smithsonian?" Brady asked, anger tinting his words. "That's not possible."

"I suppose I could have miscounted," Katie offered. "Maybe there were only ever three in the museum, not four."

"Or maybe the gray man still has three more," Richard said sadly.

Brady, once again battling his frustration, began, "Well, we do what we can and worry about more coins later. Tell us where to find this collector."

Richard paused at the hospital doors. The rain was falling heavily. He leveled a hand across his forehead in a vain attempt to keep spots off his glasses. Brady paid no mind to the rain. He barreled ahead toward the parking lot. Richard hurried to catch him.

"We gonna drive straight there?" Richard asked as he slid into the passenger's seat and Brady shoved the car into drive.

"Yep. Why not?" Brady was driving a bit recklessly, he knew, but the adrenaline in his veins was still very much present, and he wanted to get these coins before anyone else died.

"We could try to come up with a plan or a story or something."

"Here's the story we give him. A very dangerous man, dressed in gray, is after these coins, Mr. Quince, the richest man in America, and unless you give us these coins, oh very rich and powerful Mr. Quince, you're very likely to be the next one to turn up dead."

Richard turned and looked out the window and whispered, "I think he's only like sixth or seventh richest."

"What?" Brady asked, his voice raised and sharp.

Richard changed tactics, "Brady, I can see you're obviously upset, and really, who can blame you? This whole thing is..." he paused, shifted ideas, and continued, "...but storming ahead with no regard to, well, anything is not the best course of action."

"Is that your professor's voice?" Brady asked, giving Richard a sideways glance.

"Well, yes," Richard began, a little less lecture-y, but still very professorial. "When confronting an agitated person, whether a student who doesn't understand the assignment or a police officer feeling frustrated with the speed of an investigation, I have found it is best to use cool logic and calm tones."

"Well, stop it. I'm not one of your students, and I'm fine." The finality of Brady's words came into question as he continued almost immediately with much more gentle intent. "I'm sorry. I didn't mean to snap. It's just all this...whatever this is, is starting to get to me. I'm not that good with supernatural stuff, y'know?"

"I don't know anyone who is good with it. I know people who think they are, but I don't believe that they have ever really encountered it. We're both just doing the best we can."

"Why are you doing this?" Brady asked as he tried to punch in the address Katie had given them into his GPS while narrowing avoiding ramming into a parked car on the side of the road..

"Let me do that," Richard offered and took over the GPS.

"Thanks. But seriously, why are you doing this? I have...it's my job. But you? You could have just given me Katie's address and called it a day."

Richard finished entering the address and the mechanical voice of the GPS prompted them to continue for 27 miles. Richard sat back and said, with a pensive air, "That's a fair question. I'm not trained for investigating crimes. I'm trained for researching ancient stories, which I suppose is a bit similar, in intent if nothing else. It doesn't make a lot of sense for me to inject myself into this situation, does it?."

"Don't get me wrong," Brady continued. "I'm glad you're here. I mean, your background and all. The things you know. I couldn't even, I would never have thought to, y'know?" Brady could feel himself blushing. He cleared his throat and gripped the wheel firmly.

"I'm glad I'm here too." Richard offered, a smile etched across his face. His hand went out toward Brady's arm, but he pulled it back. Brady noticed. Then, Richard turned to look out of the window and said, "I need to know for sure."

Brady could hear the longing in Richard's voice. It was the same thing he felt when trying to solve a particularly difficult case. He needed certainty, he longed for answers, he hungered for resolution. He prompted, "What do you need to know?"

Richard turned back to him and Brady could feel his piercing eyes on him. When Richard spoke, there was desire in his words, "I need to know if the stories, if the myths could be, partially, true or at least based in truth." His words became plaintive, "I spend all my time sitting in dim rooms translating ancient writings or examining artifacts or trying to make sense of other people's research. But this...this is different. This is happening now. I need to know. And I think we are traveling toward answers."

"But you said that myths have a kernel of truth."

"Yes, I said that. It's a good line that nearly everyone in the field has used at one time or another, but the truth is that we doubt just like everyone else."

Brady thought for a long moment, "And this stuff, all this that's happening right now, it's, what? A way for you to justify your life's work?"

"No!" Richard exclaimed, clearly offended by the assertion.

"I didn't mean..."

"Maybe," Richard interjected, clearly deflated. He turned and stared out of the passenger side window. Brady nodded slowly and took a left turn that the mechanical voice suggested. They traveled on toward downtown.

CHAPTER 16

Abraham Quince had built a business through shady means and even shadier bank loans. He was now one of the wealthiest men in the world and also one of the most corrupt. Everyone knew his crimes; no-one seemed to care. He owned a building near the downtown area of D.C. It housed business headquarters, a coffee shop, a very successful restaurant, and a few apartments. He had a personal residence on the top floor, one of many, and one of the most secure. It was fairly difficult to get to. There was only one elevator in the building that went to the residential floors and then only one elevator from there that went to the top floor. In front of each of these elevators was a security desk.

It was easy enough to get to the residential areas. The guards made them sign in, checked their identifications, and questioned them just a bit. Soon, they were heading down a long corridor toward the second security desk, and Brady could feel his anxiety growing. His mystery sense was working overtime. Something was wrong, he could feel it, and the tingle of longing, of desire, of need had also returned.

"Do you feel that," Brady asked as they rounded a corner and saw the security desk at the end of the hall in front of an elevator.

"The coins," Richard responded. "They are here. Close."

"Yeah, and I bet..." Brady's words caught in his mouth as he saw a security guard lying unconscious behind the desk. He rushed around and felt for a pulse. There was no pulse, but there was a large pool of blood around his head. "Dead."

"The gray man?" Richard asked. "Or Quince?"

"Not sure. He was shot. That's clear enough," Brady took the guard's sidearm and handed it to Richard who held it out with two fingers like he would hold a stinky diaper on the way to the trash. "We're going to need that," Brady said, nodding to the gun. Richard frowned but took a firmer hold.

"You think they killed each other, for the coins?" Richard asked, now holding the gun like he was holding a dinner plate that he had overfilled at the buffet. Both hands flat, the gun sitting on top,, and Brady could not help but shake his head.

"Won't know until we get up to the penthouse." Brady took the key card attached to the guard's belt and used it to open the elevator. Inside, they pressed the button, the highest button. "The elevator doesn't stop at any of these floors?"

"I guess not," Richard responded. Brady watched the indicator lights flare one at a time and wondered about emergency fire routes, maybe there was a way to get off the elevator before the penthouse, sneak up through a stairwell, something, but the lights kept lighting and the elevator kept rising. They were going all the way to the penthouse, no way out of it now. He took the gun in Richard's hand, turned it, pressed Richard's hand onto the grip, pointed it toward the door, and looked firm and serious. Richard nodded and began to hold the gun in a semi-proper manner.

"Alright, so, what's the plan?" Brady asked as a muzak version of "Don't Fear the Reaper" played in the background.

"Plan? Why're you asking me?" Richard exclaimed, pointing the gun at Brady for just a second before realizing and then pointing it back at the door. "What makes you think I have a plan?".

"You said we needed a plan."

"I don't have a plan. You're the police. You don't have a plan?"

"Listen. I have been out of my depth since, well, probably since the beginning, but now I realize it. You know more about this supernatural stuff and such, so what about you taking the lead? What should we do?"

Richard clenched his teeth, but spoke clearly and plainly. Brady had to admire his composure. "We could tell him, Quince, that we have other coins."

"And if he's the one who killed the guard?"

"Then, he attacks us and you stop him. Y'know, with your police training stuff."

Brady looked at Richard with a very impassive face, then he blinked far too long and began, "Police training stuff?"

"Yeah, you're trained to take down bad guys, right? So, we tell Quince we have the other coins, maybe the rest of the coins. That would appeal to his collector's side, the curse would kick in, and when he attacks, you, we, I can probably help, take him down."

Brady stood quietly as the elevator continued to rise. One floor, two floors, Brady knew there were a half-dozen or more residential floors between them and the penthouse. He waited one more floor, "And if it is the gray man?"

It was Richard's turn to stand in silence for a floor at least.

"Katie said she thinks Quince has twenty coins," Brady broke the silence and changed the subject. They would just have to play this by ear. There was no preparing for whatever waited on the top floor. "The two of us have been having a rough time with three or four. Katie nearly died with just three."

"How has he survived with twenty?" Richard finished Brady's thought. "There was a story in Katie's journals about a rich man who wanted to collect the coins, just like Abraham Quince. The man was so consumed with amassing the coins that he spent his entire fortune trying to get more of them. He died a pauper."

"What does that mean?" Brady asked. "I thought the coins made you greedy, paranoid."

"I think it's more than that. I think they play on the holder's particular weakness, his personal vice. Most of us have a bit of a greedy impulse, a possessive nature, but not all of us. I think for Quince, it was the collecting, not the possessing."

"That doesn't make sense," Brady said, eyeing the elevator lights. They were almost to the penthouse.

"Well, I think the others, and us, we weren't even aware that there were coins in the first place. They, and we at first, thought there was just the one so they, and we, were consumed with keeping it, just it. But Quince knew how many there were."

"And Katie knew too," Brady continued. "That's why she was able to resist the three she had."

"And we know now, which might be why we were able to resist the coin on the rooftop and the stockpile we have in the trunk. Our subconscious minds are wanting to gather all of them," Richard admitted.

"You ready?" Brady asked as the final light flared, the elevator dinged, and the doors slid open. A flurry of paper and other debris swirled around them. "What the...?" he shouted over the klaxon of an alarm. He leveled his firearm and inched forward, indicating that Richard should stay in the elevator, but he jumped out as the doors began to close. He was waving his own gun haphazardly around the room. Brady had given it to him for protection but was now wondering if that had been a mistake. He grabbed the gun and held it steady out in front of Richard. Richard nodded and then let out a breath, steadied himself, and fell into line next to Brady.

"What's happened?" Richard asked.

"Stay back, be ready," Brady said and Richard slowed but continued to follow. They stepped over bodies, three security guards and at least one police officer had fallen just outside the elevator, and Brady bent to search for a pulse at each one.

"Is it the gray man?" Richard asked as they both continued to inch forward. The alarm was louder now.

Brady motioned once more for Richard to stay put. Instead, Richard crept up behind him, so close that Brady worried about tripping. Brady shook his head, but only slightly. He continued down the hall, Richard right behind him, and into the large living area. The alarm was nearly deafening now. Richard finally hung back as Brady gently pushed him against the wall. He then made his way along the wall toward the rest of the apartment. Suddenly, a shot rang out and something struck the painting hanging near Brady's head. He dove behind a nearby sofa and shouted, "Police! Drop your weapon!"

The only response was another shot. Richard hugged the wall nearer the elevator, just out of sight of where the shots were coming from. He was safe, for now. Brady continued to shout orders, but the shooter was still firing. The sounds of gunfire seemed to be getting closer. Was the shooter trying to make it to the elevator? If so, the only thing standing in his way was...

"Stop! Police!" Brady shouted again. Then, a man, wide-eyed and frantic, darted from behind overturned furniture, rounded the corner, and slammed headlong into Richard. The two stumbled backwards, one gun flew backwards, landing near one of the dead guards. A metal box slammed onto the tile floor. Brady didn't see where it came from. The fleeing man fell on top of Richard, hard, and Richard started gasping for breath. The man grabbed him, struggled into a kneeling position, and pressed the gun to Richard's temple.

Richard grabbed at the man's wrist and struggled to get the gun from his grasp. A shot rang out and Richard fell forward, the man's hand still in his grasp. The man jerked forward, fighting against Richard's pull. Brady rushed in, trying desperately to get to the gun and get Richard out of harm's way. The man's attention turned fully to Brady as Richard's grip failed and he rolled out of the way. The man straightened and held the gun in front of him.

Brady was now face-to-face with the man, and the gun. Brady used his momentum to close the distance and soon, they were each grabbing for the gun, kicking and pushing, contorted with the effort, but when Brady looked into the man's face, purple and flush with rage, he could see the abnormal dilation of his pupils, a sign of recent head trauma. He used that information, slammed his forearm into the man's temple and readjusted the grip of his right hand, closing it around the hot metal of the barrel and ignoring the pain. He pulled with all his might. The man released the gun and lunged at Brady, teeth first, gnashing and snapping like a feral animal. Brady reacted out of instinct and punched hard. The man tumbled onto his side and was still.

Brady remained on his back, breathing sporadically, the adrenaline still in effect and he saw Richard out of the corner of his eye. With effort, he sat up. Richard seemed to be trying to gather something into the metal box that lay open on the marble floor.

Brady exhaled, willed his strength back, and struggled to his feet. He shuffled over and, putting a hand on Richard's shoulder, asked, "You okay?"

Richard whirred on him, his eyes wild, before he turned his attention back to the metal box. Brady stepped back and then saw the silver glint in the light. He gasped, preparing to fight Richard, but there was something different this time. He felt the familiar pang of desire. He wanted the coins, he needed the coins, but he didn't want to fight Richard for them.

"Help me," Richard yelled too loudly, and Brady noticed for the first time that the alarms had stopped.

Turning off the alarms, Brady understood, meant that the other security guards were on their way, or the police, probably both, and the coins were exposed. Brady flung himself to the ground and began to shovel the coins into the metal box. They latched it closed just as the elevator doors opened and a host of uniformed police officers streamed out.

A cacophony of voices filled the penthouse as the officers filed in and went in every direction. They took stock of everything they could understand and scurried about until everything was under control. Richard and Brady were handcuffed and repositioned on the sofa. The man who had attacked them, now identified as Abraham Quince, was handcuffed and was lying face down on the marble floor just outside the elevator. He was snarling and trying to bite anyone who came near.

"Go over it again," one of the officers instructed and Richard cocked his head and listened intently.

"Could you speak up," Brady offered. "He had a gun shot near his ears. His hearing isn't quite back yet." Richard stared at Brady, then nodded at the officer.

"So, you just happened to come here when Mr. Quince," the officer gestured toward the man on the floor, "went crazy and killed a half dozen security guards? Wounded, what? Half a dozen more?"

"Yes!" Richard shouted, then he grimaced and said, in a normal tone, "Yes."

"And you're a sheriff from Virginia?" the officer continued.

"Yes." Brady was watching the metal box they had pushed to the far end of the area in front of the elevator. None of the officers had even seemed to notice it yet, but they would soon.

"A little out of your jurisdiction, ain't ya?"

Brady could hear the officer's reluctance to accept their story. He knew from his own experience interviewing witnesses that the officer completely knew that they were hiding something. He thought about possible explanations he could offer to help the situation, to help the officer accept the story, but he truly could not think of one that would allow them to leave the apartment with the box of coins, which they definitely could not leave in the apartment with all these people and their guns.

A second officer came over and whispered something. The first officer, whose name tag read 'Williams,' nodded. "Seems like you're mostly telling the truth," Officer Williams said. "Security in the building puts you in the elevator when the alarm starts. We have cameras in the living area corroborating your story of not being involved and just getting attacked." He bent and unlocked the handcuffs behind Brady and then Richard. "Still doesn't explain what you were doing here."

"I told you," Brady started, his exasperation showing. "We were investigating some mysterious deaths and we were told that Mr. Quince might have some information that would..."

The doors of the elevator hissed opened once again and the gray man stepped out. Brady stopped talking and tensed up. Richard shot to his feet.

"I'll take it from here, officer," the gray man said as he handed Officer Williams an open leather wallet.

"FBI?" Officer Williams said, obviously surprised.

"That's right," the gray man said. "I'll be taking these two into custody. You can deal with Mr. Quince."

"Agent Appal…Appollo…" Officer Williams stuttered, trying to read the identification card he was still holding.

The gray man took the wallet from Officer Williams and said, "Special Agent Apollyon. It's Greek."

Richard began shuffling to the side of the coffee table in front of them as if he might make a mad dash for freedom, so Brady stood and held his arm. His eyes went unbidden to the metal box and he forced himself to look away. He saw that Richard was looking straight at the box. He squeezed hard and Richard looked at him. He shook his head and Richard nodded.

"Sheriff Edwards, Professor Stanley," the gray man, Apollyon, said with a satisfied air. "I've been trying to speak with you. So pleased to make your acquaintance."

"So, you're FBI?" Brady asked, training his eyes on the man, as the other officers in the room began milling about, waiting for the investigators. They were running out of time. When the investigators got to the scene, they would find the metal box in no time. They would open it, and the entire penthouse would be filled with vicious, desperate, angry people with guns.

Apollyon merely smiled, "Where are the coins?"

"What coins?" Brady asked. He could feel Richard tense beside him. The box was against the far wall, directly in front of them, and just in front of the elevator. Brady's mind began to race with possibilities. He ran scenarios in his head and most of them ended with his death, Richard's death, both of their deaths, and some ended with just really bad injuries for each of them. They would need some sort of miracle to get the coins out of this room.

"You know," Apollyon began. "When I visited Mr. Quince last night and opened the lockbox where he kept the coins, I had no idea that he would try to murder his entire security team." The man smiled a gray-toothed smile and looked around at the remains of the pandemonium that had been raging just recently. "He nearly succeeded. I have to say, I'm impressed."

"How are you an FBI agent?" Brady asked, trying to keep the gray man's attention.

"I'm not," Apollyon admitted. "Mr. Quince had this made for me." He held up the leather wallet with his FBI credentials inside and then tossed it onto the floor next to Brady. "I bet he spent a pretty penny on it; I only paid one coin for them," the man winked. "Where are the coins?"

"Why do you want them?" Brady asked.

"They're mine," the words came out with force but no emotion. Brady instinctively shuddered in spite of consciously trying very hard to avoid doing just that.

"You," Apollyon pointed at Richard. "You touched one, didn't you?"

Richard didn't speak. He opened his mouth then closed it again and stared blankly ahead, right at the metal box. Apollyon's brow furrowed, his eyes narrowed and he began to turn and follow Richard's gaze.

"What are you?" Brady said excitedly, loudly, angrily, trying to gain the gray man's attention. A few of the officers nearby turned only briefly and then shuffled away.

Apollyon turned to Brady and smiled a very unfriendly smile, "I'm not telling. Why don't you make a guess?"

Brady looked around at the officers, still milling around the room, some were on their cell phones, some were looking at the expensive knick-knacks littering the room, and no one was paying them the slightest attention.

"Did you do something to them?" Brady asked, nodding toward a group of officers who were quietly talking in a corner.

"No need," Apollyon said with a dismissive wave of his hand. "They only see what they want. They only hear what they want. But not you."

Brady shuddered again. Apollyon's voice was like a sudden chill wind on a hot day and Brady was finding it difficult not to run to protect the coins. He knew that Richard must be feeling the same because he had been continually inching his way around Apollyon. He very nearly had a straight shot to the box and Brady could see that he was preparing to make a run for it.

"Who's in charge here?" a booming voice entered the room. Brady looked and saw another impossibly gray man, this one in a tweed sport coat, exit the elevator. Apollyon sighed an exasperated, angry sigh, and turned.

"Erastus," Apollyon said by way of greeting. "So nice you could join us."

"Apollyon," the new arrival said. "I should have known you would be here already.."

Brady moved to the side, grabbed Richard by the arm, and began a slow, deliberate walk toward the long wall leading to the elevators.

"You shouldn't be here," Apollyon said as the two gray men began to circle one another. "This isn't your concern."

Brady tugged Richard, who had become intensely interested in the two gray men. He stood, his mouth agape, and stared at them. Brady kept pulling, slowly, continuously, until they were nearly around the two men who seemed to be squaring off for a fight. When they neared the elevators, Brady pulled on Richard's arm a little harder.

"Of course it's my concern," Erastus countered. "It has always been my concern."

"No, it hasn't!" Apollyon shouted, his calm demeanor shattered and he became like a petulant child, complete with clenched fists and stamping feet.

Brady had pulled Richard very near the elevator. The box was just a bit beyond that. A mad dash could work from this distance, especially with the gray men consumed with each other, but the elevator doors were closed. He needed them to be open.

"Don't yell at me," Erastus responded calmly, with an even tone, but there was danger underneath his words. Brady watched the officers in the room, and they were acting as if the gray men didn't exist, except one or two who glanced at the men arguing and then shrugged and turned away. Suddenly, the elevator light came on and a beep sounded. The doors began to slide open. Brady shoved Richard toward the elevator and lunged for the box. Richard, once inside, held the door as Brady grabbed the box and flung his own body inside.

"Stop!" Apollyon shouted with a voice, no longer gray but full of grit and rage as he ran toward the elevator.

Richard hit the ground floor button over and over as Apollyon closed in. Erastus, momentarily caught off guard, seemed to come to a realization and grabbed at Apollyon's shoulders. The two gray men tugged at each other, wrenching and writhing, as they both advanced on the elevators.

"Push the button! Push the button!" Brady yelled.

"I am!" Richard responded and he pushed the ground floor button five more times, then he realized that pushing the button for closing the doors might work better. He did and the doors started to close..

The gray men struggled toward them. Apollyon thrust his hand through the doors just as they were closing, causing them to open once more. Brady slapped at the gray man as Erastus fought to pull him back and take his place.

"Push the button!" Brady shouted again.

"Stop telling me to push the button!" Richard was continuously pushing the button. "I know to push the button!"

Erastus won a momentary victory as he pulled Apollyon out of the elevator and flung him to the floor. He lunged for the elevator himself. The doors closed just as Erastus, his face contorted with rage, roared. His voice was the only thing that traveled through the closing doors.

"What just happened?" Richard asked as he hugged the metal box close to his chest.

"There's not just one gray man. There are two, or more maybe, I don't know," Brady admitted.

"We have all the coins?" Richard held out the metal box.

"I'm not sure," Brady took the box and sighed. "We're going to have to count them."

The two men stood in silence as the elevator descended. Brady held the metal box in front of him as if it were a delicate, fragile thing that could shatter at any moment. As the elevator came to a stop and the doors slid open, the two men walked hastily, still in silence, to their car.

"Should we count them now?" Richard asked.

"Just get in the car," Brady instructed as he opened the trunk and flung the box into it. They began to drive, not really in any particular direction, just away from the building, and more in circles than any-thing, but they were slowly gaining distance from the gray men and that was the important thing.

"What now?" Richard asked as they passed by the same gas station for the second time.

"I don't know," Brady admitted. He wanted to just keep driving and avoid having to ever stop and confront the gray men again, but he knew that was unrealistic. He needed a plan. He needed help. He had no idea how to get either.

"We need gas," Brady announced as they pulled into the familiar station.

"I really think we should count the coins. I could do it," Richard offered.

"Not alone," Brady instructed.

"Agreed."

Brady filled the tank and pulled the car to the side of the station. He retrieved both the metal box and their own lockbox from the trunk and handed both to Richard in the passenger's seat. Richard took a deep breath, whispered a calming prayer, and opened the metal box. The rush of desire was forceful. Brady watched, detached, as his hand shot forth and grasped at the coins. He pulled back quickly.

"You okay?" Richard asked.

"Yeah, I just, yeah, I'm fine now." Brady closed his eyes and recited his oath of office silently. *On my honor,* he began, *I will never betray my badge, my integrity, my character, or the public trust.* And he continued as Richard counted. He got through the oath three times before Richard interrupted his fourth recitation.

"We have twenty-seven coins." Richard suddenly said as he slammed the heaviest of the metal boxes closed. "They are here now. All of them. In this one box." He was breathing erratically, sweating and shivering, shaking just a bit.

"Okay," Brady responded.

"The other three, we think, are in the Smithsonian, right?" Richard asked. He was swallowing hard and too often as he pressed down on the top of the box.

"Yes, that's what Katie told us."

"Then I think I know what we have to do next."

"I'm listening," Brady offered. He started the car and continued to drive in ever expanding circles.

"We have to rob the Smithsonian."

Brady swerved the car but quickly recovered. "We are not robbing the Smithsonian," he said with a finality that did not allow for argument.

"No, listen," Richard prompted. "I have a plan."

CHAPTER 17

Part 2

Interlude

The warehouse annex of the Smithsonian was a large, nondescript complex of buildings near the outskirts of Baltimore, Maryland. Cherylyn Rodriguez began working at the annex soon after completing her Master's in Art History. She loved working among the rows and rows of stored artifacts from bygone eras, but her favorite spot was the secret vault where all of the most valuable artifacts were kept. That is, the vault had been her favorite spot until a couple of weeks ago when the row that housed the Ancient Roman art became her absolute, undisputed favorite.

Cherylyn now loved nothing more than to stroll down the Roman aisle and pull open drawers containing bits of pottery and pieces of mosaic; however, it was the coin drawer that always called to her. The Roman coin collection that was not currently on display featured coins of various, and expected, sizes, but it was the colors that the metals had become over the ages that entranced her. The gold had become ruddy, earthy, pitted with age; the bronze was deep, rich, like milk chocolate; but the silver shone and glittered like stars caught in water. In fact, she loved one particular silver coin above all. It was a bit larger than a quarter, with the nearly indistinct portrait of a Roma, the Roman goddess who was the embodiment of Rome. pressed into it. It amused her to think that most people would mistake the portrait for an emperor, or some other important man, but it was a goddess. The edges were roughly hewn and a bit jagged. In truth, the physical characteristics of the coin was very much like all the other coins in the collection, but there was just something about this particular one.

She had been drawn to it, seemingly for no apparent reason, from the moment she opened the drawer on her very first inventory after being hired, but in the past few months, really the past few weeks, she had found herself inventing reasons to open the drawer containing the coin, drawer number 7413. She would find a reference to a coin that had been overlooked during the last inventory, and she thought it must be in drawer 7413. She was tasked with finding some Greek pieces for a traveling exhibit, and she figured there might be some misplaced in drawer 7413. Sometimes, she just took a break and went to stare into the drawer. It was starting to affect her work.

Once or twice, she had thought about telling someone in administration about the coin and how much it affected her and how much visitors to the museum would love to see it. The appeal of the coin, the interest it prompted in her was so very strong, and she was sure that others, patrons in the museum, would feel the same. Having the coin on display could promote interest in ancient artifact preservation, but at the same time, she felt a driving need to protect the coin. Others would want to possess it, not to share it, and that was something she could not abide. Art, especially ancient art, was for everyone. It was the core of her being that told her this.

She stood in front of the drawer 7413 as she had on many other occasions, several just this past week, but something was different today. The allure of the coin was greater, the pull was substantial, nearly supernatural, and she pulled the drawer with every intent to snatch the coin, to run out of the annex and into the world that wanted her coin. She would fight to protect it, to keep it safe, and she would never stop. She shook her head. She told herself that this desire was simply her imagination, her frustration with the administration's reticence to display more artifacts, with budget cuts that suggested that preserving art was not that important. She shook her head again, more vigorously this time, and she exhaled. She whispered the line from *Raiders of the Lost Ark* that had inspired her career and had become her personal mantra, "This belongs in a museum."

She pulled her tangled mass of dark red-black hair back, which she had always seen as a stereotype of her Irish-Puerto Rican heritage, and tried to smooth it down under the hair band she used to keep the curls out of her face, but her mane, as she liked to call it, refused to be tamed. She let the strands dart out at all angles atop her head. Who was going to see her hair in the annex anyway? Her dingy white smock, stained with the remnants of ancient worlds, covered her bright floral print dress, which would have brought some welcome color to the gray, industrial space, and that made her a little sad. She loved wearing bright colors, especially when she had to work so much indoors. She longed for the archeological digs she used to go on when she first received her Master's. She loved the thrill of exploration, the joy of discovery, but she understood that her job cataloging and restoring was vitally important as well. "This belongs in a museum," she whispered again.

Her mind calmed but the pleasant memories of the ruins and excavations remained as a smile, she reached out her white linen gloved hand, without intent, and nearly touched the coin, but like always, her training prevented her from doing so. She had no reason to touch the coin, so she simply looked at it, a longing in the center of her chest rising, but then, just like so many times over the last few months, she closed the drawer and continued with her work. Today, she needed to catalog the pottery shards from a new dig site in Northern Iraq.

Cherylyn began picking up the individual shards of pottery and examining them in order to place them in the appropriate categories, but her mind kept traveling back to the coin. She couldn't understand what was different about this day, but she had no concentration. She only wanted to hold the coin. Just hold it for a minute. To feel the metal against her skin, but no, she would never do that. She would wear gloves. Of course, who would know if she took the gloves off for just a second? No, she would not do that, but the impulse was growing.

She returned to her work and then, after a few minutes she stood. She hadn't meant to stand, but she stood nonetheless. Laughing it off as just a curious tick, a restless moment, and she sat back, continuing to catalog the Iraqi pottery. One piece seemed familiar. There might be another shard nearby and she needed to check the similarities. She stood, walked directly to drawer 7413 and pulled it open. The coin glinted.

"What am I doing?" she asked the coin. She put her hand on the drawer, preparing to close it, but she found it difficult. "I need to go back to work," she said and pushed on the drawer. "I need to catalog the pottery shards, I need to get the shards numbered and filed, I need to update the inventory files, and I need to, I need." The thoughts she was expressing became muddy. She pulled the drawer fully open and took the coin in her gloved hand.

"I need to protect the coin," she said with a force that reverberated around the room.

CHAPTER 18

"Are you sure this is the place?" Brady asked as he and Richard pulled in front of the annex. The concrete exterior was plain, unassuming, and as gray as the gray man's skin. It made Brady grimace, just a bit.

"Yes," Richard answered for the third time. "I told you, they would not have a sign announcing that this is part of the Smithsonian. That's part of the security. There are some incredibly valuable artifacts in there. Trust me."

"Fine," Brady acquiesced and pulled the car to a stop across the street from the only visible entrance. The building was huge, stretching to the next intersection, filling the entire block, and filing up five stories.

"Do you feel that?" Richard asked as they both stepped into the street.

Brady felt the pull, the desire, the anger. "There's a coin in there."

"At least one," Richard agreed. "Hopefully three."

"You going to be O.K.?" Brady asked and Richard nodded. Brady returned the nod, more to assure himself than Richard, and continued to walk. *Am I going to be okay?* he thought. The feeling was there, always there, in the back of his mind, in the darkest corners. It was a constant hum, no, not a hum, a growl. It was a beast lurking in the shadows, just out of sight, ready to pounce at any moment. Yet, even with the beast a constant threat, he was still in control, he was still himself.

The security guards just inside the door accepted Richard's academic credentials and Brady's badge as the appropriate reasons for being in the warehouse and asking to see Cherylyn. Soon, the two were walking side by side through rows and rows of boxes and metal drawers. They continued in the direction the guard had pointed them. They saw the work station, little more than a long, flat surface, where Cherylyn was assigned this particular day. There were pieces of pottery scattered around but no coins. The two began to meander. They rounded a corner. Cherylyn stood near the back wall of the warehouse, her hand clenched tightly in front of her.

"Cherylyn?" Richard asked. Cherylyn turned toward the back wall and ran.

The two men stood for a moment in stunned surprise. Brady sprung into action first. He glanced quickly at the remaining contents of the drawer, coins, and he knew there was going to be a fight.

Brady cornered Cherylyn in a dead-end down one long row of drawers. She turned on him and hissed, "It's mine!"

She was clutching her hands to her chest tightly and blood was slowly trickling from her palm. He stepped closer.

"Get away!" Cherylyn screamed and began to gnash at the air in frustration.

"Cherylyn!" Richard's voice came forceful in the otherwise silence of the cavernous room. He stood behind Brady and shouted again, "Cherylyn! It's me, Richard! Richard Stanley! Let us help you!"

Cherylyn's eyes, mere slits amid furrowed brow, darted from Brady, who was inching closer, and Richard further back. Brady waited until he saw her look directly at Richard, and in that split second he leapt forward, wrapping his arms around her. Cherylyn screamed. The shrill sound sliced through the men. It shot into Brady's chest and forced him to feel his own rage. He wanted the coin in her hand. He wanted to feel the metal digging into his own flesh. It wasn't fair that she had it.

"Cherylyn, look at me." Richard dropped in front of the entwined woman and held the sides of her face to keep her from biting at Brady's arms."Listen to me, Cherylyn. Say it with me," he looked at Brady as well as Cherylyn. "Say it with me. Our Father, who art in Heaven..."

The prayer began slowly, with Richard's voice intermingling with Brady's in the tomblike quiet. Then, the two men's voices gained strength and merged seamlessly together, a unified front against the rage. Cherylyn bucked and shouted through grinding teeth, which she bared like a cornered animal.

"It's not working!" Brady called. His arms were tiring, and he knew Cherylyn would not give in, she would never give in, until she collapsed. He wondered whether his strength or hers would give out first.

Richard, still holding her face, paused in his recitation and looked directly at Brady. "Of course," he said. "Repeat after me. Hail Mary, Full of Grace..."

Brady nodded and repeated, "Hail Mary, Full of Grace..."

Richard shouted, "The Lord is with thee!"

"The Lord is with thee," Brady shouted back.

"Blessed art thou among women..." Richard said.

"Blessed art thou among women..." Brady continued and noticed that Cherylyn's body slackened just a bit.

"Um," Richard said and then his eyes grew frantic. "I don't know what comes next."

"What?" Brady asked and tightened his grip around Cherylyn. "Think!"

"I'm trying," Richard said. "Um, Blessed is Jesus?"

"Is that right?" Brady asked.

"I don't..." Richard began.

"Blessed is the fruit of thy womb, Jesus," Cherylyn offered.

"Right," Richard said and continued, "Blessed is the fruit of thy womb, Jesus."

Then together, Richard and Cherylyn said, "Holy Mary, Mother of God, pray for us sinners now, and at the hour of our death."

Cherylyn sank into Brady's arms. They all repeated the prayer, once, twice, and then Cherylyn's whole body went limp. Brady awkwardly helped her to sit on the cold floor, making sure to keep his grip around her strong, just in case. Richard pivoted behind Brady and offered what aid he could by grabbing Richard under the arms and steadying him as they all sat together. Cherylyn's hands fell open and a single silver coin tinkled to the cement.

Three sets of eyes watched the metal spin in haphazard spirals until it settled onto the gray floor. Then, a set of gray clad feet appeared directly in front of them.

"What do you think you're doing?" Erastus asked, bending down and picking the coin off the floor. The three people in an awkward bundle gasped in unison making their intertwined bodies appear like one heaving mass. "These are not toys." His eyebrows rose impassionately as he looked at their tangled bodies, "What sort of game is this anyway?"

"Who...?" Richard asked, carefully attempting to extricate his limbs from the others. Brady stood next to him and allowed Cherylyn to recline against a shelving unit. She was clearly exhausted and fell into a near-unconscious state. Brady rested his hand on his firearm.

"My name is Erastus. I believe you've met my brother, Apollyon. You left before I could properly introduce myself." Brady watched Erastus's gray lips form the words, and he saw his gray eyes staring at him. He looked amazingly like Apollyon, but it could just be that they were both incredibly gray.

"The coin?" Richard continued, clearly having trouble forming complete sentences.

"Yes, nasty little cursed objects," Erastus said, holding the coin up to the light and examining it intently. Brady could now see a bit more definition in Erastus' jawline. Apollyon had a much softer chin. "My brother uses them for...unseemly things. I try to stop him. It's a game we play."

"A game!" Brady shouted, suddenly unconcerned with the man's features. His anger was too close to the surface to be contained. "People have died! Good people! Innocent people!"

Erastus finished his passive examination of the coin and closed his gray fist around it, "Yes, people often do die when we play these games." There was a tepid tinge of sadness, regret, in the man's voice that defused Brady's anger so completely that he suddenly felt the need to sit, but he refused to show any weakness. So, he stood on shaky legs and tried to look strong.

"Who are you...people?" Richard asked, his voice unsure, timid.

"I've been known by many names over the centuries," Erastus responded as if he had completely answered the question.

"Like what?" Richard prompted, and Brady tensed beside him. Brady's mind raced with consequential ideas. *Was Richard asking questions that he didn't want the answers to? That neither of them wanted the answers to?* He wasn't sure, but they needed some answers, even unwelcome ones.

Erastus thought for a moment, "I suppose my most famous name would have to have been Utnapishtim."

Richard gasped. Brady tensed and asked, "Who? What?"

Richard grabbed Brady's arm and said, "I'll explain later." He stepped in front of Brady and then addressed Erastus. "I think I understand." Brady wished that he understood because he was convinced that he could taste the confusion in his mouth, or was that blood? He was clenching his jaw so tightly, had he broken a tooth? He wasn't sure of anything anymore.

"You are gathering the coins?" Erastus asked, still gazing at the metal disk in his palm.

"We...didn't mean...yes, we are," Richard admitted, and Brady thought about the repercussions of telling a gray man their intent, but figured the need for understanding was greater. He also understood that Richard was feeling his way through the awkwardness and confusion of this encounter, and he didn't need a clunky police officer getting in the way. "You and your brother are as well?"

Erastus nodded. "My brother has plans for the coins that are less than savory. I, on the other hand, just wish to keep them safe. They are of extreme historical importance, you know?" He appeared to direct this last statement to Cherylyn who was still sitting on the floor but was breathing more regularly.

Richard asked, "Your brother is like you?"

"You probably wish to know his other names as well, yes?" Richard nodded and Brady frowned. He was not following this conversation at all. He kept fingering his sidearm as the other men talked. "His true name has been lost to history, but he has been known as Cartaphilus and simply Joseph. There was a period of time when people called him Xerxes. That was a confusing point I can tell you."

Richard whispered breathlessly, "Ewiger Jude?"

"Yes, that was one of his." Erastus sighed. "He always enjoyed more attention than I ever got. But then again, I never really wanted that much attention. He craves it, you see?"

Brady couldn't take the passive-aggressive nature of the conversation anymore. He asked Erastus directly, "What are you trying to do exactly?"

"Who, me?" Erastus gingerly placed a hand on his chest and feigned a surprised reaction. Then his demeanor completely shifted, and he jabbed his thumb over his shoulder and asked, "Or him?"

"Yes," Brady responded. "Both of you. What are you two trying to do?"

Erastus stepped closer, cocked his head to the side, and seemed to be studying Richard's face. The movement made Brady nervous, and he pulled at Richard's arm. Richard merely covered Brady's hand with his own and remained still. "Like I said, I am trying to collect the coins to keep them safe. My brother has more sinister designs." He held the coin out near Richard's face. Brady could feel Richard holding his breath, then he realized he had stopped breathing too. "You two." He waved the coin from Richard's face to Brady's and back again. "You still want to collect the coins yourself?"

Richard and Brady both nodded and each sucked in a gulp of air.

"Good," Erastus proclaimed brightly. His gray face twisted into a pleasant smile as he produced, from his jacket pocket, a leather bag with a draw-string top. He pulled the bag open and dropped the coin inside. Then, he pulled the drawstring tight and handed the bag to Richard. "You'll need this then."

"What is that?" Brady asked. Frustration was thick in the air as Richard took the bag from the outstretched, gray hand.

"This will help as you take the coins to Judas's church," Erastus said with finality before turning and disappearing into the shadows of the room.

Brady's ears filled with silence, like being underwater, and the shadows darkened far too much. He found it difficult to breathe. He gasped for air in a stilted, ineffective manner until suddenly, the room filled with normalcy once more. It was dimly lit, but not oppressively so. The air was still but didn't fight against him. His shoulders dropped and the tension drained from him. He was exhausted, but he would not sit down. "What just happened?" he demanded.

"I think we just got some help," Richard said as he held up the leather pouch. "Can you feel the pull of the coin?"

Brady concentrated for a moment and then shook his head, "No, not even a little bit. That bag, what, blocks it?" He took the bag from Richard's outstretched hand. It was old leather but still in very good condition. He could feel the coin inside, but he had no desire to open the bag at all.

Richard nodded and bent to check on Cherylyn, who rubbed her temples, grimacing and muttering under her breath. Richard bent down and hovered over her as he whispered, "Are you okay?"

Cherlyn opened her mouth, muttered incoherently, closed it and simply nodded.

"Good. Can you sit up?" Richard continued, pulling on her arms until she rested, nearly upright, against a row of shelves.

"What happened?" she asked, still rubbing her temples, still grimacing. "Richard?" She suddenly sat up quickly. "Richard Stanley? Is that you?"

"It's me," Richard nodded and put a hand on her shoulder. "Take it slowly. The feelings are intense and can leave you pretty drained."

Cherylyn looked at Brady and noted, "Is that a police officer?"

"Yes, that's my friend, Brady, uh Sheriff Edwards. He's been helping me with, or rather, I've been helping him with a case."

"The coin!" Cherylyn was suddenly on her feet searching the floor. "I took it out of the drawer. Why would I do that? That's crazy. And I don't have it anymore."

"We have it," Richard affirmed as he now put both his hands on her shoulders and faced her. "It's okay. You're okay. The feelings will pass, or at least lessen."

"Feelings?" Her eyes were wide, glazed, a bit bloodshot.

"Desire, paranoia, anger," Richard began.

"Hunger," Cherylyn finished. "Why am I so hungry?"

"Uh, well, that does seem to be a side effect sometimes," Richard said and motioned to Brady.

"Miss Rodriguez," Brady began timidly. "Are you sure you're okay?"

"I'm confused," Cherylyn admitted. "I'm confused, hungry and confused. I'm ravenous, like I haven't eaten in days, but I had breakfast this morning. What happened to me?" She faced Richard directly.

"You...well, you...had a..." Richard stuttered.

Brady stepped forward and interjected, "You came in contact with a cursed coin that consumed you with greed." By way of illustration, he held out the leather pouch toward her. "It is safe in this leather pouch now. The curse can't get out of this, uh, magic bag."

Cherylyn stared blankly, first at Brady then at the leather pouch, then back at Brady. It wasn't until she turned to Richard that she spoke. "A cursed coin?"

"One of thirty such coins," Brady nodded vigorously.

"Brady," Richard said sharply. "I'm not sure that's helpful."

"I'm just being honest." Brady turned to Richard and held the bag out toward him, then back at Cherylyn, then he tucked the bag under his arm. "We don't have time for subtlety or easing people into this, or have you forgotten?"

"I haven't forgotten anything!" Richard said loudly and spitefully. "I think you've forgotten what it's like to just find out about these things. To just be thrown into the middle of all this crazy..."

"Holy...!" Cherylyn suddenly exclaimed. "Thirty coins!"

Richard nodded and patted her arm. "You see what you've done," he said to Brady.

"I didn't do…" Brady lined up his rationalizations but they felt inadequate when he saw the stark fear in Cherylyn's eyes. "I'm sorry," he said to her. "I should have told you more gently." Then, to Richard, "I'm sorry."

"Well, it was your turn to freak out, I suppose," Richard patted Brady's shoulder.

"Tag, you're it," Brady said and tried to laugh but it came out as a growl. He swallowed and cleared his throat.

"The old stories," Cherylyn continued, her voice squeaked and cracked. She grabbed Richard's hand. "Those Medieval stories about these coins. People consumed with greed, rage, gluttony. They're all true?"

"That seems to be the case," Richard admitted. He was watching her with careful, concerned, fretful eyes.

"And that, uh, magic bag blocks the curse?" She pointed to Brady.

"We, well, maybe," Brady responded. "Are you feeling anything about the coin?"

"Just a tiny little desire to snatch that bag and run," Cherlyn admitted as Brady shifted his posture to hide the pouch from her. "Nothing I can't resist though, and the hunger pangs are going away too."

"Good, good," Brady said, but he noticed her eyes never left the pouch as she spoke. "What about other coins that might be, uh, like this one? You ever noticed others? Anything at all?"

"No," Cherylyn began. "I had always been drawn to this coin. Just this one, but I kept repeating the steps of the scientific method in my head. That always kept me from acting unprofessionally, until today."

"And you are sure there are no other coins like this one in the building," Brady prompted.

"I'm sure," Cherlyn nodded emphatically. "Nothing even remotely like that coin." She pointed to the pouch under Brady's arm and her finger lingered a little too long for Brady's comfort.

"Then we really need to get going," Brady said and headed for the door.

"I'm really sorry about this, Cherlyn, but we need to take the coin and leave before the authorities get here," Richard said.

"Please, take it," Cherlyn responded. She stepped toward them, then she turned away, then she turned back.

Richard asked, "Are you sure you're okay?"

Cherylyn nodded, took a deep breath, and recited the steps of the scientific method under her breath. She suddenly said, "do background research," and made a dash for her office.

"What was that?" Brady asked as he turned toward the exit.

Richard shrugged, "I guess she needed to be in her office, like, right now?"

Once they were in the car, Brady drove through the deepening shadows of the city streets. He had pointed the car towards the outskirts of the city. Not knowing where to actually go, he felt it safest to just get away from people. While he drove, his mind kept returning to the gray man, Erastus. "That help you mentioned. What kind of help do you think he gave us?"

"What?" Richard asked.

"You said that, right after Erastus gave us this pouch. You said you think we just got some help. What kind of help?"

"I think," Richard began, obviously being careful with his words, and Brady recognized the technique. He appreciated Richard trying not to upset him, but he wanted to point out that they were far past the point of not being upset. "Erastus is a, well, I think he's a good guy. He gave us a clue as to what to do with the coins."

"A good guy? What clue?"

"He obviously doesn't want the coins for himself, or he doesn't seem to anyway," Richard began, holding up the leather bag. "And he mentioned a place."

"Judas's church," Brady asserted.

"Right. It seems we need to take all of the coins to this church. And then there's this pouch. It does seem to block the pull of this coin, don't you think?"

"Right, yes," Brady admitted, squinting at the pouch. "So, this pouch is even better than lead?"

"It seems it is. Then, we just need to take all of the coins to…"

"Judas's church," Brady finished. "Where is that?" Richard stopped talking, obviously lost in thought. Brady waited until he couldn't anymore. "Is it in America?" he asked.

"I don't know where it is," Richard admitted. "Somehow I doubt it is in America."

"Fine," Brady said and pulled the car to the side of the highway and stopped. He turned off the engine and got out. "Bring the pouch."

"What?" Richard stumbled out of the car and followed Brady to the rear of the car.

"We do this fast," Brady said as he opened the trunk.

The pull of the coins hit the two men like a wave from a turbulent ocean. They each began to shout.

Richard screamed the Lord's Prayer, "Our Father, who art in Heaven…"

Brady yelled his oath of office, "On my honor, I will never betray my badge…" Then, he opened the metal box.

The wave doubled, then tripled, and then came the rage. They continued to shout, each to their own mantra as the rain started. Brady grabbed at the coins, Richard held the pouch open, and they bent themselves into the trunk.

The rain swirled around them, winds buffeted them from all directions, the car offered little protection. They continued to scream into the storm and to move the coins from the box to the pouch. Every coin seemed to resist the move. Brady tried to grab a handful but only got two. He shoved them into the pouch and tried again, just to get one this time. Richard shut his eyes tightly and continued to pray.

"I can't," Brady started but then kept reciting. "I will always have the courage to hold myself and others accountable for their actions." The words gave him strength and he continued. One more coin, two more, then the cars, which had been speeding by, began to screech to a halt.

A cab driver flung himself from his car as the tires locked up, skidded across the wet pavement, and came to a shuddering stop. He began to run toward them. A woman nearly drove her SUV into them but managed to come to a stop just in the grass beside them. She struggled out of her car, forgetting the seatbelt, screaming her frustration as she undid the latch, and she began to run toward them. Tires continued to screech all around.

"Brady?" Richard asked, his hands shaking, which made Brady's job much more difficult.

"I know!" Brady yelled and continued to move coins. He gave up trying for a handful and instead was picking one coin at a time, with intent, increasing speed and accuracy. Just two more, one more, the cabby grabbed Brady's shirt and tugged hard. Brady jerked to the side. Just one more coin. He grabbed a hold of the trunk and began to slap at the cab driver's body. The woman in the SUV was just a few feet from Richard as he took the last coin, dropped it into the pouch and pulled the strings tight.

The cab driver fell to his knees, exhausted but calm. The woman stopped running with an awkward stumble that became a meandering walk. Richard dropped the pouch into the trunk and closed it. Brady stood and helped the cabby to his feet. "You alright?" he shouted to the woman, pointing at her and looking at Richard. The woman nodded and confusedly made her way back to her SUV. The cabby stumbled back to his cab. The other drivers started to inch forward, returning to their lives.

"No accidents?" Richard asked, watching the cars regain their normal pace.

"I guess not," Brady exhaled and slumped into the driver's seat. Richard slid in beside him. "What now?"

"I don't..." Richard thought for a moment, his face scrunched, his brows furrowed, then Brady saw him go into professor mode. He sat up straighter, puffed his chest out just a bit, and spoke authoritatively.

"Christian tradition tells us that Judas returned the coins to the priests who had given them to him just before committing suicide. It is believed that this stripped the coins of their curse."

"If that's true, then how...?" Brady began to drive again, in a vague northerly direction.

"I don't know what's happened since then. There are no stories that might explain what could have reignited the curse. At least, none that I know of. Most of what I know is just old stories, and I'm not a professor of literature," Richard paused in response to an alert on his cell phone.

"Richard!" Cherylyn shouted before Richard had a chance to say hello.

"Cherylyn? You should be heading home to get some rest," Richard said quickly.

"I was thinking about what you told me about the coins, and I remembered reading this story," Cherylyn continued, and Brady could hear every word of the excited woman's conversation. "Are you still close-by? There's this coffee shop. Meet me. I need to show you this."

"I ordered you coffee," Cherylyn said as Brady and Richard entered the coffee shop. There were three cups of coffee on the table in front of her, next to an ancient looking book.

"Okay, what did you find?" Brady asked as he sat down and in-stinctively lifted the coffee to his mouth. The hot liquid, laced with caffeine, was a welcome change from the frantic adrenaline rushes he had become accustomed to since meeting Richard. The coffee was comforting, calming, and absolutely normal.

"Yeah, I was looking through the passages about Roman coins," Cherylyn offered, not touching her own coffee. "There was something I couldn't quite put my finger on, something familiar about this whole thing. And then, there it was." She jabbed her finger down onto the open book on the table.

"This?" Richard asked as he looked down at a picture of a painting.

"It looks like that other painting we found at Katie's apartment," Brady observed, pointing to the little circles of silver at the bottom of the page. He assumed there were thirty even though he didn't count them. "Same little pile of coins too."

Softly, with the air of a professor telling a promising student that her ideas were not original, Richard observed, "Yeah, we already discussed the coins from the painting called *Judas Repentant.* That's how we knew there were thirty."

"Right, but this," Cherylyn said as if she had solved the mystery. After watching the men's eyes lift from the page and stare blankly at her, she continued, "It's called *Judas Returning the Thirty Pieces of Silver.*"

"Yeah? We knew that. Richard knew that the tradition said that Judas gave the money back." Brady pulled the book closer and examined it intently.

"Right, but we know that no one donated the coins to the temple," Cherylyn proclaimed. "This painting sparked a memory I had of a religion professor telling a story in class. He told us that in one story, possibly more, I can't really remember, anyway, the elders declared the coins blood money and refused to donate them to the temple. Instead, they bought Potter's Field with them."

"Wait, did you say Potter's Field?" Brady interrupted.

"Yes, it was a field where they buried paupers in ancient times," Richard answered.

"It was called Potter's Field? Truly?"

"Well, not really," Cherylyn chimed in. "It was really called Haceldama, at least according to tradition. It roughly translates as the field of blood."

"So where does Potter's Field come from?" Brady pressed.

Cherylyn took on the tone of a professor giving a lecture, and Brady wondered if everyone that Richard knew talked that way when explaining something. He didn't mind the tone, in fact it was comforting, thinking that someone, anyone, knew what was going on with some sense of certainty. "It refers to fields that were used for digging clay for pottery. They couldn't plant anything in the clay so they used the fields for pauper's graves. Potter's Field is just an English interpretation of the ancient practice."

"Why are you asking?" Richard interjected into Cherylyn's explanation.

"Because I'm the Sheriff of Potter's Field, Virginia. That can't be a coincidence."

The three fell into silence as this new revelation sunk in. Richard broke the silence by asking, "Is the name of the town symbolic in some way."

Cherylyn posed a different question, "Is it typical to name an entire town after what is essentially a cemetery?"

Brady shrugged at both of them in turn. Then he began to talk a little too fast, slightly too loudly. "How should I know? I'm the sheriff not the historian, and I just found out I moved to a town whose name is connected to a place called the *field of blood*. I'm questioning every life choice I've ever made up to this point."

"Right, well, okay, maybe we put a pin in that, for now, but I think it does need further scrutiny. Let's just focus on the facts as we know them," Richard asserted in a soothing tone. Brady had more questions, about angels and demons, about gray men, about Bible stories, about impossibly old people, but he was starting to feel a bit like a drowning man.

"Yes," Brady said, nodding vigorously. "We should just focus on what we can know, not the questions we have." He shifted tone, becoming as professional as he could in the moment. "The tradition says that they bought Pott...Haceldama, right?"

"That's right," Cherylyn said as she took the book from Brady, began turning pages, reading as she went. "But there are two different stories, at least two. One says that Judas returned the coins to the Elders and they bought the field but another says that Judas used the coins to buy the field."

"Either way," Richard proclaimed. "The coins were not given to the temple, and definitely not a church. They were used to buy a plot of land."

Cherylyn chimed in with a conspiratorial air, "A plot of land used as a cemetery."

"That's right," Richard agreed and the two began to nod slowly, each lost in their own thoughts.

"Okay, so what does that mean for us?" Brady asked, suddenly feeling left out.

"That means we have to take the coins back to the original Potter's Field, to Haceldama," Richard said, nodding his head forcefully.

"Where's that?" Brady was trying to sip his coffee but his lips were too tense to allow it.

"Jerusalem," Richard and Cherylyn said in unison.

CHAPTER 19

The only plane from Dulles Airport to Jerusalem with available seats was an Air France plane with one connection. The layover in Paris was a little over twelve hours, and Brady was restless the minute the landing gear hit the tarmac. He had always wanted to go to Paris, but he found that he was not enjoying the tips thus far. The coin pouch, now filled with all the coins they had collected, twenty-eight in total, sat heavily on his lap, and felt even heavier as he carried it into the Charles De Gaulle Airport terminals. They began a slow meandering walk around rows of seats, the shops and restaurants. Brady had to admit that this French airport was the nicest he had ever been in.

Richard stood off to the side, near a window overlooking the runways, while he talked on his cell phone, and Brady noticed, not for the first time, how handsome he was. He had a round, friendly face that was perfectly framed by his salt and pepper hair and beard. He had what his mother had always referred to as a hunter's nose, which was strong and straight. He had a build that suggested he was once athletic but now spent too much time behind a desk. Brady could commiserate with that situation. Richard turned toward him and instead of turning away embarrassed for being caught staring, Brady smiled. Richard smiled back warmly and gave a little wave. Brady felt his cheeks flush red.

"Thanks Tom," Richard said into the phone as he walked to join Brady. "I really appreciate this. I will have a manuscript ready in a couple of weeks." Richard touched the faceplate on the phone and dropped it in his pocket.

"That your boss?" Brady asked as he handed Richard his overnight bag. He took his own and they walked toward the exit.

"My dean, yes," Richard said. "I'm officially on sabbatical in order to produce a new book."

"You working on a new book?"

"Well, I guess I have to now," Richard smiled a crooked half smile, and Brady laughed a bit too loud. "Or I'll have to find another job." They stepped out into a crisp French morning. "It's a shame we can't see more of the city," Richard offered, obviously trying to sound like a normal traveler who wasn't transporting a bag full of cursed coins.

"We do have twelve hours," Brady responded cheerfully.

Richard's eyebrows rose. "I was sure that you would want to sit in the airport and guard the coin pouch the entire time."

"Nope. Never been to Paris. Wouldn't mind seeing a bit."

"We could…" Richard began slowly, carefully, a little suspiciously, "…go to the Louvre?"

"Yeah, I've always wanted to see the Mona Lisa in person."

"Okay," Richard turned and stood squarely in front of Brady. "What's wrong with you? You're acting weird."

"Y'know, I think I'm just happy," Brady began and watched as Richard's face lightened with a sly smile. "It's Paris in the Spring. Why wouldn't I be happy?"

Richard thought about it and had to agree, "You're right. We're in Paris, the weather's beautiful, the company is dashing. Nothing could be better." Richard's hand went to Brady's chest and the casual intimacy felt anything but casual.

Brady smiled broader than he thought he was capable of and said, "Yeah, so let's go see the freaking Mona Lisa."

The two men walked happily to the Metro station. They boarded the RER B train toward Massy-Palaiseau, changed to line fourteen toward Saint-Lazare to the Pyramides station. They came out of the station into the bright sunlit streets of Paris.

"How far is the museum?" Brady asked, he was looking at the buildings and the street with a transformative awe. His heart felt full and he couldn't stop smiling.

"Just a couple of minutes walk from here," Richard responded as they strolled lazily. "You've never been to Paris, huh?"

"No, but I have always wanted to." Brady pointed to a particularly picturesque building but did not say anything. Richard smiled and simply looked where Brady had pointed.

The stone buildings, each one the color of aged marble, hugged the bustling streets, while the smell of baked goods wafted through the air. The sun bathed the stone, the bricks, the blooming flowers, the faces of the crowd in a halo of warmth.

Richard spoke nostalgically, "I remember my first time in the City of Lights. When I was a graduate student studying ancient cultures. I had been so concerned with the architecture that I nearly walked out in front of a motorcycle speeding through the streets. You should watch your step. They're still pretty crazy."

Brady nodded absentmindedly as he walked, nearly stepping into the street but correcting at the last minute. "This is just beautiful," he said, his mouth agape.

The Louvre sat at the end of the street, just past a small stand of trees. They walked toward the edifice, and Brady gasped at the first view.

"Brady Edwards," Richard said as he stared at the other man who seemed to be lost in the beauty. "You continue to surprise me. I would have never thought that architecture would speak to you this much."

Brady shook his head and spoke reverently, "I've never seen anything so elegant. The columns, arches, those statues on top of the pillars, the color of the walls. What color is that even?" Something was tugging at a part of Brady's soul deep inside that longed to be more free, more refined. It was a piece of himself that he never thought about, a piece he had thought atrophied, long forgotten.

"Shall we go in?" Richard asked, flinging his arm around Brady's waist and leading him forward. They walked to the main entrance, and

Richard saw the problem first. "Brady, there's a guard looking into everyone's bags. He's going to want to look into the leather pouch."

"Maybe we shouldn't..." Brady began, but the line had formed behind them tightly. "Oh man, if we try to leave now, they might get suspicious and want to look in the bag anyway."

"Maybe if he just looks in and doesn't take one out?" Richard offered as they neared the guard.

"Your bag?" the guard asked with a thick French accent. He motioned for Brady to set it on the metal table beside him. Brady reluctantly set it down. The guard pulled open the gathered top and peered inside. "Coins?" he asked.

"Souvenirs," Richard said quickly. "From Rome."

The guard nodded knowingly, "My son collects those." He pulled the pouch closed and handed it back to Brady. "Make sure you visit the gift shop after," the guard said and waved them through.

"I can't believe that worked," Brady said during a long exhale.

"That bag is really effective," Richard nodded. "I think we can relax a bit. Enjoy the art and such. Don't you?"

"Yep," Brady said over his shoulder as he had already begun to walk through the art-filled rooms.

They walked, feeding their souls with one magnificent piece of art after another, until they came to the Mona Lisa. Brady stared over the heads of all the other gawkers and felt that pull deep in his chest turn into a longing. He waited his turn, and when the crowd parted and he came face to face with that famous smile, his eyes filled with soothing, comforting, happy tears. It was smaller than he thought it would be. Somehow, in his mind, it was enormous. In person it was intimate, precious, and fragile. His emotions swelled and he sighed contentedly. He stood there for as long as the crowd would allow before moving on.

He found Richard, who had turned his attention to another piece by da Vinci. Brady stood next to him and read the title, "Virgin of the Rocks." He gazed at the arched image of a woman, flocked by cherubs, sitting demurely under stone formations.

"It's beautiful," Brady said.

"It is," Richard responded thoughtfully. "And there's something else."

"What?"

Richard turned to Brady, his face a perfect mask of excitement. "I know where Judas's church is."

***

The plane to the airport at Tel-Aviv Yafo was not as crowded as the plane from Washington to Paris, which gave Brady and Richard much more confidence to talk openly of their quest.

"Explain it to me again, how do you know where the church is?" Brady asked, clutching the leather pouch with renewed vigor.

"I don't. Not exactly, but I believe that painting explains everything."

"Well, explain it to me. Again," Brady said, his frustration apparent.

"There was no formal Christian church in the time of Judas," Richard began. "They held meetings in houses and secret places where the elders and Romans couldn't find them."

"Right, okay, so how do we get these coins to a non-existent church?"

"The rocks," Richard said emphatically as if he was revealing something important.

"Yeah? What does that mean?"

"The caverns under the city," Richard said more excitedly. "That would have been where the early Christians would have gathered. At least some of them. Their *church* was under the noses, literally, of the elders."

"So, there are caves under Jerusalem. How many?"

"Well, quarries, really."

"What?" Brady was trying desperately to keep his voice low and even, but Richard's thoughts had been going so fast that he was having a hard time keeping up. He needed Richard to calm down and explain in simple English. "Just pretend I don't know any of this," Brady prompted. "Which seems to be the truth."

"Zedekiah's Cave was a natural formation that was turned into a quarry by Herod the Great. The cave was dug out over centuries until it formed a large cavern under the Old City walls. It's enormous."

Brady caught on to Richard's suggestion. "Then, part of it was around during Judias' time?"

"Most of it," Richard nodded for emphasis, again as if he had solved a great mystery, but Brady felt less certain that anything had been resolved. "And, the caves have been used for religious ceremonies for centuries. They have spiritual significance even with many modern Christians. If Judas had used the caves for secret meetings, or at least been present for secret meetings, then these caves have since been consecrated. Do you see what that means?"

"The caves are the church." Brady said. "I get it. The early Christians sanctified the caves so their ceremonies would be legit. So, those caverns are technically a church. But are they Judas' church, the one we're looking for?"

"I think so. If Judas was present at the beginning of this long consecration then these caves are technically his church as one of the original disciples. Judas' Church wouldn't be a brick and mortar building, not like Peter's. It would have been one of the secret places," Richard fell back into his seat, crossed his arms, and nodded.

"Okay, so we just need to chuck this purse into the caves?" Brady asked, nearly positive this easy answer would absolutely not be the correct one.

"Well, no," Richard began. He sat upright, his arms no longer crossed. "It won't be that easy. We would need to formally consecrate them to the church in order for the curse to be broken."

"So, is there a rite or a ceremony or something like that?"

Richard's face suddenly turned white and he tensed in his seat. Brady followed his friend's terrified gaze to the front of the plane where Apollyon stood directly beneath the large television screen showing some uninteresting film. The man's gray teeth glittered in the flickering light of the television as he lifted his hand. A glint of silver caught his eye as Brady stood and stepped out into the aisle.

"Welcome to Israel," Apollyon said and flipped a silver coin into the row between the passengers' seats.

Every eye on the plane followed the path of the coin as it hit one armrest and then bounded onto the worn carpet of the aisle. It came to rest nearly dead center between two occupied seats. The man on the left slowly reached out his hand to pick it up.

"No!" Brady yelled but his warning was drowned by the scream of the woman on the right side of the aisle.

"It's mine!" she shouted and dove for the coin. The man next to her piled on top and tried to shove his hand underneath her. Meanwhile, the other passengers were rising from their own seats and making their way toward the accumulating pile of people. One particularly muscular man began throwing passengers back, mostly into Brady, who tried to cushion their landings as best he could while he tried to struggle through them.

The woman who had touched the coin first appeared on the bottom of the pile long enough for Brady to recognize the frightening rage on her face. She turned, a beguiling strength suddenly evident, fighting her way free with elbows and fingernails. The muscular man lunged forward, over the others, grasping for the woman. She flung herself backwards, away from him and toward Brady. The muscular man stood, towering over the enraged woman, and bent to reach for her. She kicked, viciously, her foot landing squarely in the muscular man's stomach causing him to wretch and double over.

"It's mine!" The woman continued to scream as she kicked and flailed and scrambled awkwardly to her feet, her hands closed tightly in a ball at her chest. The others, not quite as firmly under the spell of the coin, hesitated long enough for her to flee into the back of the plane.

Richard joined Brady in the aisle, and with the added distance the coin had gained, many of the other passengers were settling down, bewildered by their own actions.

"Keep them here," Brady instructed as Richard stepped into the aisle directly in front of the mass of bodies. Then, Brady disappeared through the curtain separating the different sections of the plane.

Behind the curtain, the plane was deserted, empty rows of seats on both sides of the aisle. The woman had disappeared, obviously hiding between the seats. Or, possibly, in the bathroom at the far back. Brady felt that she had not had time to reach the bathrooms, but he couldn't tell for sure. He gripped the leather pouch in his hand tighter, and inched forward. He moved slowly through the rows, hoping against hope that the plane would land before the woman did anything too violent.

His hopes were dashed when the woman stomped angrily from the bathroom, one hand forming a claw pointed at him, the other curled tightly into a fist against her chest. Suddenly, he remembered the feel of the coin on his skin and how much he wanted to feel that again, to hold the coin, and keep it safe, but it was only a momentary flash of greed. He squeezed the leather pouch in his hand and felt stronger.

"Ma'am? I need you to calm down," he spoke as softly as he could.

"It's mine!" The woman's screams reverberated in the cabin, a wave of rage caught in a flying metal cylinder amidst the clouds.

"It is yours," Brady responded, his free hand out in front of him in a reassuring, calming posture, palm down to suggest where he wanted the emotions to go as well. He stepped forward.

"Stay back! It's mine! You can't have it!"

"I don't want it," Brady said, taking another step. He was merely three rows from her at this point. She stood in front of the restroom. He needed to get the coin before she thought to lock herself inside the bathroom. If they landed and she still had the coin, the local police would get involved and he didn't want to think about what could happen after that. *The coins. The pouch.* His mind formulated a plan, at least the rudimentary makings of a plan.

"You all want my coin!" the woman continued to scream, her eyes darting frantically around the cabin, her back firmly against the bathroom door. Brady understood that it was only a matter of time before she darted into the bathroom.

Brady lifted the leather pouch to eye level and said, "I don't want your coin. I have my own." He shook the bag and the coins inside made a tinny sound that seemed to fill the cabin.

"You have more?" the woman asked, her eyes narrowed into slits of thoughtful, yet fitful, contemplation.

"I have twenty-eight of them," Brady said and shook the bag once more. The sound was intoxicating, even for him. He felt a slight twinge of desire but swallowed hard and concentrated on his plan, his horribly improvised plan.

"Show me," the woman demanded. Brady pulled the folds on the top of the pouch and stepped forward. He held the pouch open and tilted it toward the woman. She strained her neck to peer inside, where the meager light from the overhead fluorescents shimmered against the silver inside the shadow of the leather.

"You can have them," Brady said, suddenly breaking the obsessive stare of the woman. Her eyes were frantic again, but just a bit contemplative as well. Temptation now peppered the air. Brady pressed his advantage. "Just put your coin inside this pouch and then you can have them all. No one will be able to take them from you."

"Give me the pouch," the woman hissed.

"I will. Just drop the coin inside and you can have it. The pouch and all of the coins," Brady held the pouch out as far as his arm could extend. The woman's eyes were fixed on the pouch now. There was a laser focus in her face. Brady knew that she was caught in his trap. She would do anything to get the coins, but there was still so much distrust, so much dangerous rage on her face. He slid the pouch to the end of his outstretched hand with his thumb. The pouch dangled precariously on just his fingertips. The woman snatched the leather from his hand. Brady heard the coins inside violently clang against each other and anger flared in his chest, tightened his throat, but he steadied himself, planted his feet firmly, and waited.

The woman pulled the top of the bag open as far as it would go. She stared inside and her mouth began to water. Brady held his breath and did not move. He watched as the woman's fist slowly uncurled and the coin appeared against the red, angry skin of her palm. She held the coin above the leather pouch and titled her hand. The coin joined the others inside and the air brightened. The weight, that impossible, oppressive force, dissipated immediately. The woman swooned.

Brady shot forward and grabbed the pouch and pulled the drawstring closed as quickly as he could. The woman slumped to the floor, exhausted, but otherwise fine. Brady slumped down next to her.

"You okay?" Richard's head appeared through the curtain. "Things have calmed down back here. Everyone's back in their seats. No one knows what just happened. We're about to land."

"I'm okay," Brady answered and then turned to the woman. "You okay?"

"What happened?" The woman was rubbing her temples, fear etched into her face.

"Uh," Brady stuttered and looked at Richard.

"Food poisoning," Richard offered. "The whole plane has it." He shrugged as Brady stared in disbelief. The woman nodded and lifted herself to her feet.

"I feel better now," she said. "Must have been that fish I ate in the terminal. I told the woman it smelled funny." She walked past Brady without even a glance at the coin pouch.

"Please fasten your seatbelts, we are entering our final approach path," the captain's voice filled the cabin.

Richard helped Brady back to their seats, and they waited for the plane to land as the other passengers attempted to identify what suspicious foods they had eaten recently.

"Twenty-nine," Brady said, brandishing the leather pouch at eye level before realizing he was among people who had just recently been under the spell of the coins. He dropped the pouch to his side and walked to Richard. "You okay?"

"Yes, I'm fine," Richard said. "They started coming out of it as soon as you passed through the curtain."

"Where'd the gray guy go?" Brady asked, looking around warily.

"Apollyon? I'm not sure. I didn't see him after the whole...fight."

"It might be time to talk about these guys. What are they?"

Richard seemed to consider Brady's question. "Apollyon. The name is Greek, so is Erastus." Richard mumbled as he thought out loud, and Brady recognized the technique of talking through the evidence. A tinge of pride swelled in him. Richard was becoming quite the investigator. Richard continued, "The coins are Roman. They are Judeo-Christian artifacts." He seemed to be drawing a map in his mind, his finger absent-mindedly pointing to the spots on the invisible map, which seemed to be hovering in front of him. "They showed up in Virginia after being stockpiled by a rich man and a scholar."

"What're you thinking?"

"I'm thinking, chaos."

"That's okay, I can't see a pattern either," Brady said, squeezing Richard's shoulder reassuringly on the shoulder.

"No, I mean, actual chaos. I think this Apollyon is an agent of chaos and the stockpiles angered him. He set the coins loose on your town to get you to investigate."

"Why me?"

"Good question," Richard admitted as the plane began descent procedures without any further announcements. "Erastus claims that Apollyon is Cartaphilus. That could explain things." Brady waited as they each buckled their seatbelts to prepare for landing. He wanted to prod the professor, but he felt stupid enough. He refused to ask who Cartaphilis was since Richard seemed to know immediately. Richard seemed lost in thought for a moment but quickly came back. "Cartaphilus is one of the names given to an old Judeo-Christian legend of an immortal being."

Brady nodded, "So what is the legend?"

"Cartaphilus was baptized Joseph later in the story, but he is probably best known by a name given to him even later. The Ewiger Jude, the Wandering Jew."

Brady perked up excitedly, "Wait, I know that name. He was cursed to walk the earth until the second coming, right?"

"Yes," Richard continued. "If Appolyon sees his immortality as a curse, then he might be using the coins to try and end his curse."

"How would he do that?" Brady asked and grabbed hold of the arm-rests as the plane shuddered upon approach. The flight staff huddled in the front of the cabin whispering excitedly, too concerned with the recent strangeness to follow protocols, so Brady had to assume that the shudder was normal.

Richard appeared lost in thought again, but he whispered to himself. Brady strained to eavesdrop on Richard's internal monologue. "If he can bring about the second coming then his curse is lifted. But how would cursed coins do that? He would need something bigger, much bigger." Richard fell silent as the plane made its final descent. Brady joined Richard in the silence, trying desperately to see any logic to the events, while trying desperately to not think of crashing.

The terminal at Tel Aviv Yafo was intermittently filled with waves of travelers and then nearly deserted a moment later. Richard and Brady searched for gray spots, alarming shadows, in their own particular wave. So far, there was no other sign of Apollyon.

Brady suddenly asked an impossible question, "How does he just appear and disappear like that?"

Richard shrugged and shook his head. Then, he appeared to change the subject a bit. "He only has one more coin," Richard said as they exited the airport and looked for the bus stop. The flier Brady was studying assured them they could take a bus into Jerusalem.

"Yeah, just one more and we have them all," Brady said, letting go of the mystery of Appolyon's travel talents for now as he stared at the darkening sky. Clouds were gathering on the horizon. "Maybe we should get a hotel room here and head for Jerusalem in the morning."

"No, I mean he only has one more coin. He's going to be desperate now."

Brady looked at Richard, his lips twisted to the side as he spoke, "You don't think the whole plane thing was desperate?"

"Good point, and I am tired."

"We'll get a room, sleep a bit, wake up early to go find the church," Brady offered with a smile.

"Just the one room?" Richard asked, his own smile was playful.

Brady could feel the blush paint his cheeks. He stammered, "Well, unless you would prefer to, you know, I mean, I was just thinking…"

Richard took one of Brady's hands and squeezed tenderly. "One room is fine." The two quickly caught a cab to a nearby hotel.

CHAPTER 21

The desert sun felt heavy on Brady's back. He walked, nearly doubled over, his feet sinking deeper and deeper into the sand. He struggled up a dune and then rolled down the other side. The wind whipped grainy projectiles into his skin and eyes. He tried to block the sand with his hand, but the swirl of air proved too daunting. His lungs ached and his body crumpled.

With the last remaining iota of his strength, he rolled over and gazed up at the sky, which was not blue, but white hot with the desert heat. He closed his eyes against the brilliance and felt a shadow ease over his face. He opened his eyes.

A man, gray even in the whiteness of the sun-shrouded day, stood above him, smiling a big, toothy, gray smile.

"You can't win, you know?" Apollyon said too clearly, too affirmatively, too effectively, as he stretched a gray hand out over Brady's face and silver coins began to fall from his palm. The impossible number of coins fell in a stream like water, pooling around his head and piling ever higher until only the man's gray smile was visible through the silver. Then, the coins covered his eyes and everything was dark.

"Brady?" Richard asked as he shook Brady awake. "It's time to get up. We need to get going."

Brady nodded and rubbed his eyes. The night had been wonderful; the dream had been anything but. It felt as real as a memory and much harder to shake. The morning outside the hotel room, and the presence of Richard, filled him with renewed hope. He felt lighter, happier as he drank hotel coffee and nibbled a selection of breads in the hotel restaurant. The whole morning seemed decidedly normal with travelers and locals intermingling pleasantly, with Richard smiling and holding his hand, but Brady could not forget the dream. At times, as he sipped his weak coffee, he felt like he was drowning in silver and gasped for air.

"Are you alright?" Richard asked after the third such gasp.

"I can't shake this feeling that something bad is going to happen," Brady admitted, wiping beads of sweat from his forehead with a paper napkin.

"I think that's an understatement. Of course, something bad is going to happen."

"No, I mean, it feels like something even worse is coming," Brady continued and looked around the pleasantly normal room with frantic eyes. The large picture window near their table suddenly dimmed and Brady turned. Apollyon stood between the sunlit morning and the window. "Richard!"

Richard turned in the direction that Brady was pointing and saw Apollyon step forward. The gray man lifted a gray hand and held a silver coin toward the window. "It's the last coin," Brady announced and stood up so forcefully that his chair clattered to the floor. Every other patron of the restaurant turned then and the room seemed bathed in silver.

***

Richard gasped for air in the oppressive light. He clutched his neck and pulled at his shirt collar, but nothing eased the flow of air. He struggled to his feet, nearly falling over the table, and he reached a pleading hand toward Brady. The other people began to gather round now, and one or two of them tried to pat Richard on the back.

Brady calmly turned and walked dispassionately out of the restaurant, into the sunlit morning. Richard watched through tear stained eyes, amid frantic gasps, as Brady walked with purpose to Apollyon. Then, just before Richard fell into darkness, he watched Brady hand the leather pouch over to the gray man who smiled a big, toothy gray smile.

Richard re-entered the conscious world surrounded by a circle of strangers. He blinked his eyes, trying to force any one face to be less fuzzy, more distinct, but his eyes rebelled. A kind hand lifted him to a sitting position and he realized that he had been lying on the floor. He sat for a moment longer, rubbing his petulant eyes, before the sounds of the others' voices penetrated his brain.

"Are you okay?" a voice with a thick accent asked. Richard nodded and struggled to his feet.

"My friend?" he asked, placing two unsteady hands on the nearest tabletop.

"Don't know," the accented voice responded. "You passed out and I only saw you."

Richard nodded again, more out of politeness than any understanding. He looked out of the picture window and remembered Apollyon standing there, that unearthly gray grin on his face. One of the front desk workers helped him back to his room.

"Brady!" He called out to the empty room before slumping onto the nearest bed. His head was aching, his throat was scratchy, and his heart was beating far too fast. He opened a bottle of water and drank half of it in one gulp. His throat was more than scratchy, it was constricted, tight, but returning to normal. What had the gray man done? Richard remembered choking, on the air apparently since he hadn't been eating anything at the time, and the gray man was somehow responsible. He also remembered that Brady walked outside. The coins! Brady had handed the coin pouch to Apollyon. But then what happened to Brady? This was bad, beyond bad.

"You have lost the coins?" A voice sounded from behind him. Richard jumped and nearly fell against the dresser.

"Erastus?" he asked.

"I should have warned you about Apollyon's abilities," Erastus said.

"What abilities?"

"It's just that he only uses them when he is desperate, which means you made him desperate," Erastus continued as if he had not even heard Richard ask the question.

"What abilities?" Richard repeated. His head hurt too much to deal with a gray man right now, but he was stuck. *Maybe I should just run,* he thought, but the idea made his stomach tighten, his legs weaken.

"He can control the unwarded minds of anyone who has touched a divine object," Erastus said absentmindedly as he surveyed the room, centering his attention on a framed print of the Annunciation that hung between the twin beds. "I've always liked that version," he said, pointing to the painting. "Of course, da Vinci got the details all wrong."

Richard looked at the painting and then back at Erastus. He had questions about the historicity of the painting, but they were completely unimportant, irrelevant in this moment. "Where is Brady?"

"He's with Apollyon, I'm afraid," Erastus said, sitting on the bed and obviously feigning a look of dejection. Richard grimaced at the false emotion. It made him angry that this being didn't seem to feel emotions the way humans feel them. He watched the gray man mimic a pout and felt the need, the wanton desire to pummel that face into oblivion.

He pushed his emotions down and tried to pretend he was a gray man. "What does he want with Brady?"

"He can't take the coins out of the pouch. That was a little rule attached to the curse. Pretty good, huh? It's kept the coins safe for quite a long while." Erastus smiled and let loose an odd, half-laugh that was awkward, halting, disturbing, with just a touch of something more that Richard had never heard before. If pressed, Richard would have said it was righteous indignation. "He needs a human to take the coins out."

"And he can make Brady do this?" Richard's head felt better, his throat felt normal, but his heart was still racing and his anger was bubbling, just below the surface.

"Eventually, but your friend is smart. He's reciting some kind of oath over and over in his head. It's the only thing keeping Apollyon at bay."

"Right. That. Why does that work?"

"Repeating a personal mantra can center a person, keep them from succumbing to baser desires. The coins promote baser desires." Erastus was wandering around the room, he picked up the television remote, sniffed it, then put it back down. Richard's entire face contorted with disgust, but only briefly. He was pleased that they had guessed right about the personal oaths, prayers, etc.

"Where are they?"

"That I can't help you with," Erastus said and formed an exaggerated pout with his lower lip, and anger spiked in Richard's chest. "I never could find Apollyon when he didn't want to be found."

Richard's mind began to work overtime. If he was the one trying to get Brady to take the coins out of the pouch and he was the one who was some kind of supernatural gray man, where would he go? He would want privacy, so he thought about the caves under the old city, but that seemed too close to people, too prone to interruption. He thought about another country, but that didn't seem right. Then, he thought of the desert.

"In the desert?" he asked and Erastus sat up straight.

"Well, that certainly was a popular spot for temptation in the old days," Erastus said and stood to open the door. "But I don't think so. He would want to stay close to the church."

"What church?"

"Judas' church," Erastus said in that way of explaining without explaining that he had.

Richard was no longer angry, but he was intensely curious, and he worried he was getting too used to Erastus. "But I thought you said that getting the coins to the church would break the curse."

"Yes, or, if Apollyon has possession of them in the church then the curse will be renewed. It has happened many times before."

"Wait, what do you mean this has happened many times before?" Richard asked, his frustration painting his words so much that they seemed to be in technicolor next to the gray words of Erastus.

"We've been fighting this battle for centuries." His face did the exaggerated pout again, seemingly on its own, without the gray man's conscious thought, then his face became passive again.

"So, if you've done all of this before, then you do know where he is," Richard said, stepping forward and wanting to shake the gray man until he realized what he was saying.

"Hmmm? I've never considered that before, but I suppose I do know where he is," Erastus said in his frustrating, gray tone of voice and stepped through the open door. "Shall we?"

Richard knew that Erastus was playing with him. He wasn't sure what the game was, but he also knew that he had no choice but to play. Brady needed him. "You're not going to just disappear and leave me to do this alone, are you?"

"Not just yet," Erastus smiled a crooked half-smile that looked far more like a frown, maybe a wince.

***

Brady awoke to the dim light of a torch laid on the floor of what seemed to be a man-made cave. The rough-hewn walls broke the meager light into odd, curious shadows amid damp air. But he hadn't really awakened, he knew; instead, he had come to his senses. He remembered seeing Apollyon outside the restaurant, then a darkness took control, punctuated by snippets of action and visions of life. Now, he was himself again.

He looked around at the damp stone walls and remembered, as if from a dream, walking down dark passages and climbing into tight tunnels. He shivered at the memory of doing all of this against his will.

"Do you know where we are?" a voice, cold, gray, familiar, echoed around the small space.

"A cave?" he answered.

"Not just any cave," Apollyon stepped from the shadows. He stood just a few feet from Brady, barely more than an arm's length, but that slight distance felt as if they were worlds away. "This is a very special cave. I'm betting you don't know what it's called." Brady felt a slight bit of amusement in Apollyon's gray voice. In fact, the gray man was growing more animated as he spoke, still gray, but less lifeless.

"You'd win that bet," Brady struggled to his feet. His head still felt shrouded in a dense fog that just wouldn't release him, but he was beginning to feel like his more familiar self.

"It's the Well of Souls," Apollyon announced with a flourish of his hands, looking like a tour guide presenting a particularly interesting point of interest. "I bet your friend would have known that. He is the brains of the team, yes? Do you know what the Well of Souls is?"

Brady spoke with purpose. He was not angry, more anxious than anything, but he forced anger into his tone. "No, I don't know what that is." Brady took stock of his situation. He felt the empty holster at his side and remembered giving his gun to Apollyon. The memory struck him like a punch to the stomach. "What did you do to me?"

"Oh, just an old trick," Apollyon began to circle the cave, a gray hand lightly caressing the stone as he walked. "It's how we got into this cavern too. My tricks are very effective."

Brady watched Apollyon meander slowly around the room, a pool of gray light following where he led. Brady strained to make out a narrow passageway opposite him. He could just barely see that the opening through the cave walls was shallow, probably curved. Just in front of the passageway, Brady could see a mound, like a pile of cloth, in the vague shape of a person. Apollyon paused in his stroll and took a torch from a holder in the wall. The torch sparked to life, bathing the cave with flickering light. Then, Brady could see the person clearly, a man, surrounded by a pool of dark, angry, red.

"What did you do to him?" Brady said stepping forward to check the man's pulse, to offer what help he could, he began to rip at his own shirt to provide bandages, but he stopped as the light from the torch revealed the grisly scene. "Did you do that?" Brady pointed to the man's head, which was riddled with deep, destructive gashes.

"Me?" Apollyon said with such unconvincingly feigned insult that Brady winced. "I did nothing. He did that to himself."

A vision of the man crushing his own skull between his hands filled Brady's mind, but then the image shifted to a more plausible scenario. He watched as the man in his mind slammed his head into the cave wall until he fell. A quick glance at a red smudge on the wall confirmed his theory, and the image replayed. Brady's analytical mind was quickly filled with morbid curiosity, closely followed by horror, anger, fear. Brady glared at Apollyon as the gray man unceremoniously held up a vial of yellow liquid, smiled a crooked half-smile, and slipped the vial into his interior jacket pocket. Brady watched every movement with singular interest, then he asked, "My gun?"

Apollyon produced a handgun from beneath the folds of his gray sports jacket with a flourish. He held it out. It was so close that Brady could have easily snatched it back, but he simply could not do it. "It's like hypnotism, I suppose, for lack of a better word. The trick that I do. It works pretty well on everyone, but on people who have come into contact with the coins...well, it works so much better. Of course, I don't have to tell you that."

Brady searched his memories for what he knew about hypnotism. He knew that people had to allow the procedure and couldn't be forced to do anything against their nature. If that was true, then how had Apollyon managed to get this man, who seemed to be dressed as a police officer of some kind, to bash his own head against a stone wall, and how had Apollyon managed to get him to turn over the coins? He remembered handing the pouch to the gray man outside the restaurant. He hadn't wanted to, he truly, passionately did not want to, but he did it anyway.

As if Apollyon was privy to Brady's thoughts, the gray hand caressing the wall disappeared a moment into the pocket of his gray jacket to reappear with the leather pouch. The gray man stood there, both arms outstretched, offering Brady a simple choice—the gun or the pouch.

***

"He will try to tempt him," Erastus said as he and Richard walked purposefully through the streets of the old city.

"Tempt him, how?" Richard asked. The periphery of his consciousness was noticing interesting buildings or ruins, but he kept his professorial mind at bay. Brady needed him now.

"It differs for everyone," Erastus said, his voice still as dispassionate as ever. "For some, the temptations come in the form of a sin or two or three, whichever ones to which they are most prone. Greed, gluttony, wrath...for others, it's not as simple or straight forward."

"What does that mean?"

"Apollyon prides himself on being able to turn a strength into a weakness. That's how he's won the battle all these times. He finds the hero's virtue and turns it against him or her."

Virtue? Richard's mind raced back to his philosophy classes in college. He had studied the seven deadly sins, like everyone else who read Danté and Catholic dogma, but he had been more interested in the seven virtues, the opposite pairs of the sins—liberality, patience, humility...and as his mind recounted the list of virtues, he immediately saw how easily one could be turned into a sin. He needed to get to Brady soon. "Are we close to the church?"

"Yes," Erastus said as if reciting a grocery list. "The church is through a secret entrance inside this building." The gray man pointed a gray finger directly in front of them.

Richard's eyes followed. His eyes grew wider, his mouth fell open, and his head began to shake as he recognized the octagonal building capped with a golden rotunda. "That's the Dome of the Rock!" he exclaimed.

"Yes, I believe that is what the locals call it," Erastus said and continued to walk toward the building.

"Oh man," Richard said, his shoulders slumping into a weary stance. "Can't anything be easy."

Richard stood and examined the exterior of the building. There was a wooden walkway where tourists were being directed, but not many tourists were being allowed inside, and signs that read "no entry" marked every other visible entrance. There were also several members of the Israeli police force making sure that tourists obeyed the signs.

"How are we supposed to get inside?" Richard asked, looking at the seemingly impossible task ahead.

"We only need permission," Erastus said and began to walk toward a police officer.

"Sorry, no entrance," the officer said with a thick accent and Richard felt his face flush. He wanted to grab Erastus and run away, or just run away and leave Erastus alone with all of these security personnel.

"We would like to get inside," Erastus continued, tilting his head to one side.

"You need special..." the guard began but fell silent. He tilted his head in a mirror image of Erastus. The two stood looking at each other with tilted heads for a long moment before the guard turned silently and walked toward a small group of tourists being prepared to enter the building. Erastus fell in line behind the group and Richard followed suit.

"How did you do that?" Richard asked as the tour guide began going over the proper etiquette for entering the building.

"Apollyon isn't the only one with talents. I have talents of my own," Erastus said and smiled his frown-like smile.

Richard nodded and stepped forward as the group began to enter through the wooden walkway.

***

Brady stared hard at the gun in Apollyon's outstretched hand, his mind formulating violent, impossible plans. *Grab the gun, shoot my way out*, he thought. *Even if he's immune to bullets, the distraction will work.* Then, he looked at the pouch. Those coins, those deadly, cursed coins. Allowing Apollyon to keep those coins meant more death, more chaos. He slowly reached out and took the leather pouch from the gray man's hand.

"Good," Apollyon said as he placed the gun back in his jacket pocket. "Now, just open the pouch and pour out the coins." Brady's fingers grasped the leather pull string before his mind caught up. He gripped the drawn top of the pouch in a tight fist and glared at Apollyon.

"I want out of here," he said, his voice an awkward mixture of fear and courage.

"In due time," Apollyon replied and stepped over the dead police officer and walked to a shadowed corner of the cave where the torchlight couldn't reach and lifted up a large satchel. "We have so much more to do first."

Brady left the dead police officer and returned to the larger area of the cave. His eyes were adjusting to the torchlight, but slowly. He could only see one possible exit and Apollyon was standing in it. He needed a plan. He needed time to develop a plan. He needed Apollyon to talk.

"How did you get him to...kill himself?" Brady asked, gesturing to the dead man.

"The vial," Apollyon said, stepping back over the man and entering the main chamber again. He put the torch back in its place in the wall before he set the satchel down on the stone floor and opened it.

"What's in the vial?" Brady asked, remembering the yellow liquid Apollyon had placed in his jacket's interior pocket.

Apollyon seemed to consider the question for a long moment; then, he pulled the vial from his pocket and held it up to the light. The yellow liquid glittered weakly. "It's only burial oil," Apollyon said with a shrug.

"Cursed, I suppose, like the coins?"

"Now you are starting to catch on." Apollyon put the vial back in his pocket and returned to the satchel.

"How?"

"How what?" Apollyon asked, not looking up from the satchel.

"How was it cursed?"

Apollyon paused again, his hands inside the satchel, then he made a big show of dropping what he had in his hands. "Now, that is an interesting story." Apollyon smiled a full smile, and it was not gray.

***

Erastus walked with purpose the moment they entered the Dome of the Rock. He shifted quickly, nearly too fast for Richard to follow, around a side passage that circled the outskirts of the interior room. The passage was dark, but there was just enough light for Richard to keep from tripping and to keep sight of Erastus. Soon, the gray man stepped quickly into a dark alcove, nearly invisible in the dim light.

"Here?" Richard asked, joining Erastus in the tight space between the walkway and the exterior wall.

"Here," Erastus announced and pointed downward. Richard awkwardly bent at the knees and felt around on the floor. He could only feel what seemed to be a rug of some kind. "Under the rug," Erastus instructed.

Richard pulled at the corner of the rug and waited for Erastus to step over the lifted corner. He then threw the rug back and felt the floor again. The wood of the floor was rough and uneven. Richard worried about splinters, but only briefly, until his fingers settled on something smooth and cold. A metal handle set into the wood.

The door flung open easily, Richard hadn't expected that, it seemed too easy. He expected it to be locked or blocked in some way, but it was wide open now. Richard looked down and saw flickering light at the bottom of a metal ladder. The stone walls were roughly hewn, he could still see the tool marks. He stepped on the first rung and held his hand against the opposite wall to steady his trembling legs. He descended.

Soon, he was standing in a narrow passageway, lit by torches, that led deeper into the earth. He stepped further into the darkness, closer to the next pool of light further into the earth before he turned his eyes upward in time to see Erastus silhouetted in the door.

"Erastus?" he whispered up the ladder.

"I really do wish you luck, professor," Erastus said and flipped a coin down into the shadows. Richard heard it clink and bounce, clink and bounce, but his eyes remained iced on Erastus closing the trap door above him.

***

"A long time ago," Apollyon began. "There was a man who killed quite a few people."

"You'll have to be more specific," Brady prompted, his eyes darting around the cave, trying desperately to come up with some sort of plan. There didn't seem to be any way out other than through the gray man. "There have been a lot of men who have killed a lot of people."

"Abimelech of Gideon," Apollyon pronounced as if that name explained everything.

Brady shrugged, "Sounds like a name from the Bible, but tell you the truth, I haven't read it in a while." He strained to look into the darker shadows of the cave, but the entire place seemed to be solid rock, except for the passage where Apollyon stood. There were no other options.

"Hmmm? Well, there were quite a few Abimelechs back then," Apollyon said, his head slightly tilted as if in contemplation. "That gives me an idea." He returned to the satchel and began to root around in the interior.

"What about Abimelech?" Brady urged. *More time*, he thought. *I just need more time.*

"Hmmm?" Apollyon looked up from the satchel, shook his head, and continued, "Right, sorry. I suppose I am a bit distracted. Well, Abimelek killed a lot of people and as he prepared to kill even more, by burning them alive," Apollyon pursed his lips and pretended to shudder. "Horrible, right?"

"It's pretty bad, yes."

"He trapped them in a tower, built a pyre around the base and was ready to set it on fire," Apollyon returned to the satchel. Brady could hear objects, metal, wood, maybe glass, clattering inside the leather bag.

"So, where does the vial come in?"

"The vial?" Apollyon asked and patted his jacket pocket. "Oh, it's filled with his funereal oil."

"Abimelech's?"

"Yes," Apollyon stood up straight and posed with tight lips and a tilted head. He appeared lost in thought.

"Why is that cursed?" Brady prodded.

"Why is what cursed?" Apollyon asked, turning and looking up the dark passageway as if he were listening to something. He made a move as if to head into the passage, which made Brady think that there might be something worthwhile in the passage, just out of the light, that needed more time.

"The oil," Brady said, trying to make his voice sound inquisitive and not frustrated. It was a very difficult task. "Seems like the death of a madman would break a curse not create one."

"Oh, that is an interesting story," Apollyon said, whirling around, suddenly fully engaged with Brady again. "A woman from the top of the tower dropped a stone on his head before he could set the fire. As he lay dying from the wound, Abimelek was so embarrassed that a woman killed him that he asked his servant to finish him off before he died of a split skull caused by a woman and the servant did." Apollyon again stood as if he had explained everything thoroughly.

Brady responded honestly, "I still don't get it. I don't understand why the funeral oil would be cursed."

"I was there, you see?" Apollyon began and took the vial with the yellow oil from his coat pocket, lifting it closer to the torchlight. "I saw the evil in this man. The sheer desire to cause harm to others. To murder and kill in the most horrible ways. And then I saw it..."

Brady waited for Apollyon to finish the thought, thinking that the gray man had just paused to promote suspense, but then it seemed the other man would not continue so he asked, "What did you see?"

"I saw his sin," Apollyon said, a wickedly perverse smile curling his lips.

***

Richard stood for a long moment, hoping that Erastus was just pausing before joining him, but then he slowly began to understand that the gray man wasn't coming into the passageway. He would need to go on alone, and he would need to pick up the coin that had settled at his feet. He thought about wrapping it in his coat like he had done before, but the pull on him was different this time. It seemed lesser. He simply bent down and took the coin, slipped it into his pocket, and sighed. *There's something going on here,* he thought, but knew that the answer was somewhere further down this path.

He turned and strained to see as far into the torchlight as he could. There were pools of light that didn't quite connect, but they seemed to go a very long way into the earth. Richard began to walk slowly along the uneven stone floor.

As he walked, Richard thought about how he got to this point. His natural curiosity had propelled him, but all the way to an underground cavern in Israel seemed a bit too far for mere curiosity. Why was he doing this?

Brady had asked him the same question. And he gave a very scholarly answer, but was it the truth? Was he really just searching for answers?

That seemed unlikely too. He could have just simply told the officer from some small town in Virginia to keep him informed and, if Brady had survived, then he would have gotten his answers. He would have been safe in his office back at the college and would have known the truth of the situation. So, why did he journey all this way with Brady?

He wanted an adventure. The thought came to him seemingly right out of the darkness of the corridor. He was slowly dying in his safe, little office at the college. He read about grand adventures in books and he wondered about the truths of ancient stories, but he never did anything to add to the canon, to solve the mysteries, to truly live, and to add his own adventure to the list of human adventures that had defined, and created, the world. He wanted to do something that mattered.

It was hubris. He wanted his life to be remembered for something other than teaching facts to over privileged college students. He wanted his name in a book somewhere that others like him would read and marvel at the sheer courage he had displayed. He wanted to go down in history rather than simply study it. It was prideful.

But was that the whole truth? He admitted, at least to his more prideful self, that the thought of his name being recorded for posterity was exciting, but was that all there was to his desire for adventure? He hoped not.

The passageway turned and the uneven pools of light shone on a sharp decline in the hewn stone. Richard set his foot firmly on the rock and continued his descent.

***

Brady sat in the flickering light of the torches and pondered Apollyon's latest pronouncement. His brow furrowed as he tried to interpret what the gray man was trying to say. He couldn't, not with his limited knowledge of this religious stuff. Instead of wracking his brain, he asked, "What sin would that be?"

"What do you mean?" Apollyon asked, seemingly shocked by Brady's lack of understanding.

"You're going to have to spell it out for me. I ain't exactly in Richard's league with all of this, y'know, stuff." He gestured around the cave for emphasis.

"Vainglory," Apollyon said simply and stepped forward. His eyes were intently examining Brady as if he was seeing the man for the first time.

"Not sure what that is," Brady admitted.

"An offshoot of pride, but more insidious," Apollyon stepped even closer. He was nearly outside the passageway and into the larger cave now.

"Now see, you've lost me again. I never did understand why being proud of something was a sin. Never made any sense to me."

"It's not..." Apollyon's brow furrowed deeper than Brady thought was possible. "It's not being proud of an accomplishment. It's being prideful. Hubris. It's a fault."

Brady shrugged again, this time shaking his head.

"You really don't know?"

"I really don't."

"Hmmm?" Apollyon crossed his arms and stared even more intently at Brady. "That might change things a bit."

"Change things?"

"What tempts you?" Apollyon asked. Brady just stared back, unblinking. "Exactly. This might be more difficult than I thought."

***

Richard progressed slowly down, ever down, as the passageway narrowed briefly and then expanded. There were caves, little more than alcoves, intermittently spaced throughout the passage, but still no sign of Brady.

The torches flickered as he walked, but the air was still. He felt hot and began to sweat. Then he felt cold and shivered. His nostrils were filled with must and dirt. He huffed violently, trying to clear his head.

"I should just go home," he mumbled to the shadows. He turned and faced the long passageway back to the surface. He could start climbing, the air would become more breathable, and he could just forget all of this ever happened. How had it become his responsibility to save people from their own greed? Why was it even necessary to save them?

"They should take responsibility for their own lives," he said and took a step upward. His mind felt fuzzy, like waking from a dream, but there was one thought that shone through. He saw, in his mind's eye, Brady trying desperately to keep the coins from falling into the hands of Apollyon. He couldn't let Brady fight alone. He just couldn't.

"I need to help," he said with a firm, clear voice and turned once more. Then, an image of his friend Katie, lying in her hospital bed, so tormented came to him. He saw Brady writhing in pain, desperately fighting against the darkness. He took a step forward and the road continued downward.

***

"So, that vial is filled with oil from a dead man?" Brady asked.

"It's oil from the funereal rights," Apollyon answered. Then he turned and looked at the vial with obvious pride. "I gathered it myself."

"And it can make people commit suicide?"

"Give in to despair, yes."

"Why is that?"

"What?" Apollyon exclaimed, his voice, no longer gray, no longer lifeless, was now a mixture of confusion, excitement, and frustration.

Brady smiled a short, sly smile. "Despair. Why despair? Seems like the guy in your story..."

"Abimelech."

"Right, him. Seems his sin was sexism. Shouldn't the oil make people hate the other sex, or at least discriminate against them?"

Apollyon gazed at Brady, his gray brows a knot of inquisitive examination. It was as if he couldn't tell if Brady was serious or not, worthy of an explanation or not. It was exactly what Brady was hoping for. "It's all just part of pride," Apollyon said coolly.

"So, the people kill themselves because of too much pride?" Brady asked, a real tone of confusion painted his words. He was only partly acting. He really had never truly understood the concept of the more subtle sins. Murder, yep, absolutely worthy of eternal damnation, but being too prideful? Probably deserved ridicule, maybe a slap or two, some counseling, not hell though.

"Yes," Apollyon stated flatly.

"Huh? Just like that. You're so sure that pride, uh hubris, is worthy of death? Eternal damnation?"

"Yes."

"No question? No mercy? No context? Just pride equals damnation."

"Yes." Apollyon's voice had become noticeably softer, a quiet contemplation just under the words.

"And you merely stoke the flames. That provides the chaos you yearn for?"

"Yes."

"Why do you need the coins then?" Brady asked, lifting the leather coin pouch to eye level. "Can't you just make whoever you want kill themselves? Isn't that chaos enough for you?"

"If they haven't touched the coins, I have to use a drop of the oil each time," Apollyon said and looked at the half-full vial.

"How many have you...?"

Apollyon stepped back suddenly and smiled, pointing an accusatory finger at Brady's chest. He slipped the vial back into his jacket pocket and returned to the satchel. "I think I know what you desire now," he said.

Brady braced himself for what he assumed was to come, but Apollyon only produced a piece of paper and held it out.

"What's that?" Brady asked.

"It's what you want, what you have always wanted," Apollyon responded. "And I will give it to you if you open the pouch."

***

Richard continued his lonely descent into the earth. His doubts were strengthening as his body weakened. The climb was at times steep and then nearly impossibly steep, and always down, further down. His calves ached with the effort of not falling. Another drop-off, the third such one, this one a good ten feet, greeted him and he was forced to scale down to yet another narrow ledge.

"This is hopeless," he said, sitting awkwardly on the cold stone floor. He tried to breathe the unearthly hot, then cold, air. He grew ever more tired. He wanted to close his eyes, for just a minute or two. He needed to rest. He would be no good to anyone this tired, this weary.

He reclined his head against the hard stone and sleep came to him, followed quickly by dreams. He was walking along a beach, the blue waves of the ocean were lapping at the shore, and he was happy, well rested, safe, and warm. The sun was bright and the sky was as blue as the sea, then the sky was the sea and he has floating amidst calming blue swirls of water that became light, which turned to darkness. He was alone in the unending darkness. The air turned cold, and he grew frightened. But a light shone far away, a mere pinprick in the inky blackness. He focused on the light. It grew larger, ever larger. The warmth returned to his body and he began to walk toward the light. Then, he began to run, full out, into the light that became his little office back at the college.

He smiled at the familiar surroundings, so welcome after so much uncertainty, and he sat behind his desk. A favorite book open to a favorite passage was in front of him and he read, "O, that this too, too solid flesh would melt, / Thaw, and resolve itself into a dew, / Or that the Everlasting had not fixed / His canon 'gainst self-slaughter!"

He looked down at his desk and saw a gun resting in the outgoing mail basket.

***

"Are you a demon?" Brady asked as he eyed the piece of paper in Apollyon's hand.

"What makes you think that?" There was once again no tone to Apollyon's words, only gray, lifeless sound. Brady interpreted the gray tone as professionalism. Apollyon was back on the job.

"You're offering a bargain. Isn't that what demons do?"

"And salvation is not a bargain? You don't do this, or you do that, and you get everlasting life. Isn't that the ultimate bargain?"

"Are you saying you're an angel then?"

"Is there a difference between demons and angels?" Apollyon asked and Brady thought he heard a bit of sadness in the tone. Then, Appolyon shook the paper just enough to draw Brady's attention back to it, "You want to make a deal or not?"

"What is it?" Brady asked, curiosity getting the better of him.

"I told you, it's what you desire. I figured it out as we spoke."

Brady paused. It was an interesting thought. It was something that he had often thought about—what he truly desired from life. Could it be that this...being had figured it out from one conversation? He wanted to know what was on the paper. He wanted to know desperately. His hand reached out, but he couldn't make his fingers grasp it. Every fiber of his being was screaming for him to do something different, but it was his heart that he listened to.

"No deal," he said and shoved his hands behind him.

"You are a difficult one, aren't you?" Apollyon said, dropping the paper back into the satchel. Brady watched the paper fall. He could still see a corner of white just peeking out of the top of the leather bag.

"So, what was the deal?" Brady asked, still staring at the satchel.

"You'll never know now," Apollyon said brightly and began pacing in front of the dead security officer.

Brady tore his eyes from the satchel and watched Apollyon walk the width of the cave. He paused briefly at the walls on either side and poked a finger at the stone as if he were examining the strata.

***

Richard's dream-self reached for the gun. He picked it up and examined the black-gray metal. It would be so easy to just...give up. What was he fighting for anyway? Did anyone care? The whole world was just one person after another looking out for themselves and no one else. Even those who thought they were selfless only really looked out for their own—their children, their relatives, no one else. No one cared about Richard Stanley. Why should he care about them?

His parents were dead. He didn't have children or a spouse to miss him. His friends, what few there were, would get over his death pretty easily. In fact, his death might inspire one of his writer friends to include him in a dedication to a book. That was a form of immortality after all. It would be better than dying in a cave underneath Jerusalem. The cave. He was suddenly back in the cave.

The gun was heavy in his hand, but it felt inevitable. He dropped it to the stone floor and it clambered loudly, so loudly that the sound reverberated in the cave. Over and over he heard the crash of metal on stone, louder and louder, until...he awoke.

"That wasn't just a dream," he said into the dim torchlight. He sat up and leaned against the jagged rocks. His brain felt fuzzy, detached, absent. He rubbed his temples and closed his eyes.

"These are tests of some kind," he said emphatically. "The caves, the visions, whatever happens next. Tests. Like..." He thought about the stories he had read about demons, devils, even angels, gods, testing mortals. "Just tests." He whispered and tried to remember that he was a very good test taker.

***

"Why are you doing this?" Brady asked as Apollyon leaned against the cave wall and stared off into the shadows.

"Doing what?"

"This, all of this," Brady gestured to the satchel and then to the dead guard.

"We all have our roles."

"What does that mean?"

"From the dawn of creation," Apollyon started to pace again, but this time further into the cave. The passageway was clear for several steps each time he passed. Brady counted off seconds in his mind. "There were prescribed roles that we all had to play," one one thousand, two one thousand, three..."But some of us didn't like our roles."

"What was your role?" Brady counted barely three seconds of space when the man was clear of the passage.

"I guarded a tree," Apollyon said with a snort. "And not the tree you might think needed guarded, nope. Just a tree. An ordinary tree."

"I don't get it."

"Neither did I, you see."

"I'm gonna need more."

"Creation!" Apollyon said with a flourish of his hands. "All of it. It needed to be guarded. Protected. And we each got a small piece. Some smaller than others."

"You were assigned to guard just one tree?"

"Yes! Do you get it now? One tree! Not one species of tree, no, that would be too much. One single, solitary tree."

"What happened to the tree?"

"What happened....?" Apollyon began and took several steps angrily toward Brady. The passage was nearly clear now with just the gray man standing a bit too close to him for comfort. "Who cares what happened to one tree?"

"So, you thought you desired what? More responsibility?"

"Yes!" Apollyon's voice reverberated off of the stone. "And when we were refused our demands, well..."

"You revolted," Brady prompted, as he stood and faced the gray man. His legs tensed, ready for action.

"Of course we did, wouldn't you have done the same?" Apollyon turned and walked to the nearest wall. The passage was completely clear now. Brady shifted his stance slightly so that he could feel a toe hold through his shoes. He tensed his legs as Apollyon continued, "Here, look at this layer of rock. Did you know that one of us was assigned to guard this bit of rock right here?" Apollyon held his index fingers about five inches apart on the stone. "Just this bit. Nothing more. And look at it now. Buried under tons of other rocks that no one guarded."

"Why did no one guard the other rocks?" Brady asked.

"Ah, you start to see it now, don't you?" Apollyon turned and looked at Brady. He kept an index finger poised just above the rock he had indicated before. "This rock was important and this one," he lifted his finger a half inch higher. "Not as important. Why?"

"I don't know," Brady answered honestly.

"Neither did we," Apollyon said sadly and turned back to the wall.
***

Richard was forced to feel his way along a section of the corridor where the torches had died. He could feel the stone, jagged and cold against his palms, but he couldn't tell if he was heading in the right direction anymore. He had walked straight, but there should have been other torches by now, right? Had he turned a corner? Was he heading back the way he came? He stopped walking and doubt flooded his thoughts.

Maybe I should turn around, he thought. *I could go back to the spot where the torches were still lit and grab one.* The idea seemed sound. He shifted his weight to turn, but couldn't bring himself to make a step.

The passage hadn't curved. He was almost sure of that fact. He had been walking in a steady, downward line. There had been slight curves along the way, but he had always been able to see the next pool of light up ahead. Why would that no longer be the case?

"Things change," he whispered into the pitch blackness.

Of course things change, but there is comfort in certainty too, right? Some things are dependably the same. The sun rises in the morning and sets in the evening. The force of gravity is pretty consistent throughout the planet, although there are slight variations he had read about where gravity exerted less force than...no, that wasn't productive. Gravity is pretty consistent. Very consistent. And walking in a straight line with a consistent downward flow will not allow you to accidentally go back the way you came. It isn't possible.

"I just need to keep going," he said firmly and turned back again. He began inching his way along until he felt warmth on his face. He touched his cheeks and then held out his hands toward the source of the heat. He immediately felt the warmth become too hot. It was a torch. A lit torch.

He put his hands back to his face and realized that his eyes were shut so tightly that his lids were beginning to ache with the strain. He forced his eyelids to relax and then he slowly opened his eyes. He was standing in a part of the corridor that was identically lit as all the rest. He looked back toward the area where he had been convinced there was no light and the pools of light were flickering just as they always had been.

He slumped against the wall. *How can I do this all by myself?* He began to sit, to lower himself to the ground, to shut his eyes against the loneliness, to sleep, just to rest for one minute, just a minute. Then, a new flood overtook him, a thought out of seeming darkness, so strong, so powerful that he stood immediately. He saw, in his mind's eyes, Brady fighting for his life against the gray man. He was alone too. He started to walk faster, with renewed strength, with meaningful purpose, further down the pathway.

***

"All of this death is because you didn't like your work assignment?" Brady asked. "That seems a bit, I don't know, childish, don't you think?"

"Oh, extremely." Apollyon nodded and Brady could barely contain his surprise. "I agree. It's all childish. Just a childish game, and I started a long time ago to ignore the rules. I'm now playing my own game. Do you like my game?"

"Not even a little bit," Brady said sternly and glanced up the passage-way, past the dead guard. He thought he could see a shadow moving just beyond the first bend in the corridor. The shadow grew larger. He just needed a little more time. "So, the other guy told us your name was Carta, something."

"Cartaphilius," Appolyon said. "Yes, that was one of my names."

"So, how does that work?" Brady asked. "If you were at the beginning of Creation, then how are you also the Wandering Jew guy?" There was a distinct movement in the corridor. Someone was coming. Just a bit more time.

"Just a game we all played once we abandoned our assignments." Appolyon appeared to be lost in thought again as he rubbed his fingertips against the stones. Brady flung himself into a sprint. He ran as fast as the small space would allow, jumping over the corpse, and darting around the corner.

***

"What!" Richard screamed as Brady nearly bowled him over.

"Run!" Brady shouted back and pulled the other man's shirt sleeve. The two began scrambling up the steep passageway. They ran until the air caught in their throats, and then they both slumped against the walls.

The torch light flickered as always in the damp air as the two men tried to catch their breaths.

"What are we running from?" Richard asked, looking frantically back down the passage.

"Just keep going," Brady instructed and started to walk upward, ever upward.

Richard paused, wondering if this was another test. If so, what sin, or failings, was it designed to exploit? Trust? Was he not supposed to trust Brady? That seemed unlikely, but he doubted whether anything was real at this moment. He looked back down the passage and saw the identical pools of torch light he had been seeing this whole time. He felt the air, both hot and cold, slowly swirl in meek circles all around him. He felt the pangs of mistrust tug at his stomach. He wanted to accept that Brady had somehow gotten away from the gray man, and that this was his friend, but the visions the cave prompted were...disorienting to say the least.

"Stop!" Richard called and Brady turned.

"Come on," Brady pleaded. "Apollyon is probably right behind me."

"How did you get away?" Richard asked, trying to identify some trait, some feeling, that would reveal the truth of this situation.

"I ran. While Apollyon explained why he was doing what he was doing," Brady said, still backing up the corridor. "Please, just come on."

"How do I know...?"

Brady heard the sadness in Richard's words, and then another thought struck him. "How did you get here?" he asked, stepping toward Richard.

Brady looked into Richard's eyes and recognized the doubt. "Erastus," he responded simply.

"Another gray man?" Brady nearly spit the words out.

The two men stood a few feet from each other, but the distance seemed to be growing by the minute.

"You don't trust Erastus?" Richard asked.

"You do? Why?"

"I...he's...I don't know. What did Apollyon say?"

"A lot. He told me a story about a mass murderer and funeral oil. Something about not liking his guard duties. Other crazy stuff. What did Erastus say?"

"Not much. He was...somewhat detached."

"That's not how I would describe Apollyon. If anything he's too involved."

"I think I should go on into the cave," Richard announced, pointing back in the direction they had come.

"There's nothing down there except Apollyon and a guard he killed."

"I still need to see," Richard took a step away from Brady.

"You want me to come with you, don't you?" Brady said with an obvious tint of suspicion as he held up the leather pouch. "I have the coins. We should just go."

"Not all of them," Richard responded and pulled the coin from his pocket. Brady gasped and stepped back. "It's alright. I think this one is inert or something. It doesn't have the same effect as the others."

Brady nodded and held the pouch open until Richard dropped the coin inside. "Now, we have all the coins. All thirty of them. Let's just go."

"No," Richard said. "You should take the coins and go."

"We should take the coins and go," Brady corrected.

"And then what? We just keep running around the world, hoping to stumble on another way to break the curse? This is it, Brady. This is the cave that Erastus said would..."

"Erastus?" Brady said with disdain. "How can you, we trust him? He's one of them."

"I just trust him. I can't explain it."

"So, what? You want to take the coins back to the guy who wants us to bring the coins to him? The guy who uses the coins to kill people?"

Richard paused. Brady was right. How could they chance taking the coins anywhere near Apollyon? Was it the right move? He had no idea, but his eyes were open and he knew what he had to do, and he knew why he wanted to do it.

"We have to try," Richard said. "If not us, then, who?"

CHAPTER 22

Richard stepped over the body of the guard. Brady had warned him about the gruesome scene, but he still wasn't prepared. He closed his eyes tightly and then opened them to see Apollyon as he stood patiently in the flickering light, his hands extended in greeting.

"Welcome," he said in that strange gray tone that was not welcoming, nor frightening, nor any emotion really, but all of them as well. Richard noticed, in that moment of intense focus, that there was a stark difference between his voice and Erastus'. Whereas Erastus appeared to have difficulty displaying even the simplest human emotion, Apollyon oozed emotion, but the emotions were too much, too many at once, and the effect was unnerving. With one word, Richard felt fear, excitement, doubt, guilt, and other emotions that weren't so easily identified, and he had no idea how Apollyon's voice inspired these emotions while still sounding as dull and lifeless as Erastus.

"Thanks," Richard responded, cautiously making his way closer to the gray man. The satchel Brady had described was now at Apollyon's feet. "Is it my turn for your presents?" he asked, pointing to the bag.

"Do you want a present?" The words felt like an accusation, and Richard could feel a tinge of guilt rise in his chest.

"I want you to stop all of this," Richard said, still slowly circling the room. Apollyon had not moved. His arms were still outstretched as if he were expecting an embrace. "Brady told me that you were...rational. Can't we come to an agreement?"

"Rational?" Apollyon sneered and turned suddenly to face Richard who had walked behind him. The gray man's back was now to the passageway. "Somehow I don't think that is the word he used."

"You got me," Richard smiled. "He said you were crazy, but that you made some interesting points."

"Oh, yes? Like what?" Apollyon crossed his arms and stood very casually as if he were an old friend Richard had met on the street. As unnerving as Erastus' lack of emotion was, this man's demeanor was much more frightening. There was a defiance in Apollyon that made every interaction feel like a challenge.

"He agreed that it was unfair that you were assigned a tree," Richard began, trying to keep his eyes off of the shadowy figure creeping into the cave behind Apollyon.

***

Brady inched as quietly as he could along the rough hewn floor. He crouched and nearly crawled at times, painfully aware of how far his shadow extended into the cave. He nearly put his hand into the pool of blood at the guard's head before he realized what he was about to do. He glanced at Apollyon as he repositioned his hand and felt the relatively bloodless stone of the damp floor and shuddered at what this gray man was capable of doing.

Richard had done his job. Apollyon was facing away from the entrance, and he had gotten him to start talking, moving him as far to the back of the cave as was possible, and as far away from Brady as they could get him. Apollyon wanted to tell his story, he wanted someone to listen, and he needed people to understand and commiserate with him. Brady had identified that desire to be heard as the gray man's own secret desire. The one thing he could not resist.

According to Richard, the only thing Brady needed to do was to consecrate the coins inside this cave. But to do that, he needed to spread them out on the stone. Once inside the cave, he pulled the leather pouch open and slowly reached inside. Carefully, he felt for the edge of a coin. The jagged metal was cool to the touch as he closed his forefinger and thumb around it, lifting it silently from its siblings.

The silver glinted sharply in the torch light and Brady felt the need to take the coin and run, but he keep repeating the phrase Richard had suggested over and over in his mind, "I consecrate these coins to the Lord's use. May they serve His purpose."

The desire to possess the coin was strong. It tugged at him like a rope around his throat. He wanted to scream, to run, to throw the pouch, but he forced a tepid calm onto his mind. He exhaled silently through his mouth and concentrated.

I consecrate these coins to the Lord's use, he thought loudly and wished that he could speak the words out loud. Maybe that would help. *May they serve His purpose.*

His thumb and forefinger were white and pinched together so tightly that they ached. He willed them to relax, but they simply squeezed tighter. He exhaled through his mouth again and forced his jaw to slacken, then his shoulders to drop, then he thought about his arm, then his fingers. With effort, and many more deep breaths, he was able to place the first coin onto the stone floor and release it. He exhaled, almost making an audible sound but catching himself in time. He had done it. He had touched a coin and released it. He had resisted the curse. Now, just twenty-nine more to go.

***

Richard watched over Appolyon's shoulder as Brady struggled with the first coin. *This is not going to be easy*, he thought as he continued with the plan. "Maybe you could tell me what it is you really want, and I can help?"

"Psychoanalysis?" Apollyon snickered. "Better than you have tried, but why not? I'll let you have a go." He sat unceremoniously, cross-legged, onto the floor and motioned for Richard to begin.

Richard lowered himself, much more gently and awkwardly sat with his legs curled under him. "Okay, let's see. From what I understand, you were one of the beings tasked with guarding creation. Right?"

"That's right," Apollyon nodded and smiled broadly. "We were two of the chosen few who were elevated with power and extremely long life. Mostly because we had done something bad. You see, immortality is a curse. I've been cursed."

Richard paused to consider. "You're not an angel?"

"Angel?" Apollyon's laugh was as colorless as his words and the monotonous echo was truly unnerving. Then, he suddenly stopped and looked pleased with himself, "You know, now I think on it, maybe I am after all. Huh?"

"But you were given a task like an angel, right?"

"Yes, that's right. More curses."

"How many of you were there? Guarding creation?"

"Hosts. Did you not learn that in Sunday School?"

"Hosts, right. And each of you were given a piece of creation to safeguard."

"And I was given a tree, and maybe the tree was more than it seemed, or maybe the tree would spawn other trees that were then chopped down to build a great cathedral, or maybe the pulp of the tree was used to craft the paper that drafted the Declaration of Independence, or maybe, maybe, maybe…I've heard it all."

"And none of that matters to you?" Richard asked as Brady laid another coin on the stone. *What is taking him so long?* Richard thought. *Just get them out of the bag and do it.* He was nervous, more frightened than he had ever been, and still trying to provide counseling to a disgruntled angel. "What could the tree have been that would matter to you?"

"Nothing. The answer to that is nothing. What could possibly matter to me? That I spend thousands of years guarding a tree that might later give way to something more important? And then the guardian of that more important thing would be praised, not me."

"So, you want acknowledgement."

"Yes!" Apollyon shouted and Richard watched Brady jump, glance their way, and continue to pull coins from the pouch. "Why shouldn't I get just a little praise? I followed the rules for eons. I was penitent, truly penitent.. I was on-board with it all. All the curses, all the menial tasks, all of it. But when does it end? Why didn't I even get a mention in the texts?"

"The texts?"

"The texts, the texts, the Holy Books, the tablets. I would have even settled for a footnote on a papyrus scroll, but nothing. No one knows or cares that I was assigned to guard some tree."

"Where was the tree?"

"Why do you care?" Apollyon said and placed his hands on the floor as if to rise.

"I would like to know. Is it still around? Could I maybe see it one day?"

"No, it's not still around. It was a tree, just a normal tree," Apollyon said and settled back down to the stone. "It grew, it aged, it died. The end."

"Didn't you get another assignment after that?"

Apollyon smiled a big, toothy, gray smile. "I did. And I'd like to get back to it now. So..." He placed his hands on the ground again, preparing to rise. Richard watched Brady freeze, a coin in his hand.

"What happened to the tree after it died?" Richard asked, his hand outstretched, trying to will Apollyon to remain seated.

"What do you mean? It rotted." Apollyon had settled back down. His plan was still working, but Richard knew that time was short.

"I mean, it is a law of nature that matter can neither be created nor destroyed, so the matter that made up the tree, where is it now?"

"What?" Apollyon seemed legitimately surprised. His gray features twisted in thought.

"Can you find it? Are you still connected to the stuff that made up the tree?"

"I..." Apollyon's gray eyes became unfocused, distant, and Richard waited. The gray man fell into a shallow trance.

***

Brady was able to pick up the pace after the first few coins. The consecration was working, evidently, because the pull of the coins was lessening with each one he laid on the floor. The curse was dissipating; he could feel it happening.

He placed another coin on the floor and let out a long, halting breath. He caught himself and tried to silence the breathing as he chanced a look toward the others. Apollyon was still facing away from him, Richard caught his eye and made a series of slight motions, a raised eyebrow, a nod of the head, a slight jerk of his hand, all of them calling for him to continue. He returned to his work, *I consecrate these coins for the Lord's use.*

Richard sat as still and silently as he could, not wanting to break the spell that Apollyon seemed to have put himself in. He waited, breathing in and out, daring a glance at Brady's progress from time to time. Then, a slight movement of Apollyon's head drew his focus.

"Interesting," the gray man said as his gray eyes danced over Richard's form. "I had never considered this before. I suppose because I really am not that well grounded in the sciences, more a philosophical bent you see? The matter, the atoms, the stuff of existence, it is still here, most of it anyway. I think there's a smidge floating out near Mars. Not important. You've given me a lot to think about. Thank you, Professor Stanley."

"Wait. So, where is it? The matter?" Richard prodded, trying to extend the conversation just a bit more.

"That is an interesting development, that is," Apollyon said. "And I will be sure to ponder the significance later. Right now, I really should get back to work."

"But you have to tell me." Richard failed miserably at his attempt to keep the panic out of his voice.

Apollyon stared at him, his brow furrowed with consideration, his lips twisted in thought. "You," he finally said.

"What?"

"Well, not all of it mind you, but a large chunk is right inside you," Apollyon pointed a finger at Richard's chest. "Isn't that fascinating? But there's more." Apollyon stood and Richard scrambled to his feet as well. They stood face to face, Apollyon stepping closer and whispering,

"There's also a rather large bit in your sheriff friend over there." He jabbed a thumb over his shoulder in Brady's direction.

Richard opened his mouth to say something, anything to distract Apollyon, but then he chose to simply grab the man's arm. He was shocked at his own momentary audacity. Then, the fear set in. His eyes grew wild and his legs began to falter.

"Well," Apollyon said with an amused grin. "You caught me. Now what are you going to do with me?"

Richard couldn't move. He glanced over at the dead man and Brady. His breaths came in fluttering gasps. He let go of the man's arm, but he forced himself to stand taller.

"Good choice," Apollyon said. "Now, I appreciate the conversation. Truly. You really have done something no one else has ever done. You gave me something to consider after I finish reactivating the curse."

"But..." Richard tried to speak, but there was a rushing sound in his ears, a drumming in his chest.

"Now, now, don't fret," Apollyon began. "You did your best, and you gave him lots of time to perform the ceremony." Then, over his shoulder Apollyon called, "Are you finished yet, Sheriff?"

"You're too late!" Brady yelled as he finished placing the final coin on the stone. "The coins have been consecrated! They're just coins now!"

"That's true," Apollyon agreed as he turned to face Brady. "But they were soon going to revert to normal coins anyway."

"What are you talking about?" Richard chimed in as he flanked Apollyon, ran to Brady, and helped him to his feet.

"The curse," Apollyon walked slowly toward them and was soon standing eye to eye with the other men. "It has a shelf date, you might say. Most do, but not all."

Brady's breathing was returning to normal as he asked, "Okay, so we didn't need to go through this consecration stuff?"

"Not really, but it was a great help to me," Apollyon said and stepped forward. He knelt down and picked up one of the coins and held it to the torchlight. "Just a coin now, but still really beautiful, don't you think so?"

Richard watched Apollyon suspiciously as he grabbed coin after coin and dropped them into the leather pouch Brady had left beside them. "The tests in the passageway, the dream that was really a vision," Richard began. "What was all that for?" The air suddenly turned cold and then immediately hot, as Apollyon stood and pulled the drawstring tight.

"You wanted us to consecrate the coins," Brady said simply. Apollyon blankly stared at him. "But why? I thought the thing you wanted most was chaos and these coins certainly did cause chaos."

"Chaos? Yes, I suppose you would see it that way," Apollyon began, his gray eyes sparkling with amusement.

Brady pulled at the back of Richard's shirt, hoping the other man would realize they were going to have to run soon. He backed slowly toward the passageway, tugging at Richard's shirt as he moved. Richard got the message and stepped back with him. "If not chaos, then why?"

"Chaos is such a simplistic way of looking at it though." A voice, cold and monotonous, sounded behind them. Brady and Richard turned in unison to see Erastus standing squarely in the middle of the passageway, the only way out of the cave. "Was that necessary?" Erastus asked, pointing to the guard's body at his feet.

"It was absolutely necessary," Apollyon responded with an insidious sneer.

"I'm sorry about my brother," Erastus said, stepping over the guard and stopping directly in front of Brady. "His enthusiasm for our work often causes him to be messy."

"And you are too neat," Apollyon offered from the back of the cave. "You never want to get your hands dirty."

"What is this?" Brady asked, stepping backwards, and looking from Erastus to Apollyon and finally to Richard.

"It's another test," Richard answered.

"Very good," Apollyon said, clapping his hands much too loudly in the small space.

"What kind of test?" Brady asked, his back now against one of the walls.

Richard was still standing in the center of the cave, Apollyon stood in a pool of light near the back wall, and Erastus stepped out of the passage. The two gray men turned to stare at Brady while Richard stayed with his back to him. Brady's breathing became erratic. Something was very wrong here. The air had gotten so hot, but his skin was shivering. His head felt fuzzy and he had to put a hand against the stone to keep from falling, or fainting; he could no longer tell what his body might do.

"This test is just for you, Sheriff," Apollyon said, passing the coin purse to Erastus who held it out in front of him, sitting equally on both of his upturned palms, like an offering. Apollyon then thrust a hand into his jacket pocket and produced the vial of yellow liquid. He popped the small cork out of the vial and held it out. "It's a simple choice really."

The cave seemed to shrink as Brady watched the two gray men standing on opposite sides of Richard. He looked at the torches, and they appeared the same as they had been, but the cave was much darker. He was having difficulty seeing beyond the row of men in front of him. Why couldn't he think clearly? His thoughts were vague, indistinct, gray.

"What are you doing to me?" Brady asked.

"Just a little nudge," Apollyon responded, his voice dripping with so much false sweetness that it made Brady physically ill.

"That is right," Erastus added, his voice sounded like the voice feature on Brady's smartphone, but with less personality. "We cannot make you do anything that you do not inherently want to do. We can only nudge you to make a choice."

"Believe me," Apollyon added. "It would be so much easier if we could just make you do what we want you to do. Like at the restaurant. You remember?"

"Richard, what is going on?" Brady asked Richard's back. The other man seemed not to notice. "What did you do to him?"

"He's not going to be much help I'm afraid," Apollyon said, patting Richard on the shoulder as he spoke. "He's had a long day and we thought he might want to sit this one out."

"Besides," Erastus added. "He already passed all of his tests."

"Now, Erastus," Apollyon chided. "This isn't a competition. But if it was, you're right. Richard is way far out in the lead. But not to fret, Sheriff. This last one is a doozy and could potentially tie up the score."

"It is a choice, like so much of life is a choice," Erastus said.

"You'll have to pardon my brother this time. He always thinks things have more meaning than they do," Apollyon interrupted.

"A choice of two roads," Erastus continued, ignoring Apollyon.

"Mine first!" Apollyon said enthusiastically. "If you choose my road, then I will just pour one little drop of this oil on Richard."

"But that's the..." Brady began.

"That's right. But wait, there's even more," Apollyon pointed to the leather pouch in Erastus's hands and continued, "If you choose me, then the coins are yours. Thirty pieces of ancient silver, with, well let's be clear, significant historical value. I'd wager a collector or a museum would pay half a million each for them. Conservatively speaking. You could probably ask for more. Start a bidding war. That's always fun."

"And Richard?" Brady asked.

"Oh, he'd most likely be dead," Apollyon said, pooching out his bottom lip in mock sadness. "But that just means more for you."

"You think I would kill him for..."

"You wouldn't be killing anyone," Apollyon interrupted. "Remember the oil's curse? He might not even give into despair. He might be one of the few who could easily withstand the oil's influence. There have been others to survive. Not many, mind you, but others. And if he does give into despair, then he would kill himself. You would be long gone."

"There is no way that..." Brady began.

"Wait!" Apollyon interrupted. "You haven't heard the other offer. You should have all the information before making such an important decision."

"I'm not going to let you kill Richard," Brady said emphatically.

"I would certainly hope not," Erastus interjected, holding up the leather pouch. "Would you like to hear my offer?"

***

Richard opened his eyes to a bright day full of warm breezes and sunshine. He stood in a field of wildflowers, and the reds, yellows, and oranges of the blooms mirrored the brightness in his chest. His heart felt light for the first time in days. His lips formed a smile effortlessly, easily. He was happy for just a very brief moment. Then, he remembered that he was actually in the cave with the gray men.

His mood changed, but the scenery did not. "Where am I?" he questioned the breeze. A warm gust was the only response.

He bent and touched the closest flower, a poppy, he thought, although botany was not a speciality of his, and it felt so real. He flicked at the petals and broke the stem. He lifted the entire flower to his nose and sniffed. An earthy scent tickled his nostrils and he closed his eyes. When he opened them again, he was facing a large stone castle. The field of flowers, maybe marigolds, he really did not know flowers, led to the entrance gate.

He took the flower with him and walked through the gate. The interior of the castle was cool with dim light seeming to flow from the stone walls. He found himself in a great hall with white and red banners adorning the walls and columns. He walked toward the end of the hall where an ornate chair sat on top of three stone steps. He paused at the steps and waited.

***

Brady paused. His eyes darted frantically around the cave. The situation was dire. Even if he got past Erastus, which did seem likely because the gray men were obviously more about psychology than physicality, he couldn't leave Richard. And Richard was in some kind of trance. How could he break the trance?

"I think he's ready for your offer," Apollyon said.

"My road is simple as well," Erastus began. "You take your friend and leave the cave."

"Wait, what?" Brady exclaimed.

"That is the entire offer," Erastus said. "You take your friend and leave the cave. After that, what you do is entirely up to you."

"What's the catch?"

"No catch," Erastus said in his gray voice that felt so lifeless, so color-less that it made Brady shiver. He held up a key. "The key is to the trap door that will allow you to leave this cavern." Brady looked at Erastus and then at Apollyon, who just shrugged and held out the vial again, shaking it slightly.

Brady waited for the other shoe to drop, but the two gray men fell silent. They stood patiently, each holding their respective objects in front of them. Brady knew that the choice of the vial was out of the question. He would not risk Richard's life for money, even a whole lot of money, but the other choice was too easy. Brady had learned long ago that the easiest choices often turned out to be the worst ones. "What about the coins?" he asked Erastus.

"They would stay with us," Erastus answered in that same monot-onous tone that gave no indication of excitement or confusion or any-thing helpful.

Brady eyed the coin pouch and pondered the implications of this choice. If the coins remained with the gray men then what would be the outcome? They were consecrated, right? The curse had been broken. They were just coins, right? That's right, yes? Is it? He really needed Richard's advice on this one. The obvious choice seemed much too obvious, and even though Erastus said there was no catch, there was always a catch. He needed to identify the catch before, and then a question came to mind. "And the curse on the coins?"

"You deactivated the curse," Erastus said.

There's more. There has to be more, Brady thought. "Then why do you want them?" he asked.

"You do not get to know that," Erastus said.

"Tell me or I won't make a choice at all."

Erastus looked at Apollyon who merely shrugged again and smiled. Erastus shook his head slightly and jiggled the pouch just enough to hear the coins clinking softly inside.

***

Richard stood in front of the steps until two doors on either side of the room opened. He looked at each one, identical rectangles of light in the dim room. He stepped to the left and tried to peer through the light. He could not make out anything of distinction past the threshold. The same when he stepped right.

"What is this?" He asked the empty room, but he knew the answer. "What kind of choice is this? I should have at least a little information or it's just a guess."

Silence answered him.

He continued to stand in front of the steps and a memory from his childhood came to him. He remembered reading a story in elementary school about a man faced with a similar choice—two identical doors. Behind one was a beautiful woman, and behind the other was a vicious tiger. The man was forced to make a choice with no further information. It was a story about fate, luck, destiny, whatever you want to call it.

But the gray men were all about temptation, weren't they? What was tempting about two identical choices? Another thought came to him, a poem about two roads in the woods. The two roads were fairly identical as well, only one slightly more traveled. That poem was about the choice, making a choice instead of standing still. Was that the temptation? To make a choice, or not?

Richard stood in the middle of the room, he looked at the left door, then at the right, then back at the left. He sighed deeply, sadly, expelling frustration and anger into the musty air. He stepped toward the right and walked close to the light. It was a solid thing, or very near it. He touched it and felt what he could only describe as a membrane, like the skin of a pudding. He pushed his hand through and a tickle of wind fluttered in his palm. He walked to the left door, repeated the process, and felt the same tickle.

"This is an impossible choice!" He shouted and his voice echoed off the stone walls, swirled around the steps, settled into the chair on the dais. Richard nodded as the sound of his own voice died slowly in the dim light. He walked back to the center of the room, looked once more at each door, then he climbed the steps, turned, and sat in the chair. He looked back onto the great hall and waited.

***

Brady looked at the gray men. There was no way he was going to choose the vial of oil. He would not, knowingly, put Richard's life in danger, but the pouch? He couldn't let these beings keep the pouch either. There was something he was missing about this choice.

"You need to choose or we'll choose for you," Apollyon said, pulling the cork from the vial.

"Then, you'll just have to choose," Brady said, his anger flaring. "I'm not playing this game."

"Choose!" Apollyon shouted and his voice echoed through the cave and into the corridor.

Murmurs flowed back through the passageway.

"What is that?" Erastus asked.

Apollyon stepped closer to the passage and listened. Brady strained to hear. Shuffling, like feet on stone floors, and whispers. Several different voices, maybe four or five people.

"Someone's coming," Apollyon announced and replaced the cork in the vial. He slipped the oil back into his jacket and stepped around Richard, still entranced, and pushed Erastus to the side of the cave.

"You killed a guard," Erastus said as he dropped the coin pouch at Richard's feet and started rummaging through his own jacket pockets. "They're coming to investigate."

The gray men began to whisper and Brady tried to listen to the words, which now sounded like hisses, clicks, an occasional grunt, and some other sounds that were too odd, too alien, for Brady to label.

The gray men stepped into a deep shadow near the back of the cave and they became nearly invisible. Erastus was still rummaging through his own pockets and Apollyon was agitatedly trying to help him look for whatever he was looking for, but he was only making the search more difficult.

Brady took a tentative step forward and, when the gray men didn't notice, he rushed forward, snatched the leather pouch from the ground, grabbed Richard by the arm, and pulled him into the corridor. To his shock, Richard began to run.

"Are you alright?" Brady asked as he jerked Richard through the passageway, around corners, but the question died in the air as they were suddenly face-to-face with several automatic weapons pointed directly at them.

CHAPTER 23

The Israeli police office was stark and utilitarian, but bustling with people. Richard had been ushered into a holding room while Brady sat at an officer's desk waiting for his credentials to be verified. The officer on the phone behind the desk was asking questions in a thick accent but Brady understood that he was talking to someone at the Potter's Field police department. He hoped whoever the officer had reached was being helpful because the zip-tie securing him to the chair he was sitting in was beginning to dig into his wrists.

The officer hung up the phone and looked at Brady's badge once more before lifting his eyes. He stared at Brady with intense curiosity. "You are very well out of your jurisdiction, Sheriff." The officer stated.

"I...we were following clues that..."

"And the two men in gray?" The officer asked and Brady noted that the name badge said Peretz.

"Officer Peretz," Brady began.

"Inspector Peretz, but you can call me Aaron," the man said and Brady recognized the technique. Humanize yourself, while maintaining distance and authority, make yourself appear to be a friend who has power. It was effective. Brady found himself wanting to trust Aaron with the whole story.

"Thank you, Aaron," Brady began again, opting to play along for the moment. "The gray...the men in gray, kidnapped me and my friend, Richard, he came to..."

"That's Professor Stanley?"

"Yes, Professor Stanley." Another technique. Interrupt the answer so that the suspect has to start again. Improvised answers would falter, rehearsed ones would repeat. "He came to save me. The men in gray kidnapped me, killed one of your officers and were trying to make off with valuable artifacts," Brady chose each word carefully, trying neither to falter nor repeat, and hoping against hope that Richard would make a similar statement.

"That's right, the coins," Aaron said and pulled the leather pouch from a box next to his desk. He placed it in front of Brady and the coins rattled inside.

"Yes, those. We managed to get the coins and to get away from them. The men in gray."

"And you believe they are responsible for three other murders in the States?" Aaron asked, but the question seemed accusatory.

"Yes," Brady said simply. One more technique. Lay out the evidence to show how crazy it all sounds. Brady wanted to explain about the coins and the curse but he didn't see any way that this man, who was following police procedure to the letter, would believe him.

"Well, I just have one more question then," Aaron said and lifted the coin pouch. He placed it in his open palm and seemed to gauge its weight. "Why is it that we only found you, Professor Stanley, this pouch, and a dead Inspector in that cave?"

"What?" Brady exclaimed. "The gray, the men in gray were there! We had to run from them! They were right in the cave!"

"No, there were no others in the cave," Aaron said and stared directly at Brady's eyes. "And no other exits. We searched. How do you explain that?"

Brady thought back to the cave. Apollyon had pulled Erastus to the side, which gave Brady the opening to escape. Erastus was, what was Erastus doing? He had dropped the coin pouch. That was an odd move. Brady hadn't considered it at first. The coins were what this whole thing was about. Why did he just drop them? Because he was searching for something in his jacket pockets. That's right. Erastus was frantically looking through his jacket pockets. Apollyon had the vial of oil and

Erastus must have had something that...what? Made them disappear? Made them invisible? He suddenly wished that explaining the cursed coins was the only thing he needed to do.

"Fine," Aaron said as he gathered papers together, took the leather pouch, and stood. "I'll let you think about that while I go submit these to the evidence vault." He motioned for another officer, who cut the zip-tie on the chair and lead Brady to an interrogation room. On the way, he spied Richard tied to a chair on the other side of the room. He tried to get his attention but to no avail.

The officer shoved Brady into a holding room with just a metal table, two chair and a mirror on the wall. Then, he left, closing the door behind him. Brady watched him leave and felt a wave of hopelessness. He slumped into one of the chairs and wondered what the prisons were like in Israel.

He glanced at the mirror, obviously a two-way mirror, and wondered if anyone was watching him right now. He also wondered if Richard was all right. He sighed wearily and put his head onto the table.

How had he gotten to this point? He was in a police department in Israel being held for suspected murder and theft of antiquities. How had that happened? The gray men. That was how. They must have disappeared from the cave somehow or he would have seen them. The officers had carted Richard off immediately, but they had kept Brady separate, at the scene, while they searched. No gray men. They obviously had all of these supernatural powers. They probably just told the officers to let them go and forget they were ever there. They might have even planted the suggestion that the whole mess was the Americans' fault.

The door opened slowly and a police officer walked into the room. Brady lifted his head and tried to look at the officer's face but he couldn't make out any distinct features. He tried to look at the name plate but couldn't identify any readable word on it. The officer slowly lifted his hand, like a magician performing a trick, and pulled at a strip of cloth wrapped around his palm.

The cloth unraveled slowly and the officer began to become less distinct, if that was possible. Then, all of the color drained from the man and his uniform became gray. Brady gasped as he looked up into the gray face of Erastus.

"How?"

"The Bandage of the Prophet," Erastus said by way of explaining but doing absolutely no explaining. Brady didn't need any further commentary. It was yet another supernatural object, probably related to disguise or hiding. It didn't matter.

"That's how you escaped the cave," Brady said.

"Yes," Erastus offered as he folded the strip of cloth and shoved it into his jacket pocket.

"What do you want now?"

"You," Erastus said and pointed toward one of the walls, evidently in the direction of where Richard was being held. "Your friend is out there and you have not made your choice yet." Erastus said while standing aside and holding the door to the room open. "You should go get your friend."

Brady rose slowly and walked through the open door. He watched the gray man with suspicion as he went, but Erastus merely smiled and nodded.

Once outside the room, Brady looked down the hallway and saw Apollyon standing and pointing toward an area of the building where desks were positioned haphazardly, with no discernible organizational strategy at play. Brady walked down the hall and past Apollyon who smiled an identical smile to the one Erastus had presented, but for some reason, Apollyon's gray smile made Brady's skin crawl.

Brady watched the police officers mill around, presumably going about their daily business, but he knew that most of them were just trying to catch a glimpse of the Americans who had murdered one of their own. He could feel their judgments all around. He tried to see things from their perspective—a cave under an incalculably valuable religious site, a dead Israeli officer, an American college professor, and an American sheriff holding a leather pouch filled with extremely rare coins. He had to admit that, in their shoes, he would be thinking murder and tomb robbing too. In no circumstances would he have imagined thinking that there were two supernatural entities controlling the entire scenario.

He stepped from a hallway and caught Richard's eye. Most of the officers were engaged in hushed whispering sessions and hadn't noticed him yet, but Brady knew that would change soon. If the gray men were trying to orchestrate a prison break, they were doing a poor job of it. Suddenly, an alarm sounded from outside the building.

The room nearly emptied as most of the officers, who apparently were only hanging around this area out of curiosity, which proved Brady's theory correct, hurried out of the building. There were now fewer than a handful of officers in the room, three that Brady could see easily, another couple behind a column. Had the gray men set off the alarm? It seemed too coincidental not to have been part of their plan.

Brady used the sudden departure to rush to Richard's side. "The gray men are here."

"I figured," Richard responded as Brady tested the zip tie. It was solid and effective.

Brady shuffled to the nearest desk. "I'll look for something to cut this. Keep an eye out." He gestured toward the other side of the desk and looked around at the remaining officers. They were gathered near the exit. One was holding open the door and the others were talking and pointing outside.

"What's that alarm?" Richard asked.

"I thought you might know. It sounds like a fire alarm, maybe?" Brady found some industrial scissors and hurried around to cut Richard free. "I'm not that familiar with Israeli alarms."

Richard slipped his hand free. The two stood and marveled that none of the officers had noticed them yet. Richard asked, "Are the gray men doing something to them?" He pointed to the officers who seemed too engrossed in the commotion outside to even glance around.

"I have no idea," Brady responded. "But they were back there." He pointed down the hallway where the holding rooms were. "Both Erastus and Apollyon."

"Both of them? Another way out back there, maybe?"

Brady shrugged and the two men headed down the hallway that he had just exited. The gray men stood shoulder to shoulder in the hall. Erastus's arms were crossed on his chest in a defiant stance while Apollyon held out the vial of yellow liquid.

"Time to choose," Apollyon said and shook the vial in front of him and he held the pouch in his other hand. Erastus uncrossed his arms and produced another key, obviously to the security door behind him.

"What are they doing?" Richard asked. "The police are, and we need to, they can't just, what are they doing?"

"They want me to choose."

"Choose what?"

Brady looked at his friend and then at the vial of liquid. It was the same problem as before. If he chose the vial and the oil was used on Richard, then the chances of him committing suicide were completely unacceptable, and if he chose to leave? He still couldn't see the pitfall. He needed advice. He turned to Richard, "They said we could leave. Just give up the coins and we can leave."

"What?" Richard eyed the gray men, each one was impossible to read, but Apollyon did seem to be enjoying himself more than Erastus.

"Back in the cave when you were out of it. They said I can choose to take the coins or we could just leave."

"What am I missing?" Richard asked, watching the gray men intensely. "What are you not telling me?"

Brady thought again for a long moment before he responded, "We can just leave. The other choice is not an option."

"What's the other choice?" Richard prompted.

"It doesn't matter, it's not..."

Richard grabbed Brady by the arm and squeezed hard, "Tell me."

"They would use the vial on you," Brady responded, his eyes staring down at the green tile floor.

Richard held his breath for a moment before he let it all out with his voice. "Use the vial," he said with determination.

"No!" Brady shouted. "You saw what the vial did to the man in the cave. We can't chance it."

Raised voices began to sound behind them. Apollyon cocked his head to one side and cupped a hand around his ear in an exaggerated motion that made Brady think of mimes. He suddenly disliked the gray men more, which he thought would have been impossible. "Sounds like they have discovered their prisoners have escaped. Time is running short. You need to choose."

Brady wracked his brain. What was he missing? It couldn't be this simple. If he chose to just leave and he and Richard walked out, leaving the coins, then they were still just old coins. Really old coins. Coins worth a fortune. Brady's mouth began to water at the thought of all the money he could have by selling the coins. And then a thought, brief and frightening, shot through his mind. He could just take all of the coins and leave Richard with the gray men. After all, Richard was a successful college professor. He didn't need the money. And Richard said he was willing to chance the vial. Greed, raw and powerful, encased him. He felt it, tasted it, longed for it, then he whispered, "It would reactivate the curse."

"What? Taking the coins? How?" Richard eyed the leather pouch suspiciously. "What about me?" he began. "Can I take the coins? Can I snatch the coins and run? After all, you don't need the money they would fetch. You're a sheriff. You have respect and admiration. A college professor who has devoted his life to studying ancient artifacts deserves the money." Richard shook his head and gasped. He turned to Brady. "I'm so sorry. I don't know where that came from."

"I get it, trust me, I understand." Brady nodded his head toward the pouch.

"Greed," Richard said. "The sin of greed would reignite the curse. If either of us takes the coins, then we would be betraying the other, just like Judas."

Brady asked, "And if we just leave the coins with them?"

"They would find someone else to tempt. Eventually, someone would betray a loved one for the money."

"Then we're stuck," Brady sighed wearily.

The voices down the hallway were growing louder and angrier. Brady had an idea. It was probably stupid, it probably wouldn't work, and it would probably end with them in a prison cell, but it was also something he could live with.

"Not much time now," Apollyon announced. "Time to choose."

Brady crossed his arms defiantly, nodded to Richard who did the same, and everyone waited.

"Make your choice!" Apollyon shouted, the fragile veneer of politeness eroding with each passing second.

"We choose neither," Brady said firmly, suddenly enjoying the fact that Apollyon seemed so frustrated. He felt he was winning somehow.

"That's not a choice," Erastus said in the same gray tone he always had, but the words were tinged with something neither Richard nor Brady could easily identify.

"It is a choice!" Brady suddenly shouted and stepped forward. The voices from behind rose louder as his words echoed against the cinderblock walls. "Everything is a choice!" Brady flung his whole body, with abandon, at Erastus and grabbed at his gray jacket.

***

Apollyon nearly doubled over in laughter as Brady tried in vain to push Erastus against the wall. Erastus simply stood still, his gray face a mask of something resembling confusion. Then, with a slight wave of his hand, Erastus shoved Brady against the opposite wall. The illusion dissolved and Brady slumped against the back wall of the cave. The damp stone was cold and sharp against his shoulders.

"I told you that wouldn't work," Apollyon continued to laugh as Brady became aware of the vision. They had never left the cave, and he could see the impossibility of the scenario now.

"That was a test," Brady said as he struggled to his feet. Richard was still in his trance in the center of the cave, near the dead security guard lying in front of the only way out. Brady looked into the passageway, half-expecting to see the flashlights of the Israeli police coming closer. Only the same torchlight as before illuminated the passage. "It was all some kind of dream."

"A vision," Apollyon corrected. "A vision in the desert," he lifted his arms in an exaggerated flourish. "An age old technique, which I told him wouldn't work."

"It is the way this sort of thing is done," Erastus said.

"Maybe we try it my way now?" Apollyon took the pouch from Erastus and tossed it to Brady. "Here, take these."

Brady caught the pouch and stared blankly.

"No catch, no worries," Apollyon stated. "Just take the coins, take your friend, get out of here."

Brady watched as Apollyon took Erastus by the arm and pulled him toward the passageway.

"I do not believe in this plan," Erastus said as the two disappeared into the shadows beyond the torchlight.

CHAPTER 24

"Richard?" Brady said softly, an unsure hand on Richard's shoulder. "You okay?"

Richard began to blink, shifted back and forth on his feet, swayed a little too much so that Brady helped steady him, and finally said, "I'm back. I'm awake. What happened?"

"I truly have no idea," Brady admitted. "I was in this vision where I, we, got arrested and had to escape from the Israeli police."

"I had that vision too," Richard said. "But mine started in this weird throne room and then you grabbed me and pulled me into the passageway and we were arrested."

Brady rubbed his eyes with the palm of his hand. "So, what was real and what was, you know, not real?"

"I don't think any of it was real," Richard said and pointed to where the security guard had been lying. There was just a vague damp spot on the floor.

"For Pete's sake," Brady was pacing back and forth. "The dead guy wasn't real?"

"I think he was supposed to provide motivation, scare us a little, maybe."

"Are we, uh," Brady began, breathed in, looked frantically around him, touched the stone wall, and continued. "Are we actually in a cave in Israel right now?"

"Yes," Richard nodded. "I think the visions started when we entered this cave. You with Apollyon and me with Erastus. Seems like they're gone now."

"So, we passed the tests, we won?"

"I don't think so. It doesn't feel finished," Richard took the leather pouch from Brady. "We still have these to deal with."

"Can we get out of this cave now?" Brady asked as he walked toward the passageway. The torches were dying quickly as they hurried through the tunnels, climbed back up the rock faces, slipped through the narrow bits, and gazed up the ladder at the closed trap door. "Do you think they really locked it?" Brady asked, thinking back to the key Erastus had offered.

Richard admitted, "That might be their plan, to trap us under the Dome of the Rock for a couple hundred years or so."

"Yeah, that would be bad," Brady added as he looked up at the door. He was absentmindedly twining a piece of cloth around his fingers, then unwinding it, and wrapping it around different fingers. As he did this, he faded from sight, then reappeared, then parts of him faded, then reappeared.

"Where did you get that?" Richard asked, taking the cloth from him.

Brady shrugged. "I picked Erastus' pocket. Right at the end of the vision back there. I thought I'd try to get the pouch, but I missed and figured if Apollyon had a magic vial in his pocket, then maybe, but all I got was this old piece of cloth."

"Old cloth?" Richard took the scrap and wrapped it around his hand and disappeared. His disembodied voice continued, "This will make getting out of the Dome of the Rock unnoticed much easier."

After a trap door seemed to open by itself, and a few visitors felt the odd sensation of someone standing close to them when no one was there, and others felt a slight rush of air as if someone had just passed by, even though no one had, Richard and Brady dashed behind a pillar and unwrapped their hands.

"That's a handy thing," Brady said, admiring the yellowed cloth.

"Yes it is, but I think we might have created a ghost story or two with some of those visitors," Richard responded.

"Naw, they'll chalk it up to something spiritual or something."

Richard nodded slowly, "So, what do we do now?"

"Well, we have the coins," Brady offered, holding up the leather pouch.

"And we're sure we didn't make a choice?" Richard asked.

"Only one way to be sure," Brady said and tugged open the drawstring. He took a deep breath and reached his hand into the pouch. The cold metal, ragged against the skin of his fingers, greeted him. He closed his thumb and forefinger around a coin and lifted it free. The two men held their breaths, waiting, anticipating. Nothing happened. "Looks like we did not make a choice," Brady said and easily dropped the coin back into the pouch. "So, what do we do with them?"

"I think the choice thing proved that the curse can be reactivated," Richard began, pulling the drawstring tight. "If we sell the coins, or give them away, the gray men will find them and tempt whoever has them."

"And someone, somewhere, will make the wrong choice," Brady agreed.

"We have to get them somewhere the gray men can not get to them and no one else owns them."

"Like a museum," Brady offered.

"That sounds like a good plan," Richard agreed. "We could donate them to a museum and make sure that the curator knows not to let anyone touch them."

"You think that will work?" Brady asked, concerned with Richard's own concerned look.

"Souvenir?" a gravelly voice asked suddenly from beside them. Richard turned and saw an elderly woman. "They are made right here," the woman said, pointing an old six inch nail at them. "Same as what crucified the Lord."

Richard took a nail and looked closely. The edges were not smooth; they were rough and flaky with jagged peaks that cut into his skin. "What kind of metal is this?"

"Pure iron," the woman said proudly. "Straight from the smithy here in town."

"Iron," Richard whispered, a thought tickling the back of his mind.

"What are you thinking?" Brady asked.

"How far is the smithy?" Richard asked the woman.

The blacksmith turned out to be a historical reenactor who had developed a mobile blacksmith stand that he could erect in various places around the city, but always near tourist attractions. He made trinkets that were historically accurate, at least as historically as he cared to make them, and his number one seller was the nails. They were fashioned from iron and worked to resemble, as closely as anyone knew, the nails used for crucifixion during Roman times. The old woman collected the nails from the smithy every morning and then sold them to tourists, but the blacksmith was selling his wares very near the old wall today. It would be just a quick fifteen minute walk to the smithy.

"We destroy them," Richard said after the old woman told them all about the smithy and where to find it.

"In the forge," Brady agreed, immediately understanding Richard's plan.

"Thank you," Richard said to the woman and offered her a ten dollar bill for the nail. She smiled and handed him a handful of nails. Richard took the metal spikes and dropped them into the leather pouch where they intermingled with the coins.

"This can't be that easy," Brady began as they started walking toward the smithy. "If someone could have just thrown these coins in a fire then wouldn't they have done it a long time ago?"

Richard thought for a moment, then spoke with finality, "You're right. Someone probably has thought of this plan before now, possibly long before now, and possibly multiple times before now. Will this time be different? I don't have an answer, and I don't see another idea."

"What about the museum idea? That sounded good."

"It might work, but I fear it would just prolong the process of the coins getting out into the world. You saw how they affected Cherylyn. The curse built up on her until she couldn't resist. Putting this in a museum would give us a few years respite at most. Then, we, or someone else, would have to start all over again, from the beginning, with all the death and violence.."

"And that's what the gray men want, isn't it?" Brady offered and Richard nodded in agreement. "So, we destroy them."

"We destroy them."

They walked faster now. The day was stretching into night, and the gray men always seemed to appear whenever they were on the cusp of making progress in this quest. The gray men were overdue.

CHAPTER 25

Part 3

Interlude 2

Amos Baumer had been reenacting ancient Roman smithy techniques to entertain tourists for years. He had discovered a particular talent for it as a teenager. His skill was such that he could forge a novelty sword, tiny and delicate, by hand that could be worn as a necklace, but the tourists only seemed interested in the nails. It was child's play to forge iron nails. They were simply six inch long spikes of iron. He had baskets and baskets of them, and the tourists kept buying them.

He also had candle holders, crosses, elaborate decorative hangings, along with the delicate jewelry, but he understood that the tourists did not appreciate the fact that he could work a piece of metal with such finesse that the finest machine made metal art seemed clumsy by comparison. They wanted the nails.

"Your forge," a voice sounded beside Amos. The sun was dipping below the horizon and the tourists were nearly all gone back to their hotels. The empty streets seemed as gray as the man's voice. "How hot does it get?"

Amos looked up in the direction of the gray voice and saw a gray face looking back. He tried to stifle a shiver but failed miserably, and quickly, in order to cover his rudeness, said, "I try to keep it at 760 C, or about 1400 F."

The gray man nodded, "Can it get hotter?"

"Yes."

"Enough to melt silver?"

"Do you need some silver melted?" Amos asked, suddenly more curious about the man's words than his gray appearance.

"Can this forge melt silver?"

Amos felt the gray man's gray words more than he heard them and they were forceful, demanding. He nodded.

"That's a shame," Erastus said as Apollyon stepped from the shadows, a vial of yellow liquid in his outstretched fingers.

***

Richard and Brady rounded the corner just in time to see Erastus holding a man's arms behind his back while Apollyon held a vial above the man's head.

"No!" Brady shouted and sprinted forward. Apollyon smiled a wicked, gray smile and replaced the cork in the vial. Erastus released Amos and the two gray men turned and casually strode down the alley, disappearing into the deepening shadows of the city.

Brady ran forward and took the man by the shoulders. He could see the tears flowing freely down his soot-stained cheeks. He yelled over his shoulder, "This is the blacksmith we were looking for." He lowered the man to the ground and held his head against his chest as the sobbing became convulsive. Richard joined him and tried to wipe the yellow liquid off with the tail of his shirt. The liquid smeared, mingling with the soot, and formed a grotesque blotch. "Is that the funereal oil?" Brady asked.

"Yes! Hold him," Richard responded, trying to capture the flailing arms and restrain the kicking legs.

Brady held the man from behind and the three awkwardly sat in a strange huddle. "What do we do?" Brady asked. He was thinking about the guard in the cave, the pool of blood, the angry gash in the man's head. But that wasn't real. This is. "I don't..." he began. He frantically searched for something, anything that would help. He saw a photograph of the man with a woman and a child, and the immediacy increased. He saw a certificate of appreciation made out to Amos Baumer. "Amos," Brady shouted to Richard. "His name's Amos."

"Amos, can you hear me?" Richard cooed as he held Amos' hands, trying desperately to keep him from clawing his own face. He had faltered a couple of times already, which had resulted in bright red lines near his eyes. "You need to calm down. Everything will be alright, I promise. Just try to calm down. Breathe. You'll be alright."

Brady winced at Richard's promise. He had long ago learned not to promise something you had no way of delivering. He wrapped an arm as securely around Amos' chest as he could and used the other to search the storage area under the cart. He found little swords, nails, and crosses. He lifted a delicate metal cross attached to a rosary and remembered Katie Share's suggestion. He took the rosary and pressed it into Amos' hand and said, "A prayer. We need a prayer

Richard thought for a moment and then said, "Bless us, our Father..." Amos bucked underneath them, but the men held him tightly. Richard continued, "With the light of Your Countenance."

***

Amos fell deeply into darkness. He was surrounded by shadows, ugly and vicious, biting at his hands, his feet, his face. He fell further. There was no light, no hope, no point to living. He wanted so desperately to give in to the darkness, to simply lie back and let it bury him, overtake him, consume him. Then, a light, small as a pin prick, shone through the shadows.

"...all of us as one." Richard continued and Brady found himself reciting his oath of office in his head. He was also wishing with all his might that this prayer, or whatever it was, would work quickly.

***

The light pulsed brighter. Amos remembered the death of his mother. She had developed cancer when he was far too young. He remembered her wasting away in a hospital bed they had put in place of her regular bed. Her bedroom was the same, except for this bed, this unnatural bed, marking the comfortable memories with deep sadness. She had died in a bed not her own. The darkness deepened.

"For by the light of Your countenance..." Amos remembered the day his daughter had been hit by a car. She had been playing with friends and a speeding car slammed into them and then sped away. He remembered the anger, the rage, at the driver. How could anyone do that to children and then just go on with their life? His daughter slipped into a coma before she finally succumbed to her injuries. He remembered the funeral procession. He had barely been able to walk to the gravesite. The darkness overtook the pinprick of light.

"You gave us the Torah of life and..." Amos saw his wife, still so sad a year later. He could do nothing to lessen the pain. He tried, but she kept falling deeper and deeper into despair, until it became necessary to get outside help. He remembered the white hospital room where his wife tried desperately to overcome her sadness. The shadows oozed around him like ink from an endless well.

"...loving-kindness, righteousness..."

Then, the pinprick of light returned. Amos remembered his mother's smile, before the cancer, before the unnatural hospital bed. Her face was luminous, alive, and beautiful. She was holding her granddaughter for the first time.

"...blessing, mercy, life and peace."

He remembered his daughter's laugh. It was a combination of sheer joy and breathless excitement. She was playing in the water at the beach, her grandmother watching over her. The day was bright and warm. The pinprick of light grew brighter. He remembered his wife leaving the hospital, finally able to move forward, not forget, but not succumb either. She had triumphed over the worst pain, the deepest hurt, and she had survived. The sun outside the hospital doors was invigorating. The light was so very welcome after such a long, miserable night.

Amos let out a deep sigh and the tears slowed.

***

"I think, I think that did it," Brady said, as Amos slumped into his arms.

"Are you sure?" Richard asked, noticing that BRady was still hugging the man close.

"Yes, I think so," Brady said, relaxing his grip and slowly lowering Amos's head into his lap. He released his hug and sat back, exhaled a long, renewing breath, and looked at the forge. The fire was completely dead. "They did this to keep us from destroying the coins," Brady offered.

"Yes, which just proves that this might be the right path," Richard said, still trying to wipe the oil from Amos's forehead.

"So, what now?" Brady asked.

Richard sighed wearily and looked down at Amos who had fallen into a peaceful sleep. He looked back at the forge. It was mobile. They could take it away from people, maybe back to the caves, but first they needed to make sure the blacksmith was okay. As if on cue, Amos opened his eyes. He looked up at Richard's worried face and smiled, "Hello, my name is Amos."

"Nice to meet you Amos," Richard responded.

Brady dragged the forge behind him as Richard helped Amos through the narrow streets toward his home. Amos was unsteady but getting stronger with each step. He asked, "You said a prayer back there. What was it?"

Richard tensed, "It's the only Jewish prayer I know. You don't know that one?"

Amos shook his head, "It sounded vaguely familiar."

Richard flashed a curious look behind him and Brady returned the confusion. Richard asked, "You don't have a similar prayer in your religion?"

"I'm an atheist," Amos said as he pointed to the door painted bright blue.

They walked up some narrow stairs to a small but comfortable sitting room. Amos sat at the small dining table in the corner near the front window that overlooked the alley between buildings, but a sliver of sky could be seen just in the top right hand corner. Brady sat across from him as Richard paced in front of the small sofa.

"Is he alright?" Amos asked, indicating Richard.

Brady shrugged and asked, "Are you alright?"

"Why did it work?" Richard said and it did not sound like a question with an answer. He continued to pace.

Brady understood that Richard was lost in a mystery. He thought he had solved the secret of overcoming the artifacts, personal oaths or beliefs, but that was shaken a bit by Amos' atheism. So, Brady helped out the investigation by asking, "Back there, when you were, you know, in trouble, what were you thinking when you heard Richard's words?"

Amos shook his head, "I was suddenly consumed by everything I had lost in life, the people who died far too early. It was such a weight."

Richard stopped pacing and stood next to the table. His foot was tapping though, and Brady recognized his own sign of anxiety, a desire for fast answers. He reached up and squeezed Richard's hand. The other man took a deep breath and squeezed back as he asked, "And the prayer didn't give you strength to fight it?"

"Not the prayer, no," Amos admitted, "but the words. I heard 'love' and I thought of my mother's smile. I heard 'life' and I thought about my daughter's laugh. That's all I remember."

"Hmm?" Richard scratched his chin as he started to pace, but then he stopped and turned back to them. "It's not the words, it's the intent. I was trying to help Amos and he felt me trying. It didn't matter what I said."

Brady shook his head, "No, I think it did matter. The specific words mattered. I think maybe prayers and oaths and such use words that prompt the feelings that we need to overcome the curses. In Amos' case, it was reminding him of the love he has for those he's lost." He paused, realizing he was completely out of his depth here. "Right?"

Richard's mouth hung open and Brady tried not to be offended by how shocked he looked. "That's it, you solved it." He rushed forward, leaned down, and gave Brady a deep, passionate kiss. They returned to themselves quickly, realized where they were, and turned to Amos, ready to apologize.

Instead, they were greeted by a friendly smile. "You two are well-matched. I'm pleased you found each other. Do you want tea? Coffee?"

They both nodded and Amos went into the kitchen space and turned on the electric kettle.

CHAPTER 26

They drank their tea and tried to plan their next move. They had the forge. Amos told them they could use it for as long as they needed.

"We still need to find the church," Richard said as they poured over the map that Amos pulled up on his computer.

"I thought," Brady asked. "Well, wasn't that the church under the Dome of the Rock?"

Richard shook his head, "No, I don't think so. It was a church, but not the one we need."

"Which church do you need?" Amos asked suddenly from the kitchen where he was pouring Brady a second cup of coffee.

Brady walked to him to retrieve the cup and answered, "Evidently, we need to find Judas' church, which is not really a church but a cave or something."

"It's a cave," Amos said definitively as he handed Brady the coffee.

Richard interjected, "Are you sure?"

"Sort of," Amos explained, "My mother used to take us into the caves. She would show us a particular spot that she called Judas' church. I don't know if it truly was, but she thought so."

"Where?" Both Richard and Brady exclaimed and after a quick lesson in getting around the city, they went in search of the Church of Judas.

Amos's forge was little more than a metal oven fixed atop a cart. Richard and Brady were easily capable of pulling the cart along the city streets. The road to the caves was much harder. Amos had pointed them toward a place where they could enter the caves without much chance of being seen. There were fewer and fewer of these places, where tourists were not directed, but there still were entrances that only the locals knew about. Without pavement, or any sign of attempts to smooth out the road, the going became harder, but the cart's wheels traversed the uneven earth well enough with some pushes and shoves, a couple of tugs from the men. The interior of the cave was even more difficult going. They had to lift, shove, and pull hard to get the cart completely inside. Then it was a matter of finding the right spot, which AMos was not sure of, but there were rumors, which had to be enough.

The cave was pitch black, lit only by their two flashlight apps on their phones, until Brady lit the fires of the forge. A soft orange glow bathed the stone walls in a semblance of warmth..

"Thank goodness Amos isn't a purist," Richard said as he opened up the propane tank. "Otherwise, we would be here all day trying to light this thing."

"Agreed," Brady said as the fires of the forge speedily grew in intensity. He watched the gauge in order to make sure the fires were hot enough to melt the silver. The temperature began to rise steadily. "Still, it's going to take a bit."

Richard nodded and began to stroll around the cave as Brady pretended to watch the fire but was actually watching the handsome professor examine the walls. He watched him tenderly touch the surface, obviously reciting something in his head, and then scratching his chin. Obviously lost in thought, he turned and their eyes met. Brady smiled, "FInd anything interesting?"

Richard smiled back, "It's fascinating. We just walked in, you know? I've toured these caves before. At least a different part of them. It's a tourist spot. This place that will hopefully help us save the world is open for tours. It's crazy."

"That's the crazy part?" Brady asked, a mischievous smile etched across his face.

Richard laughed easily, beautifully, "Fair point." He walked over and hugged Brady, kissed his cheek, and asked, "So, how's the fire?"

Brady answered, "Just a few more minutes and I think we'll have a hot enough fire."

"Really?" Apollyon's sinister gray voice echoed off of the cave walls and the two men tensed and prepared for a fight.. "I don't think you have the time."

Brady grabbed the metal poker he had been using to stoke the fire and brandishing it like a sword, he took a defensive stance in front of the forge. "We're going to destroy the coins," he said defiantly.

"So many like you have tried," Erastus's gray voice entered the dimly lit cave from the opposite side. Brady turned toward him as Richard kept facing Apollyon. "They all failed. What makes you think you can do better?"

Brady chanced a glance at the temperature gauge. It was close, but they needed more time. "We're going to beat you," he said, pointing the poker at each of the gray men in turn.

"I know you think that, but you are incorrect," Erastus said, his gray voice turning somber. "Humans, at least the mortal ones, are such flawed creatures."

"It's true," Apollyon chimed in. "They always fail. They mean well, of course, but they are just so very, very weak. And young. They're mere children playing games they don't even understand." He reached into his jacket pocket and pulled out the vial of yellow liquid. "Speaking of, you still need to choose."

"We made our choice," Brady said, holding up the leather pouch.

"Not hardly," Apollyon said and shook the vial.

"I will not tell you to use that on Richard," Brady said emphatically. "It's not happening, and we have the coins." Brady shook the leather pouch, mimicking Apollyon's gesture.

"Choose," Erastus said, his gray voice taking on a slight air of anger as he inched closer. Brady decided the meager emotion was a compliment to his ability to annoy.

"No!" Brady shouted. "We're going to destroy the coins!" Brady turned and lunged at the forge, the leather pouch in his outstretched hand. Impossibly, Erastus stood between him and the fire. The gray man reached out a gray hand and casually took the pouch from Brady.

"You will choose," Erastus said and the gray had left his voice almost completely. It was now filled with danger, red and black.

"You have nothing left to bargain with," Apollyon said, his own gray voice filled with amusement.

"That would be true," Brady said. "If that pouch was filled with coins."

Erastus's face changed from angry to confused. He glanced at the pouch in his hand, then he pulled the drawstring and thrust a gray hand inside. He began to scream.

"What is it?" Apollyon asked and rushed forward. He took the pouch from Erastus as the other fell to the ground, writhing in pain, the tips of his fingers engulfed in black smoke.. Apollyon turned to Brady, "What did you do?"

"Just replaced the coins," Brady said, shocked by Erastus's reaction, but pleased with the results.

"With what?" Apollyon shouted and tried to look into the pouch.

"It's the iron," Richard announced from the forge. "The nails are made of pure iron with jagged edges. I think your buddy must have pricked a finger on one of them."

Brady couldn't help but think of Sleeping Beauty and wondered if the princess in that story was really a gray person who was cut by an iron nail, which would explain a lot about that story that he never understood, but then he returned to the task at hand, reached into his pocket, and pulled out another one of the iron nails. He held it like a knife and then jabbed at Apollyon. The spike pierced the gray man's skin, just above his wrist. Apollyon screamed as the skin just below his palm began to smoke and burn, the nail still hanging from him.

"What have you done?" Apollyon screamed, joining Erastus on the ground. The two gray men writhed in unison, engaged in a grotesque dance of pain and fire, until they finally, thankfully, fell silent.

"What was that?" Brady asked, turning from the unconscious gray men to Richard.

"Iron," Richard simply said and continued to stoke the fires of the forge.

Brady nodded, although he had no idea why iron had worked the way it did or how this plan had actually succeeded. He bent forward and tried to find a pulse on Apollyon's wrist, the one not smoking, and found nothing. He tried to find a pulse in his neck and found nothing there too. "Do these guys even have pulses? You know, when they aren't unconscious from whatever the iron did to them?" he asked.

"I have no idea," Richard responded. "Leave it, I think the fire is hot enough now."

Brady nodded and reached into the pocket of his pants. He pulled out a package wrapped in rough canvas and tied with a string. He pulled the string, and the canvas splayed open revealing thirty silver coins. "And this will do it? This will end it?"

Richard nodded, but his eyes betrayed a deep worry. He bent his head to the forge. Brady stepped forward and flung the canvas, complete with the coins, deep into the heart of the flames.

The night was heavy and full of sinister sounds of small animals scratching, skittering, slithering, and wind, whipping, swirling, growling, as Richard and Brady alternately continued to stoke the forge and gaze inside at the coins. Just outside the cave, they heard the calls of the night birds and, once or twice, Brady was convinced he had heard a lion's roar. Amidst it all, the gray men lay unmoving.

"They still haven't moved, or breathed," Brady said, pointing to the gray men. "Did we kill them?"

Richard shrugged and continued to watch as the fire licked at the metal. The canvas had long since turned to ash. The temperature gauge read 926 C. Richard performed a calculation in his head and interpreted the reading as 1700 F, plenty hot enough to melt the silver, but none of the coins were even starting to bend from the heat. This plan was not working, and the propane tank was nearly out of fuel.

Richard and Brady sat and listened to the wind and birds until the propane completely ran out. The fire quickly died after that. They continued to wait until the night air grew chill, and the morning sun was just beginning to rise over the horizon. Brady touched a tentative hand to the side of the forge. It was still warm, but the damp night air had cooled it sufficiently. He used the metal poker to scrape some of the ashes onto the stone floor. There was an unmistakable tinkle of metal on stone. Richard bent forward and picked up a shiny silver disk.

"It doesn't look damaged at all," Richard observed as he took the coin from Brady's fingers.

"It looks shinier," Brady noted. "I think we just cleaned them."

"This doesn't make sense," Richard proclaimed, frustration causing him to wince. He went over the calculations in his head. "The melting point of silver is well below 1700 F. We maintained 1700 degrees for hours before the propane ran out. The silver should be slag at the bottom of the forge."

"We can't destroy them, can we?" Brady asked and began to gather the coins back into the leather pouch. The heat of the metal was uncomfortable in the palm of his hand, but he ignored the pain. They had failed. These coins were still here, still whole, still capable of killing people. He finally drew the leather strap tight and stood looking at the sunrise. "What now?" he asked.

"I guess," Richard began. "I guess we go with our first idea, the museum."

Brady nodded. A gust of wind brought an unearthly silence into the cave. The silence grew and pressed on their ears as if they were in the depths of the ocean, deep underwater, drowning in the quiet. Brady held his hands to his ears to try and block the silence. Richard shook his head in a vain attempt to expel it. Then, as suddenly as it began, the silence ended with a gasp of air from behind them. They turned and watched as the gray men drew in long gulps of air and began to sit up.

"I have had just about enough of you two," Apollyon said as he pulled the iron nail out of his wrist and dropped it to the ground. "Ouch, that stings."

Erastus struggled to his feet and rubbed his hand. He looked at the small, red dots on his fingers. "That was a good try, but the effects of iron ebb after a few hours."

"Yes, and you should have been running the whole time," Apollyon sneered.

"We're not making a choice," Brady said, shaking his head and holding the coin pouch.

"I think you've made that abundantly clear," Erastus said. He loudly sucked on his fingertips.

"Well, I say we let them go," Apollyon offered and he made an awkward raspberry sound. "It might be the leftover iron poisoning, or maybe the fact that they are made up of my tree, I don't know. I think they earned it."

"It seems we have no choice but to wait," Erastus agreed and turned.

"Wait for what?" Richard called after him as Apollyon joined and they strolled toward the city. "Wait for what?"

"They're not going to tell you," Brady said. He picked up the leather pouch and then placed a reassuring hand on Richard's shoulder. "Let's just go home."

CHAPTER 27

The plane ride back to the U.S. was uneventful. Brady had been so nervous for the first couple of hours that he nearly threw up his dried out chicken, luckily his overpriced beer helped keep it down as he constantly scanned the aisles for any sign of the gray men. He didn't want a repeat of the trip to Israel, but he also didn't fully expect to see them, unless letting them go was another one of their tests.

"You think the Smithsonian?" Brady asked after nearly an hour of silence.

"Yes, I think Cherylyn would know how to protect them," Richard said between anxious hiccups.

"Do you really think that or are you trying to make me feel better?"

Richard shrugged and closed his eyes. "I don't know, and I'm too tired, and nauseated, to come up with any meaningful answer right now." Richard allowed his head to slump onto Brady's shoulder and he drifted into a fitful sleep.

Brady liked the weight of Richard's head on him. It felt like home. He began to breathe a bit more deeply.

"Templar?" Richard whispered.

Brady whispered back, "What?"

Richard was obviously asleep, but whispered again, "Knights Templar?"

Brady sat a while longer, pondering Richard's words and coming to the conclusion that whatever he was dreaming about was something professors of history dream about. He could ask later. He leaned his own head against Richard's as his energy gave out and he joined Richard in sleep. As he slept, he dreamed. In the dream he saw the old woman who had told them about the nails, but this time she was even older and her eyes were no longer the deep brown he remembered. They were white. No color at all, simply white. And she spoke without words.

"You have proven yourself worthy," the woman said without moving her lips, her white eyes glowing.

"Worthy of what?" Brady asked, strangely aware he was in a dream and that this dream was more than it seemed.

"You can gather and protect the artifacts," the woman said and smiled a big, toothy, gray smile. "You are very good at it."

Brady awoke with a start. The plane was approaching Washington D.C. and the pilot had just announced the weather.

"You okay?" Richard asked as he returned his tray table to its upright and locked position.

"I think so." Brady responded sleepily, then he asked, "So, what's a Templar?"

Richard responded, "A Templar? Why do you ask?"

"You kept whispering it in your sleep. Templar. Night. Something like that. I had this weird dream. I thought maybe you had one too, about Templars or something."

"The Knights Templar?" Richard answered breathlessly.

"Yeah, that's it. What's the Knights Templar?"

"Huh," Richard huffed and shook his head. "It's a long story."

Once in the taxi headed to the Smithsonian Annex, Richard recounted what he knew of the Knights Templar, especially the part about them protecting important religious artifacts. He also mentioned the Friday the 13th massacre.

Brady offered, "The old woman in my dream said I was good at protecting artifacts."

Richard added, "And in my dream we were being inducted into the Knights Templar."

The two men fell into contemplative silence for the rest of the taxi ride. Cherylyn met them at the door to the Smithsonian annex. She was anxiously kneading her hands. When they walked up to the steps, she hopped down several steps to greet them.

"You have all thirty?" she asked before they could even say hello.

"Yes," Richard answered and handed her the leather pouch. Cherylyn began to take the pouch but hesitated. "The curse has been removed," Richard reassured her.

"These are magnificent," Cherylyn said as she lifted coin after coin from the pouch.

"They have to be protected," Brady warned.

"But if the curse is gone..." Cherylyn began.

"It can be reactivated," Richard began. "Or we're pretty sure it can. In any case, we need to make sure that the coins are secure and no one, and I mean no one, can get to them."

"That brings up a question I've been meaning to ask," Brady interjected and pointed to the coin pouch. "Why did they let us deactivate the curse?"

"What do you mean?" Richard asked. "I do not think they let us, I think we beat them."

"Do you?" Brady continued. "Really? They are...whatever they are. They've killed so easily before. Why didn't they just kill us and take the coins?"

"They, I mean, we, they..." Richard stumbled over the words and Brady understood the problem.

"Exactly!" Brady said. "They could have beaten us at almost any time, but they didn't and they let us deactivate the coins. Why?"

"I do not know, but I do know that we have to put these somewhere safe," Richard said, waving off Brady's arguments and turning back to Cherylyn.

"The vault," Cherylyn said, a proud glint in her eyes as she turned and led them into the building. They walked down a long corridor to a service elevator. Cherylyn pushed the button for sub basement 3.

"Are you sure the vault is the safest place?" Brady asked as the elevator began to descend.

"It's the safest place I've ever seen," Cherylyn smiled. "And I've been to Fort Knox." She pushed a key into the keyhole above the numbered buttons. A metal panel sprung open on the opposite side of the door. She stepped over as Richard and Brady watched with interest. She pulled the metal panel and revealed a second keyhole. She reached into her pocket and produced a large, very ancient looking key.

"That looks like," Richard began. "Is that the ChiRho symbol?"

"It is," Cherylyn responded and held up the sturdy metal key so that they could see the design on the head.

"It looks like an X with a P over it," Brady said.

"It is," Cherylyn offered as she put the key into the lock and turned. A shudder, as if some huge gears had been activated, shook the elevator. Cherylyn didn't seem to notice. "The X is the Chi and the P is the Rho. The first two letters of Christ in Greek. Also, the first two letters of gold in Greek, but that's neither here nor there. It's a very famous symbol. You've never seen it?"

Brady shook his head and Richard smiled. The elevator continued to descend to the last light on the numbered panel and then the lights on the panel went out completely.

"Are we still going down?" Richard asked.

"Yes," Cherylyn answered, keeping the key turned in the lock.

"How far down does this elevator go?" Richard prompted.

"I'm not sure," Cherylyn answered. "To be honest, this is only the second time I've gone down to the secret vault."

"Why only the second?" Brady asked.

Cherylyn shrugged, "I only just learned about it after you guys left the last time. I had a dream about it. When I woke up, I knew where the key was and how to operate the elevator, and a few other things."

Richard stood agape as he asked, "What other things?"

"You'll see. It's pretty cool," Cherylyn smiled mischievously.

"Seriously," Brady interrupted. "How far down does this go? I've, we've had some recent experiences with deep holes in the earth and I would really just like to know."

Cherylyn nodded, "I've tried to calculate the time it takes to drop between floors and extrapolate from there, but I think the elevator slows after it passes sub basement 3, so my best guess is another five floors or so."

"What's between the sub basement and where we're going?" Brady asked, suddenly feeling a bit claustrophobic and a little anxious.

"I think it's just solid rock," Cherylyn said, tilting her head to the side and looking up at the ceiling. The elevator shuddered again and stopped. "Might be some dirt too. Maybe water. There used to be a lot of swamp land in D.C. Anyway, we're here."

The doors opened and automatic lights flared to life along a corridor that ended in a metal door. Cherylyn led the way, and at the door, she pulled her cell phone from her jacket pocket. She pressed on the face plate and held the phone up to a digital panel next to the door. The locks clicked loudly in the small enclosed space of the corridor.

"Digital key?" Brady asked.

"Yes," Cherylyn said as she pulled against the heavy metal door. "It's crazy, but evidently the last curator who had been assigned to the Annex installed it himself, like last year. He retired shortly after and I became head curator here. Before that, it was this old lock from the 19th century that looked like a barrel attached to one of those nose ring things they put in bull's noses. You know those big metal hoops. I swear I thought I saw a guy the other day with one of those things in his ear. That has to hurt."

Richard and Brady nodded confusedly and followed Cherylyn through the door into another corridor, this time the walls were solid rock.

Richard asked, "You learned all of this from a dream? Did you learn how old this vault is?" He was rubbing his hand along the stone and feeling the tool marks. Brady did the same although he had no idea why.

"I'm not sure," Cherylyn admitted. "In the dream, I was told that it was here before America was founded. That might be just my own wishful thinking, but it might be true too."

They walked down the corridor in the glow of Cherylyn's cell phone held like a flashlight. At the end of the stone corridor was another door. This one was ancient looking and wooden with rough hewn metal hinges.

"Can you hold this?" Cherylyn asked Brady and handed him her cell phone. Brady held the light up to the door. He tried to find a key hole but there didn't appear to be any, at least any that he recognized as a key-hole. Cherylyn was rummaging through the back pack she was carrying. She finally found what she was looking for and pulled out a dagger.

"What is that?" Richard asked, eyeing the spike of aged metal.

"This?" Cherlyn asked and brandished the dagger. "It's a dagger."

"I can see that," Richard continued. 'What's it for?"

"It's the final key," Cherylyn said and handed the dagger to Richard while she continued to rummage through her backpack.

Richard looked closely at the dagger and began to examine it out loud,

"It's old, very old. But that seems impossible. The metal is still in such good condition. It looks like it could have been forged just a year or two ago. How old is this?"

"Pre-Roman, I think," Cherylyn said as she pulled a piece of paper from her backpack. She unfolded the paper and held it up to the light from the cell phone. She began reading silently.

"That's impossible," Richard began. "A dagger this old, made of what? Iron? Couldn't possibly be in a condition this good. The corrosion pattern should be much more advanced, even if it was kept indoors this entire time. And..."

"Got it!" Cherylyn announced and took the dagger from Richard. She held it up to the door and began to chant.

"What language is that?" Brady whispered to Richard.

"I'm not sure," Richard admitted and strained to hear individual words. "Maybe, maybe ancient Hebrew?"

Cherylyn continued to chant and then the glow from the cell phone intensified. The light grew stronger and stronger until it seeped into the wood of the door. Then, the door began to glow. It was an eerie, greenish-yellow glow that filled the entirety of the corridor with a haunting light. The light grew in intensity until it was painful to look at, and then it dimmed rapidly dissipating into the shadows.

"What was that?" Brady asked, looking at the cell phone with distrust.

"There's not a modern word for it," Cherylyn said as she watched the door closely. "The closest word we have would be prayer, but that's not an exact translation."

"A prayer?" Richard exclaimed, but his next question was swallowed by the loud clicks of tumblers falling into place. The wooden door shifted on its hinges and then popped open with a loud hiss.

"There we go," Cherylyn said cheerily. She turned on the flashlight app on her phone and pointed the light at the wall. "The last curator also put electric lights in the vault complete with their own generator. Get ready for a shock." Cherylyn held her hand out and flipped a switch on the wall.

Richard and Brady blinked rapidly, forcefully, in response to the flood of light, until their eyes adjusted; Brady had to wait a bit longer for his mind to catch up. He wondered if Richard was feeling overwhelmed, but then the man's giddy expression suggested something entirely different.

Behind the wooden door was a large, cavernous room filled with what could only be called treasure. Richard immediately began dating the objects in his mind, calling out dates as he pointed at objects, "Pre-Roman, 10th century, pre-Columbian?"

Brady was happy that Richard seemed to be having the time of his life, but he was simply awestruck by the piles and piles of gold. He stood with his mouth open, tenderly stroking some of the artifacts, and whistling involuntary catcalls.

"When you said vault, I'll be honest," Brady began. "I wasn't thinking this. I was thinking a big room full of dusty boxes and files."

"What, this?" Cherylyn snickered, a mischievous bounce in her step. "This is just the outer vault. The good stuff is behind that." She pointed to a part of the wall decorated with carvings.

Richard immediately went to the section and began an excited attempt to decipher the carvings. He called out, "There were some obvious Egyptian hieroglyphs. I recognize many of the symbols from my observations of the pyramids of Giza. There were also some Celtic runes. I encountered them on a particularly rewarding dig in the north of France." He fell silent and began to rub his chin as he pointed to a few of the symbols. "I can't identify these. I'm not even sure what region of the planet these come from. This is..." Richard stretched a hand toward the carvings, careful not to touch them.

"Incredible?" Cherylyn offered and then she lifted the dagger once more. "Just wait." She pointed the dagger at one particular symbol.

Richard offered, "Is that Roman?"

Cherylyn nodded and she slid the blade easily between the lines of the carving. "Grab that chalice," she said to Brady. Brady turned and began looking around, a bit wildly. Richard picked up a nearby chalice and handed it to him.

"You mean this old cup?" Brady asked.

"That's the one," Cherylyn said, taking the chalice from Brady and inserting the base into another symbol.

Richard called out as if he was answering trivia questions at the local bar, "That one is Celtic."

"And I need that arrow head. The stone one." Cherylyn pointed behind Richard.

"Is this Native American?" Richard asked, handing her the stone arrow head.

"Meso American. So, yeah," she took the arrow head and inserted it into a third symbol. The oddly modern sound of gears springing to life filled the chamber followed by a rumble as the section of wall slid open to reveal yet another chamber. She took her cell phone out again and turned on the flashlight app. "I almost didn't find the switch last time," she said as she felt along the side of the doorway.

"You have electric lights here too?" Richard asked, stepping forward. Brady saw that he was barely able to contain his excitement. He looked like a child at Christmas.

Cherylyn offered. "The previous curator was spending so much time down here that he was afraid he'd go blind from the candlelight. This room has its own generator too."

"More cataloging?" Richard asked, stepping forward again. He squinted into the dark room.

"Translating," Cherylyn responded. "Here it is," she announced and turned the switch. Lights flared to life and Richard gasped.

"Scrolls?" Brady asked as he stepped close behind Richard.

"Yep," Cherylyn began and she pointed to an unrolled parchment on the singular table in the center of the shelves overflowing with yellowed scrolls.

"How old?" Richard asked as his hand instinctively reached out to touch a roll of parchment on the nearest shelf.

"You ever hear of the Library of Alexandria?" Cherylyn asked.

"No!" Richard exclaimed loudly, pulling his arm back in shock.

"Alexandria, Virginia?" Brady asked, acutely aware that he was out of his element.

"Egypt," Cherylyn answered without even a hint of sarcasm. "The attacks by the Others destroyed a vast quantity of the works, but these represent the bulk of what was saved."

"Who are the Others?" Brady asked. "Sorry I keep asking stupid questions."

"Don't be sorry," Richard interjected. "I appreciate the company." His mouth was still open most of the time and Brady squeezed his shoulder tenderly.

"The Others are a mysterious group that has been around since, well, no one knows. When I had the dream that revealed the location of this vault, I knew the answers to a great many questions were down here. I have learned so much in such a short time. Anyway, the Others attacked the Library out of jealousy or maybe pride. It could have been greed," Cherylyn said as she took the coins to the table and began to read the unrolled parchment. "They used powerful weapons that nearly succeeded in destroying the only works that could have stopped them.

Luckily, some of the more important scrolls were saved. Like this one." She pointed to the parchment on the table.

"But history says that the library was completely destroyed," Richard offered, joining Cherylyn at the table and looking over her shoulder.

"A cover story," Brady interjected. "To throw them off track."

"Right!" Cherylyn shouted with far too much enthusiasm. "And it worked for centuries. We had the scrolls to keep the Others at bay, but then..." Cherylyn's voice trailed off as she began to concentrate on a passage of the scroll.

"But then what?" Richard asked from behind her.

"What?" Cherylyn held up the coin pouch and looked at it.

"What happened that caused the Others to become active again?" Richard pressed on.

"Where did you get this coin purse?" Cherylyn asked, completely ignoring his question.

"Erastus gave it to us. Why?" Brady asked, sensing something was wrong.

"It shouldn't work, you know?" Cherylyn said more to herself than to anyone else. "Iron can weaken the curse, but leather?"

"We figured it was part of the curse somehow," Brady continued and stepped forward. The three of them stood and stared at the pouch. "Maybe the original pouch?"

"Judas' own coin purse," Cherlyn began. "Made of leather more than two thousand years old. Impossible."

"Forgive me for saying this, but most of what we've encountered is impossible," Richard offered.

"True, but," Cherylyn began then screwed her face up toward the men standing behind her. "Who's Erastus?"

"One of the gray men hunting us," Brady offered.

"Oh no!" Cherylyn exclaimed and grabbed the pouch and ran from the room. Richard and Brady followed her. They hurried through the treasure chamber and through the stone corridor, but they were stopped at the metal door by the sight of Apollyon and Erastus standing shoulder to shoulder, blocking the passage.

"What is this place?" Apollyon asked. He ran his hand over the metal door, gazed into the stone corridor, and licked his lips expectantly.

"It's okay," Cherylyn said, but her tone suggested the situation was something other than okay. "They can't break the seals."

Appolyon stepped forward, held out a hand, and whispered, "Hello. Nice to see you again. We'll just take what's ours and go." He pointed to the pouch in Cherylyn's hand.

"They tracked the pouch," Brady said, mentally kicking himself for not thinking of the possibility sooner, and for trusting Erastus at all, and for still trusting the pouch after finding out that Erastus was a jerk.

"What are you doing?" Richard asked as Cherylyn held the pouch out to the gray men and stepped forward. He pulled her backwards but she fought him. Brady joined in, grabbing the pouch from her, and then wrestling her into the treasure chamber. He closed the wooden door behind them.

"What just happened?" Cherylyn asked as she shook her head in disbelief.

"They can control people who have touched the coins," Richard explained.

"Why didn't they control us all?" Brady interjected. "We've all touched the coins."

"The vault," Cherylyn said, gesturing all around her. "There are wards against...well, nearly everything. It must weaken their abilities."

"So, they still want the coins. Why?" Brady pressed forward with his train of thought. "The curse is deactivated."

"They can obviously reactivate it," Richard said. He seemed frustrated and Brady understood that he was asking the same questions over and over, but it was his process. He needed to get the questions firmly in his mind in order to answer them. That meant repetition.

"Yes, I know that," Brady said, trying to mentally tell Richard that he wasn't an idiot, but his own frustration was showing. The words came out a bit too pointedly. He softened them. "I mean, they said they would just wait us out. I thought that meant they had given, oh, of course..." He stopped talking and began to pace around the vault.

"What?" Richard asked.

"This place," Brady exclaimed. "They tricked us into bringing them right here. They obviously have never been here before, and they knew someone was stockpiling their cursed objects. They just needed some sucker to lead them straight to the vault."

"Oh," Carylyn interjected. "The people who originally built this vault must have hidden it from them. This could be bad. If they get in here, well, these things are dangerous." She looked around at the various artifacts and frowned deeply.

"What about all this stuff? Is there something we can use to help us?" Brady asked.

"Maybe," Carylyn said and then began pacing in the opposite direction of Brady. "I'll need to concentrate, I think the book is..." She walked to a nearby table and rummaged through a pile of books. "Yes, it is here. Then, I just need to..." She wandered off into a corner of the room, sat cross-legged on the floor, and began to read.

Brady shrugged in Richard's direction and Richard shook his head.

"I guess we'll wait?" Brady asked and stood next to Richard who was examining a table filled with oddly shaped cups.

"This is a lot, huh?" Richard asked as he lifted a wooden goblet.

"I am sorry, you know? That I got you into all this. I really am," Brady offered, his hand on Richard's arm.

"You have nothing to be sorry for," Richard said, handing him the goblet. "Look at this. This artifact, I think, might be the Holy Grail."

"What?" Brady took the cup and held the carved wood with reverence.

"I know, right?" Richard said. "This is the adventure of a lifetime. I should thank you for getting me into this."

"Well, then, you're welcome." Brady carefully set the goblet back onto the table.

"And I should apologize for being so rude to you," Richard began.

"When were you rude to me?" Brady asked earnestly, honestly.

"Well, I'm sorry anyway." Richard nodded, "So, they still want the coins? It makes sense, kinda. Whoever broke the curse is more than likely the strongest candidate for reactivating it."

"Yeah," Brady said, mentally checking off boxes in his head. "That explains why they haven't killed us...yet. But why let us deactivate them in the first place? Erastus mentioned a time limit for curses. Is that a thing?"

"A time limit?" Richard asked. "The curse might have been running out. That would make sense." He seemed to realize what he had said and shrugged. Brady nodded. He knew what Richard meant, and he agreed silently that none of this really made sense. Richard continued, "Lots of curses in literature have time limits, or quotas, or the like. Maybe the coins had done enough over the past millennia to make up for the initial deed, so they needed a new deed to reactivate the curse."

"A new betrayal," Brady said and the boxes in his head were nearly all checked.

"One of us," Richard interjected.

"I got it!" Cherylyn shouted and ran back to the library. Richard and Brady quickly followed her. They found her scanning the scrolls until she uncovered the one she was looking for. She slipped it from its resting place and unfurled it. Then she began to chant.

"What language is that?" Brady asked.

"I have no idea," Richard admitted and the two fell silent and listened to Cherylyn make sounds that felt like words. When she finished, she carefully rolled up the scroll and replaced it.

"There," She said emphatically.

"There, what?" Brady asked.

"I just activated some treasures," Cherylyn explained and pointed out into the room where several artifacts had begun to glow.

Beyond the large, thick, closed wooden door, Brady thought he heard the sounds of a vicious argument. Raised voices, filled more with volume than emotion, carried through to their sanctuary. At one point, Brady even thought he saw a flash of light as if a silent bomb had exploded.

"What kind of stuff did you activate?" Brady asked, backing away from the sturdy-looking door that he no longer trusted.

"Here," Cherylyn said and handed him a breastplate of armor. It was glowing green. "Put this on. Richard!" Cherylyn called and tossed a dark gray helmet, which was somehow shining with a white light, to Richard. "You put this one on."

Richard caught the helmet and slipped it over his head. He vanished.

"What the...?" Brady exclaimed as Richard took off the helmet and became visible. He held out the green armor he was about to put on and looked at it more closely.

"Magic," Cherylyn said forcefully. "Get used to it." She grabbed a length of golden cloth that was adorned with golden metal and fastened it around her waist. Brady pulled the leather straps affixed to the breastplate and fastened them around his own waist. He felt strangely powerful.

Cherylyn began to rummage through the artifacts looking for other glowing items. "What else, what else?" She picked up a gnarled stick roughly the size of a ruler, which seemed to be just really clean rather than glowing. She tucked it under her arm. She looked around as a loud bang shook the room. "Sword!" she shouted and pointed to the opposite side of the room, behind Brady.

Brady ran to the sword. It was glowing a bright white. He picked it up and it was far lighter than it should have been. Another loud bang and the door to the room slipped from one of its hinges. It hung awkwardly, allowing Brady to clearly see the face of Appolyon on the other side. The gray man was smiling a large, gray smile.

Cherylyn pointed to Richard. "Put on the helmet."

Richard slid it over his head and he was gone. When he disappeared, Brady could see a wooden pole behind him that seemed to be very clean. He shouted, "Richard! That pole...!" His words were cut short as Erastus shoved the door from the last hinge and it fell with a clatter.

"Ready?" Cherylyn asked.

Brady thought, *Not even a little bit*, but he nodded emphatically.

Erastus stuck his head into the room and sneered. "Here's Johnny!" he said through gray teeth.

"Really?" Brady asked as he raised his sword.

Erastus snickered, "Where's your sense of humor? This doesn't have to be difficult, you know?"

Brady set his feet firmly on the stone floor. His muscles tensed, his stomach fluttered, and he focused his mind. He watched as the two gray men stepped cautiously over the remnants of the door. Erastus licked his gray lips as he looked over the treasure trove.

"My, my," Erastus began. "Haven't we been busy?"

Appolyon reached out for a golden box. A flash of electricity flared and he snatched his hand back. "Protected," he said with a wince.

Erastus smiled, "Protections fall when the caster is dead." He began to slink through the tables, around the displays, his hand hovering just above the artifacts. Every so often a spark would flash and he would smile. "Let's see." He pointed to Brady who lifted his sword a bit higher. "You're not a caster. That's clear." He twirled his finger toward the inner vault. "The professor could be a caster. Is he hiding back there? But I don't get the sense that he knows the spells. Not yet." He continued to twirl his finger as he turned to Cherylyn. "Now, you. You're new. Where have you been hiding?"

Cherylyn held the glowing stick in her outstretched hand. Brady stepped toward her but stopped when she held up a hand to him. She took a deep breath. "I surrounded myself with books. I figured the threat of education would keep you away. I was right."

"Ha!" Erastus exclaimed through a big smile. His gray face seemed almost loving as he said under his breath, "Kill her."

Appolyon sprung forward. He moved so swiftly that Brady froze for a moment. He tried to focus on the blur moving toward Cherylyn, but his eyes simply could not focus. Cherylyn whispered something. Suddenly, the stick in her hand was a spear, golden, shimmering in the light. She swung the spear and connected with the blur in front of her. Appolyon flew sideways and slammed into the wall. He struggled to his feet as Erastus shot toward Cherylyn.

Brady sprinted to her side and swung his blade wildly. Erastus dodged, only barely, and punched Brady square in the chest. A thud rang out and Brady fell backward. He was not hurt, but he was winded. The green armor covering his chest was vibrating. He tried to get to his feet, but the armor was clunky. He could only watch as Erastus closed in on Cherylyn.

A flash of light appeared near Erastus' head and a stream of snakes fell from seemingly nowhere. They swirled around the gray man, covering his face and half of his torso. He tore at them as he stumbled around. Cherylyn took advantage and swung her spear. Erastus screamed as he flew across the room, landing on a tabletop filled with artifacts that began to shoot electric fire directly into him. His screams became silent spasms of pain. His gray skin began to blacken and smoke. Appolyon, now on his feet, hissed at Cherylyn before turning and dashing toward Erastus. Brady could see a blur enwrap the writhing gray man before they both disappeared into the silent darkness of the corridor beyond the broken door.

Cherylyn slumped to the ground as she let out a haltingly tense breath. Richard suddenly appeared next to her as he lifted off his helmet. "Is it over?" he asked. He dropped his helmet and brandished the staff in his hand like a sword.

Brady looked to the door and then to Cherylyn. "Is it?" he asked.

Cherylyn nodded and began to chant in a language that made Brady's skin crawl. A red glow surrounded the open doorway and then irised closed, creating a curtain of light before dissipating into nothingness.

"Was that...?"

"A protection spell," Cherylyn said as she fell back onto her hanches. Her breathless voice was weak and her head was lolling to one side. Richard knelt and caught her as she fell forward.

The stone corridor was eerily silent. The dim light from the vault shone only so far into the space, and beyond the small stream of light was a deep, foreboding darkness. Brady stepped forward into the small pool of light and tried to see into that darkness. The gray men were gone.

CHAPTER 28

The floor of the secret vault far below the Smithsonian Annex was anything but comfortable as Brady rolled over on the pile of robes and cloaks they had amassed as a makeshift bed. He closed his eyes and tried to sleep, but there was no rest. His mind was still replaying the recent battle, and his churning stomach was still waiting for the gray men to return. He gave up on the idea of sleep and sat up.

Cherylyn breathed softly and rhythmically beside him. Richard sat on a bench facing the shattered door. He still held the glowing staff in his hand. Brady joined him. "Anything?"

"Nothing," Richard responded. "You should really try to sleep. It's only been an hour since I took over the watch."

Brady patted Richard's knee jovially. "I'm fine. Can't sleep. You could..." He stopped as Richard shook his head. "Well, then, we can have a little talk." He closed his hand around the staff just above Where Richard was holding. "What does this thing do?"

Richard looked at him and smiled, "It conjures snakes." Brady jerked his hand away. Richard laughed, "I'm not sure how it works. I walked one of the gray men on the head and a bunch of snakes appeared."

"I saw that," Brady admitted. "I thought it was something Cherylyn did."

Richard tapped the staff onto the stone floor. "Nope, it was me."

"Huh," Brady said and took hold of the staff again, this time his hand was touching Richard's. "So, how are you doing?"

"Ha!" Richard let out a too-loud laugh. The men turned to look at Cherylyn who jerked a little bit but fell back into rhythmic breathing quickly. "Shh, sorry. Was that a line?"

Brady tried not to laugh out loud. "Maybe a little," he admitted. "But I also want to know how you're handling all of this."

Richard turned to face Brady. He became earnest, serious. "I'm good as long as you're here."

"Good," Brady said and leaned toward him.

"Good," Richard repeated. Their kiss was loving at first, then passionate, then a bit too passionate. A sudden snore from Cherylyn made them both break away.

"Maybe not the time," Brady said.

Richard nodded, "Probably not."

They sat close together, hands intertwined around the magical staff between them. Brady suggested, "Want to sum up everything? Lay out the evidence?"

"Sure," Richard said. "We just fought the gray men. They appeared to have supernatural strength and speed."

"That's true," Brady agreed. "The way Appolyon slammed into the wall and just got right back up, and the way they moved."

Richard made a sweeping motion with his free hand. "And all these things, they hurt them somehow."

"Yeah," Brady looked around. "Why is that?"

"Well," Richard began as he retrieved a parchment that he had draped over the bench beside him. "While you were resting, I tried to read, well, decipher, one of these scrolls."

"Yeah?" Brady took the scroll and held it up to the light. It was obviously old, there were symbols on it that could be letters, or words, or something. "So, anything?"

"Yes," Richard leaned over as Brady held the scroll. He put his head close to Brady's, cheeks nearly touching. Brady could feel the heat of his skin and his mouth was suddenly dry. "Here," Richard began, pointing to one of the symbols. "This part is a history of some sort. It seems that the gray men have been doing their little tricks for centuries." He pointed to another part. "This section recounts battles that people have had with them. Every time, the people used enchanted objects to win."

"Wait," Brady interrupted and leaned a bit toward the scroll even though he had no idea what it said. "I thought the gray men were fighting each other."

Richard took the scroll and unrolled it a bit more. He handed it back to Brady and then leaned in again. He was even closer now, his arm around Brady's back, their shoulders pressed together. Brady swallowed hard and tried to concentrate. Richard continued, "That seems to be part of the game, or scenario, whatever. The gray men always appear as if they are enemies, but they are working together to destroy humanity."

"Why?" Brady asked. "Aren't they angels or something?"

"I don't think so," Richard pointed toward the rolled up part of the scroll and Brady unrolled it further. "Here, it seems to suggest that they are celestial in nature, but not angels nor demons. The ancients had no word for what they are. I don't think we do either."

"Weird," Brady said as he turned to face Richard. They were so close that He felt Richard's breath on his face. He smiled and they kissed again. This time the passion came quicker, more fiercely. A moan from behind them caused them to stop again.

"What time is it?" Cherylyn asked as she stretched and struggled to her feet.

"Nearly six," Richard answered, his lips still very close to Brady's. They stared into each other's eyes as Cherylyn stumbled over to them.

"That means the staff will be arriving soon," she said as she continued to stretch. "I think this is over, for now."

The two men stood together and they all looked at the shattered door.

Brady asked, "What now?"

The three of them exchanged looks and then they all frowned deeply.

***

"You really can't stay longer?" Richard asked as he held Brady's hand. They were leaning against Brady's police car, trying to say good-bye, finding it difficult to do.

"I want to," Brady responded, lifting Richard's hand to his mouth and kissing tenderly. "But I have duties…"

"As sheriff, I know," Richard interrupted resignedly. "You'll come back soon though?"

Brady smiled and put his head on Richard's shoulder. "Absolutely."

Cherylyn bounded out of the Smithsonian Annex and approached, half-skipping. "It's all done, all official." She handed a stack of papers to Richard. "You are officially employed by the Smithsonian Annex."

"That was fast," Richard took the papers and began flipping through them. "I haven't even given notice at the college yet."

Brady took the papers and flipped through them as well. "So, the funding for this place?"

Cherylyn said, "Right, that." She indicated that Brady needed to keep flipping. When he got to the second to last page. She pointed to the stack. "There. At the bottom. See that budget breakdown?"

Brady read the list of agencies that provided funding to the Annex. Some were expected like the Smithsonian Institution provided a large chunk, but nowhere near enough. There were private funding sources that were a bit suspect. Brady's eyes went directly to Abraham Quince. "He funded the annex?"

Cherylyn just nodded, her eyebrows raised conspiratorially.

Richard leaned over and perused the list. "I guess he figured he could get his hands on pieces for his collection if he funded the storage and cataloging of those pieces." He pointed further down the list. "Who are all these people?"

"That's the weird thing," Cherylyn said as she pulled a folded piece of paper from her back pocket. She handed it to Richard. "I found this in the protected files, the ones we aren't even allowed to put on the computer. It's a list solely for the eyes of the senior curator."

Brady read the list of names and organizations. Nothing jumped out at him. "And that's you now, right?"

"Yes," Cherylyn said excitedly. "I haven't even begun to scratch the surface of all the secrets in this building. I mean, I've been on the job for less than six months and I've been cursed, discovered a secret vault with enormously powerful magical weapons, fought what can only be described as supernatural beings, and now learned that my salary comes from really sketchy places."

Brady handed the papers back to Richard as he hugged and kissed him one final time. "Well, I've put this off for long enough. I should go." He shook Cherylyn's hand, but she went in for a hug anyway.

"I'll be working on that thing you asked for," she whispered as they hugged.

Brady winked at her and then at Richard. As he pulled the car onto the semi-busy streets, he looked in his rear view mirror, half-expecting to see a gray man there. He only saw Cherylyn waving animatedly and Richard, his hand high in the air.

CHAPTER 29

Potter's Field, Virginia, had never seemed a large place, but since his adventure, the town was so small that Brady feared he had developed some type of claustrophobia, maybe small town-a-phobia? He did all the things he had done before the coins. He walked around town, he answered calls, he caught the occasional shop lifter or jay walker, but he felt so much bigger than the town now. He wondered if he was being prideful, which he now knew to be a problem, but he decided it was something else entirely. It was restlessness, and a need to be of more use. Then, there was Richard.

They had shared something. Something meaningful. Richard suggested that it might have been adrenaline, or fear, and that they should really think about it before making any rash decisions. Brady had agreed that they would take some time, keep in touch, and plan for the future later. It had barely been three days but it felt like a lifetime to him. He decided a phone call was overdo and he would make that call right after work.

"Good morning, Sheriff," Elizabeth Woods said as she paused in front of him on the street.

"Elizabeth?" Brady began and stopped walking. "How's Lonnie?"

Elizabeth turned and smiled warmly, "He's much better. Thanks for asking."

"So, it was just exhaustion?"

"Yep, just working too hard, I suppose," Elizabeth responded. She shook her head as she spoke. "I'm so sorry he gave everyone such a scare. I'm making sure he gets plenty of rest now."

"Good. Good," Brady said and watched as Elizabeth continued on, but he couldn't shake the feeling that he should tell her the truth, that her husband had nearly been killed by an ancient curse, that he and a history professor had traveled the world to break the curse, and that a woman he met, Dr. Katie Share, had also been nearly killed by the same curse, that a very rich man named Abraham Quince had not fared any better than Katie or Lonnie, and that a young graduate student named Carrie was now in a psychiatric hospital because of the very same curse. He could go on and on and on, and he so wanted to tell someone, anyone, about his adventure. Instead of saying any of that, he just smiled and shook his head. After all, who would believe his crazy story anyway?

His deputy, Pete Daily, had handled things very well while Brady had been galavanting all over the globe. In fact, Pete had convinced himself that he would make a better sheriff than Brady. He was even planning on running for the position in the fall. Brady thought that was a splendid idea and he wondered if making Pete the interim sheriff for a while right before the election would help matters. He decided that it would, and having Pete win would free him up to...what?

He sat behind his desk in the little office near town hall. He thought about Richard and wondered what he was doing right now. Maybe he had just uncovered another dangerous artifact that needed to be housed in the Annex. Maybe he was practicing with the snake staff. Or maybe he was sitting at his own desk and thinking about the sheriff of Potter's Field. He daydreamed and waited for something, anything, to happen. It didn't, so he rose and said goodbye to the night staff he had been able to hire just to answer phones since the deaths and Lonnie's episode put pressure on the mayor's office to do something about the 911 situation. He went outside, sniffed the cool evening breeze, got in his car, and drove home.

His little house was still as cozy as it had ever been, but it was so much smaller now. Too small. He made a simple dinner, ate it in front of the television, washed up, and got ready for bed. Then, he sat on the side of his bed and sighed. Was he an adrenaline junky now? He wondered if that was anything like being too prideful. He had heard of people becoming addicted to danger, and he had experienced his fair share of danger over the last couple of…no, that's crazy. He was still just Brady. He was just tired, that's all. He just needed to rest, but first, he was going to talk to Richard.

He picked up his cell phone and was about to dial the number when the phone rang. It was Richard. "Hey, I was just about to call you," he said happily.

"Brady," Richard's voice was even more excited. "I just got off the phone with Cherylyn. She just got a communique from someone claiming to be part of something called the Administration."

Brady interrupted, "What's a communique?"

Richard answered, "In this instance, a telegraph."

"You're kidding?"

"No," Richard responded, his voice even more excited. "It was a telegraph. I didn't even know you could still send a telegraph, but she got one that said there was a new artifact that we needed to find."

Brady shot to his feet. He began to gather clothes from drawers and the closet before he realized, "Wait, I can't just…"

"Oh," Richard interrupted again. "And they gave you a job. Double your old salary."

"Thank goodness," Brady sighed and smiled excitedly. He collected his badge and placed it next to his gun on his dresser. He would drop them off at the station tonight, then he would call Pete in the morning and let him know he could take over as sheriff, permanently. "I'm on my way."

"I can't wait to see you," Richard said.

Brady finished packing. He closed the door to his cozy house behind him and pointed his car north.

CHAPTER 30

Epilogue

Room 413 of St. Mary's Hospital just outside of D.C. had been turned into a makeshift apartment while Dr. Katherine "Katie" Share continued to convalesce. She had convinced her colleagues from various colleges who visited to travel to her apartment and gather materials for her to continue her work. Richard and the Sheriff, what was his name, she thought. Brady something. Had left her laptop and a couple of her notebooks, which was a tremendous help. Her friends brought books and more notebooks.

"They're cleaning out your apartment," the secretary from the college where she taught online classes full time had told her. "They hired a professional service. We tried to get everything that we thought you'd want to keep. We're storing them in one of the vacant offices on campus."

Katie had thanked the secretary profusely for going out of her way to make sure she could still work, and then had wished she had taken the time to learn the woman's name. She thought about going on the college's website and looking in the directory, but something had been nagging at her since she finally woke up without the pull of the coins tinkling in her brain.

She searched through the pages of notes she had entered into her laptop. Nothing. There was something she was missing. She pulled one of the rolling tray tables toward her. The nurses had allowed her to keep several in her room so she could pile books on top of them. She lifted one book and tried to remember the contents of it. No, that's not the one. She lifted a second. No. A third. No, none of these would help with the uneasy feeling she had developed. She pushed the tray table away and looked around the room.

There, on the chair near the window. A book that had once been bound in a deep red material, but the spine was now bleached by the sun, sat amidst other books and file folders full of paper. She tried to lift herself off the bed but she fell back, her arms unable to support her added weight. How had she allowed herself to get into this condition? She began to chastise herself, but then the memory of the hunger filled her mind. The unrelenting, uncontrollable hunger. She closed her eyes against the pain of the memories.

When she opened them, one of the nurses was standing by the side of her bed.

"How are you feeling?" the nurse asked, her name badge read "Cathy." Katie made a conscious effort to remember that name.

"I'm fine," Katie began. "Would you be so kind as to hand me a book from that chair?" Katie pointed to the chair and the sight of her swollen hands made her shiver.

When the nurse left, after handing her the book, Katie got to work. She flipped through the pages quickly, a half remembered page stuck in her head. She searched the book quickly and then there it was, the very page she had been looking for.

"You never cease to amaze me, dear Katherine," Apollyon's gray voice sounded from the doorway.

"What do you want?" Katie hissed. "I don't have the coins."

"I'm aware of that," Apollyon said as he oozed around the room, his gray fingers touching on various books as he went. "But that doesn't mean you're no longer useful to us. You've been researching artifacts for so long, and you are so very good at finding them. Amazingly good in fact considering you do it all using a keyboard and a library card. Truly inspiring."

"I'm not going to help you!" Katie nearly shouted. "I'll fight you!"

"You'll try," Apollyon said, his gray voice like a snake slithering through tall grass. "Just like you did before. How did that work out for you?"

Katie felt tears flowing down her face. She tried to be strong, she tried to be brave, but the memory of Apollyon visiting her every night, whispering in her ear, and propelling her already ravenous hunger to ever greater intensity. She swallowed hard and realized the book was still on the tray table in front of her. She tried to close it, but a gray hand slipped in between the pages.

"What do we have here?" Apollyon asked as he lifted the book and opened it to the pages that Katie had been reading. "Oh my," he said in his lifeless, gray voice. "Do you know where this is?"

"No, no, no, no," Katie repeated over and over as she tried desperately to remember the Lord's Prayer. No other words could penetrate the fog of fear that Apollyon had created around her.

"Katherine, Katherine," Apollyon whispered as he bent near her ear. "Tell me what you know about this." He held the book open in front of her and Katie couldn't help but look down at the page. It was a reproduction of a nave mosaic from the Basilica Santa Maria Maggiore.

"I won't tell you," Katie said, her voice weak and shaky.

"Even if I help you get back on your feet?" Apollyon asked.

Katie's eyes left the page and fell on Apollyon's gray face. "How?"

"I can take the hunger away," Apollyon cooed. "You could get back to your old self so quickly."

Katie, her face streaked with tears, looked back at the book splayed open in front of her. She knew what Apollyon wanted, and she knew his power. He could help her. She placed a swollen hand on the page with the picture. Her fingers were tingling from poor circulation, so it felt like a phantom hand, not her own doing his bidding. She tried one more time to recite the Lord's Prayer, but the words would not come. Instead, she began to speak without fully intending to, "It's a mosaic called *The Fall of Jericho and Priests Bearing the Ark of the Covenant.*"

"Really?" Apollyon moved even closer to her ear, speaking softly, liltingly, "Good. And, have you found the Ark of the Covenant?"

Katie's eyes grew large and fresh tears fell.

"No, not the Ark," Apollyon smiled a grim, gray smile. "The horn." Katie blanched as he asked, "So, where is it?"